ENFLAME

A TANGLED LOVE STANDALONE

STACEY LYNN

Copyright 2015

Enflame, A Tangled Love Standalone
Stacey Lynn
© 2015 Stacey Lynn

All Rights Reserved. This book may not be reproduced, scanned, or distributed in any printed or electronic form without permissions from the author, except for using small quotes for book review quotations. All characters and storylines are the property of the author. The characters, events and places portrayed in this book are fictitious. Any similarity to real persons, living or dead, is coincidental and not intended by the author.

Trademarks: This book identifies product names and services known to be trademarks, registered trademarks, or service marks of their respective holders. The author acknowledges the trademarked status and trademark owners of all products referenced in this work of fiction. The publication and use of these trademarks in not authorized, associated with, or sponsored by the trademark owners.

Editing provided by: Amy Jackson Editing

Proofreading provided by: Emily A. Lawrence

Cover design provided by: Shanoff Designs

Table of Contents

One 1
Two 10
Three 22
Four 38
Five 50
Six 63
Seven 75
Eight 86
Nine 98
Ten 112
Eleven 122
Twelve 133
Thirteen 145
Fourteen 161
Fifteen 172
Sixteen 184
Seventeen 195
Eighteen 204
Nineteen 217
Twenty 227
Twenty-One 241
Twenty-Two 251
Twenty-Three 262
Twenty-Four 267

Synopsis

Enflame, Tangled Love - Book Three

Talia Merchant dropped the idea of a forever kind of love after the first guy she loved stole not only her heart, but he also took her virginity....and then he took off.

Now, busy with caring for her father and trying to save her teen shelter, Talia doesn't need the messy entanglements that come with real relationships she doesn't have time for.

But after a mysterious benefactor saves her free clinic and reveals himself...everything changes.

Donovan Lore doesn't just want in Talia's bed, which is the only thing she offers —he wants inside her heart and he doesn't care what type of fight Talia puts up. He's determined to break through every one of her walls until she's pliable and needy in his hands and writhing beneath him.

And Donovan always gets what he wants.

*To all my readers
I couldn't do what I love
Without you.*

Chapter One

My fingers hesitate, running down his cold, pale skin. He no longer wears a tanned and healthy look. His skin is sallow, sunken in and dark around his eyes. His cheekbones protrude too far and his lips are too dry.

Everything about him feels and looks wrong, regardless that I've seen him like this almost every day for the last month.

"Get better soon, Dad." My hand leaves his cheek and moves to under my eyes, wiping away my tears that slowly begin to fall.

His eyes are open but unresponsive.

I should be used to it, but I would give my right arm for the outer edges of his eyes to crinkle, the corners of his lips to turn up, just one more time.

"See you tomorrow." I brush my lips across his forehead, forcing myself out of the chair and out of his room.

The nursing home he's in has a constant musty smell to it that clings to my clothes.

I would give anything for a shower. Maybe a glass of wine and a Skype date with my best friend, Laurie.

But neither of those are on the agenda for today.

I still have a business to save. And no funds to do so.

"Miss Merchant?"

My heeled boots pause on the cracked linoleum floor and I close my eyes, blinking slowly and praying for patience.

Why couldn't I have afforded a better place to send him?

"Yes?" I turn and look at the sharply dressed woman. A clipboard is in her hands and black plastic frames surround her eyes. Her lips are bright red and in a familiar pinched expression. I'm not ever sure I've seen the Administrator of Centerville

Nursing Facility do anything other than purse her lips.

"Your father's bill is past due."

"I know." I swallow, twisting my lips, stalling for time and an explanation. The problem? I have neither. Nor the money she's seeking. "I'll get it to you as soon as I can."

"Yes, well, you see…" Clicking heels echo in the hall as she walks closer. "We are not a governmentally funded facility, and if you can't pay this bill, we're going to have to look into transporting him elsewhere."

Like hell, I want to say, but press my lips together.

I hate this.

My hands ball into fists and I nod briskly. "I understand. It won't happen after this."

She eyes me warily. More like an eagle searching for prey.

I hate her. This place.

I despise the fact that my dad took amazing care me of me, his only daughter, on his own for most of my life, and only thirty days after his stroke I'm already struggling to care for him. But there's no way he's going anywhere. I can barely afford this piece of crap place, but it's an exotic retirement resort compared to the government-funded long-term care facilities I locked at while he was in the hospital.

"See that it doesn't." She turns on her heels.

When she's gone, my head falls back and I glare at the stained circles on the ceiling tiles.

Before my eyes can fill with tears, I take several deep breaths, forcing down the tsunami of emotions threatening to pull me under the force of its heavy swells.

I have too much to do. Too much is at stake.

I don't have time to huddle in a corner and cry.

* * * * *

"We have a problem."

I shoot invisible daggers from my eyes to my assistant, Marisa, as I step through the door of our nonprofit, teenage counseling center. "Not the four words I need to hear today."

She nods once and points toward my office with her thumb. "I know. But Jeremiah is here."

My eyes fly wide open and my hand covers my heart. It's beating rapidly. Thank goodness.

"How long?" I ask, walking past her and tossing her a look over my shoulder.

Jeremiah's been one of my most frustrating young teenagers. At thirteen, he thinks he's got the world figured out already. Thinks he knows everything. I don't know what his family situation is, but I know he often shows up bruised and bleeding from his lips or cheeks. His assurance that it doesn't come from his family has assuaged my concerns for the most part. The fact that he's usually dressed in designer clothes—jeans more expensive than I can ever hope to own—doesn't play a part, but it does make me curious about him. I wonder about him and why he shows up, comes regularly for a week or two, and then we don't see him for months.

I'm always terrified that we might never see him again.

Plastering on my most friendly and nonthreatening smile, I walk through my door. "Hey there, stranger. How are you?"

Jeremiah turns his head, looking at me over his shoulder.

I fight the urge to gasp or rush to him. His left eye is swollen. His bottom lip is cracked, and there's some dried blood. Glancing down, I see his knuckles on his right hand are equally cracked and bleeding.

Fighting.

I shake my head before joining him in my sitting area. Most of the time, the majority of the teenagers who come to my center are homeless, struggling in school, or running from abusive homes. We've found several of them dealing drugs on the street corners of Grand Rapids.

It doesn't stop me, ever, from bringing them here and loving on them, though—as long as they don't do drugs on the property. That's my most important rule.

My second: be honest.

It's not a big list of rules, but it's amazing how even those two are difficult to adhere to.

Jeremiah always follows the first. Occasionally, the second.

"Hey, Miss Merchant," he mumbles, a typical greeting by teenagers.

I don't take offense to his lack of manners.

Sitting down, I brush my hands down my jeans, thankful I dressed casual today. It helps with the kids—young adults—I'm desperate to reach.

"What's up?" I ask, quirking a brow.

Jeremiah and I play a game frequently. I like to call it Wait. Essentially, I ask a question. And then I wait.

Sometimes I wait for an answer the entire time he's here, but by avoiding it he's not lying, so I allow it.

He's a smart kid, figuring out how to stretch the rules in his favor when he needs to. He must be desperate, because it's only when he needs a place to stay that he does this.

"Got a room?"

"Need ice for your eye?" I counter, giving him a look that says he needs to start talking.

He brushes back his sandy brown locks and looks down at his knees. He flexes his injured hand, trying to stretch his fingers, and I see him grimace.

"I'm good."

I scoff and point my index finger in his direction. "Stay here."

Shooting him a scolding look, I'm not surprised when Jeremiah chuckles. I'm not very fierce, and my scolding looks are typically used when I'm trying to fight a smile. All the kids know it, but despite that, very few of them take advantage of me or my kindness. I've always hoped my genuine love for the kids who walk through the doors of our center is what helps them relax around me, but I could be blowing smoke up my own ass.

Walking out of my office, I quickly head to our kitchen to grab a couple of ice packs and our small medical kit.

When I return, I take note of Marisa as she talks on the phone. She's speaking tensely but quietly and her eyebrows are raised significantly. She holds up a hand, telling me to wait for her to get off the phone.

"That was the bank." Her bottom lip finds its way between her teeth.

I hold up an ice pack and the medical kit. "I can only deal with one emergency at a time."

"I know." She pushes off her chair and takes the few small steps to me, lowering her voice so no one can hear us. Not that there are many people here besides us—Jeremiah, and a handful of kids watching some ghost hunters show in our common area. My other counselor left her job months ago, when we stopped making enough money to pay her already meager salary. I can't blame her, either.

"We have forty-five days," Marisa says, resting her hand on mine. "That's it."

A cold chill of fear slithers down my spine. I'm failing at everything despite trying to maintain control.

"I'll get on more fundraising as soon as I'm done here."

I turn my back to her, knowing the woman who's been more like a mother or aunt to me over the last few years is watching me walk away.

I'm not avoiding.

I'm procrastinating.

There's a huge difference.

"Here." I hand Jeremiah the ice pack and watch as he gingerly presses it over his eye.

He hisses in a breath when the cold hits his skin, and I take a seat next to him, opening the medical kit.

"Let me clean you up," I tell him, not giving him time to say no. With his scraped hand in my lap, I clean his wounds quickly and then cover them with an antibiotic cream. "Are you ever going to tell me what the fights are about?"

I look up from my position and into the boy's light green eyes. They're so bright—a complete contradiction to the general heaviness and darkness that fills the rest of his young features.

Jeremiah might only be thirteen years old, but he has the intelligence of an adult. Coupled with the looks and body of a cover model and the recklessness of a MMA fighter, he has so much going for him; but he's also a walking disaster.

He's going to end up in huge trouble someday with all of this fighting, and while I never admit it to anyone else out loud, I have a larger soft spot in my heart for Jeremiah than for some of the other kids who walk through my doors.

It could be because he vaguely reminds me of someone I used to know. Even though that guy turned out to be a grade-A prick, he was still the only guy I ever thought I loved, and there's something about Jeremiah that makes me think of him.

It could also be because even when he's scowling and sullen, there's sadness in his eyes that I want to help erase.

"Bad day at school," he finally mutters, looking directly at me.

I smile faintly, not showing my surprise for the honesty.

"What school is that?" I ask, and press an alcohol wipe to his cut lip.

He sucks in a breath.

"Sorry. I should have warned you that it stings."

"I can take it."

"School?" I ask again.

From the corner of my eye, I notice his backpack slung on the floor haphazardly. It's open, and as I catch a hint of deep red fabric, I no longer need him to answer.

Raising my gaze back to meet his, I say, "You go to Western Prep."

He scoffs and looks away. His hands, which are resting on his thighs, ball into fists. "Only the best for me."

Leaning away from him so I can reach my garbage can, I throw away the wrappers and wipes, tossing them in with a flick of my wrist.

"Nice shot."

I sit up and take in his faint smile.

"Thanks, I played basketball for a while."

And just like that, his smile disappears and is replaced by his familiar scowl.

"Look, Jeremiah. I don't mind that you come and hang out here. In fact, I want you to be here. But if you want my help, you're going to need to give me a little bit more than you have in the past."

I almost hold my breath waiting for him to answer. I don't typically push him for information because I haven't wanted to scare him away. But I've never seen him this injured before, either. It worries me, and when he slowly turns his head and our eyes meet, his light green eyes to my baby blues, his lips twist.

He licks his lip and his shoulders roll forward. Shaking his head, his hair falls over his forehead and into his eyes. I hate that I can't see them. It's true that eyes are the windows to the soul. I can almost always gauge everyone's emotions by them.

"Just a shitty day," he mutters.

"Manners," I remind him with a smile. No swearing isn't one of the rules because it'd be fruitless, but I still try to teach them what's best when I can.

"Sorry." He looks up and at my wall. It's full of inspirational quotes I've painted onto broken pieces of wood. It looks chaotic, but I like spending time finding meaningful quotes, preparing the wood by sanding and distressing it, and then painting the words and sealing it to the boards. My dad's hands were made for working with automobiles. Mine were made for woodworking and caring for people.

Today I catch him looking at the sign that says You were given this life because you're strong enough to live it.

"What does that make you think of?" I ask cautiously.

His lip curls at one end, and I've lost him, I know it. I don't know what he thinks about when he goes silent, but Jeremiah has a way of closing down completely.

I'm about to push, to ask for more, when I see Marisa walking toward my office.

She doesn't knock when she reaches the doorway but nods her head toward the front waiting area.

"There's someone here for Jeremiah."

My head snaps toward him. "You called someone?"

"Fuck no," he snaps and jumps to his feet. His closed-off expression has been quickly replaced with a fury I can feel rolling off his body as he quickly reaches down, snags his backpack, and tosses it over his shoulder.

I don't have time to reprimand him for cursing before he's pushing past me.

My eyes go wide as I shoot Marisa a look. "Who is it?"

She shrugs. "Don't know, but he's damn fine to look at."

I snort. Of course she'd notice. "Nice."

Quickly, I follow Jeremiah to the front entrance to meet whoever has come to get him.

I'm shocked, and I feel my adrenaline kick in as I make the short walk down the hall.

"His suit is designer and the man comes from serious money," Marisa whispers, hot on my heels.

I'm just about to ask her what in the world she's talking about when I see him.

It can't be.

But…oh, shit. It is.

Time begins to move in slow motion as I watch the man turn, his gaze fixed on Jeremiah as he approaches. Everything happens as if I'm watching a movie: seeing it, but detached—like I'm only an observer and not in the same room. I'm not five feet away from the man who filled my heart with his love and then crushed it with his silence.

His large hand comes out and clasps Jeremiah's shoulder, shaking him slightly. A line digs deep in between his brows, and I watch as the man I've never wanted to see again is standing in the entryway to my office.

My safe place.

My feet shake in my heels and I reach out to steady myself with one hand on the wall.

"Holy shit," I gasp.

"What?" Marisa asks.

I turn around, hissing at her to be quiet, when that voice…

A voice I loved—a voice I never thought I'd hear again—calls my name. "Talia?"

Chapter Two

Donovan Lore.

The man who slid his cock inside of me—the first person to do so—and whispered my name in the most tender manner.

It can't be him.

But I already know it is.

Closing my eyes, I inhale a deep, steadying breath before letting it out through my lips.

This is really happening.

I can't believe the man who took my virginity and then took off is standing in front of me.

And damn it if he doesn't look even better than he did eight years ago.

His golden brown hair, which reminds me of brown sugar, is perfectly styled and cropped short on the sides, slightly longer on top. His green eyes are staring directly at me. I notice as he drops his gaze and slowly brings it back up until our eyes meet.

I don't know how long we stand in the entryway, the silence and tension growing thicker with each bated breath that pounds wildly in my chest.

I swallow, knowing I need to speak, but words have failed me.

Plastering on my fakest smile, one that instantly begins making my cheeks ache, I take a step toward him and stop. One is enough.

"Hello, Donovan." I watch his gaze dart between me and Jeremiah.

"I'm surprised to see you," he says and his voice is firm. It's also deeper than it used to be, but I'd recognize the timbre of it anywhere.

His presence rattles me to my core, and while there are a

thousand things I could say to him, number one being "I wished I'd never see you again," I stop myself.

This is still my place of business, and I'm a role model for the half-dozen teenagers who are now surreptitiously watching my interaction with this man.

This man who happens to be dressed in a designer charcoal-colored suit, just like Marisa told me. It's not hard to figure out that Jeremiah is related to him in some way, and now I realize why he always held a hint of familiarity.

"You know Jeremiah?" I ask, ignoring the unspoken question in his statement. What am I doing working at a teenage counseling center? He shouldn't be surprised. I always knew I wanted to do something like this with my life. But the fact that he is surprised stings. As if he doesn't remember the times we shared, the nights I lay in his arms and spilled my dreams in whispers.

Donovan looks at Jeremiah. Jeremiah's scowling at Donovan.

Donovan slides his hands into the front pockets of his dress pants. It opens the bottom of his suit coat, and if my eyes were to look lower than his full lips, I'd get a great view of his crotch.

Somehow, I find the willpower to avoid it and keep my eyes on him.

"Yeah," Jeremiah finally huffs, his sarcastic and angry tone clear. "I know him."

Donovan shoots him a look and nods toward the door. "Go get in the car. Bentley's waiting for you."

"Fucking great," Jeremiah grumbles. "Just what I need—a sixty-year-old babysitter."

"If you stayed in school and stopped beating the crap out of everyone—" Donovan stops his rant and scrubs the back of his neck with one hand. He releases an exasperated sigh and Jeremiah rolls his eyes. Donovan's voice is softer when he says, "Just go get in the car, J. We'll talk in a minute."

I'm pretty sure I hear him mutter "fan-fucking-tastic" before he looks back at me. "Bye, Miss Merchant."

I smile and lift my hand. "Manners," I remind him gently.

A slight smile tugs at the edges of his lips, and I know we're both thinking of his cursing.

"See you soon, Jeremiah. Come by whenever."

"That won't be happening," Donovan clips.

With another teenage angst-filled huff, Jeremiah charges past Donovan. The front door bangs against the wall as it opens and then again when it shuts.

I cringe at the sound. I don't have the money to replace the old, rickety door.

"You work here?" Donovan asks when Jeremiah is gone. "Not the place I'd ever expect to see you."

I ignore the faint reminder in his tone that we know one another, and that he's apparently forgotten what's always been important to me.

"Talia started this place three years ago. It's a fantastic and caring place for teens who need some help staying out of trouble to come to. She's done amazing things for the community and for the hundreds of our kids who have walked through these doors since the time we've been open," Marisa says, choosing this moment to speak up.

My mouth is gaping wide by the time she's done rambling.

Shooting her a silencing glare, I look back at Donovan.

"You own this place." It's a statement, not a question, so I don't bother confirming.

"You can go now," I snap, and instantly chastise myself. The last thing I want is for him to know how painful it is to be standing in front of the man I had saved myself for.

What a bunch of crap.

Five months spent dating me, trying to get in my pants—all

ENFLAME 13

while promising he could wait until I was ready—and the second I give it up, thinking I'm falling madly in love with Donovan and that nothing could tear us apart—not the gossip on campus, not the fact that we came from completely different worlds, and not the fact that his mother hated me—he just took off.

I woke up, a tender ache at the apex of my thighs and a smile on my face, only to roll over and find an empty spot next to me.

And I didn't get anything. Not a note. Not a phone call.

Today is the first time I've seen or heard from Donovan Lore since that very night, and the reminder of how much it hurt then, how much that one night changed who I am...

I can't handle it.

"Good day, Donovan." I nod and turn to leave, but my feet freeze when he asks me a question. It's the pain, the hesitancy in his voice that has me stopping and looking at him over my shoulder.

"Does he talk to you? Jeremiah, I mean. Does he say much when he's here?"

"He shows up for a few days every couple of months, bruised and bloody." I arch a brow, silently asking a question.

"Fights at school," Donovan says, and if I'm not mistaken he's trying not to growl at my silent accusation. "I wouldn't touch him."

"I wouldn't know. I don't know a thing about you."

He flinches slightly. I blink, and when my gaze is refocused on him, I see a completely different Donovan in front of me from the one I dated in college and the one I was just speaking to.

His features have hardened and there's a glint in his eye. His gaze drops and rakes down my body as if he's moving in slow motion. I feel it like he's touching me everywhere, even though he's several feet away and a desk separates us.

When he finally blinks, his expression says he's decided

something—only I have no idea what. It seems as if he's just made a plan and chosen a way to accomplish a set of goals all while staring at my body, which is clothed in skinny jeans, high-heeled boots, and a long cream-colored sweater.

He slides a card onto the counter of Marisa's desk and taps it once with his index finger. "If he escapes his driver again, call me."

I'm not given another chance to speak before he turns on his heel and walks out the door.

Marisa hustles to the desk and picks up the card. When she glances at me, our eyes meet and I cringe again. I know exactly what she's seeing.

"You know Donovan Lore? CEO of Lore Enterprises?"

The implication in her tone, coupled with the one arched eyebrow, is clear.

Leaning in, ensuring I keep my voice at a whisper, I hiss, "I am not asking that man for money to save this center. I'd rather lick dirt."

Marisa's eyes sparkle and she waves the card. "How do you know him?"

"I don't." My hands rub the sides of my jeans. My palms are sweaty and hot, and I hate that seeing him for mere minutes can elicit such reactions in my body. My heart is beating fast. My skin feels tight.

It all feels wrong.

"Sure didn't look that way to me," she says, and wiggles her eyebrows.

"This isn't up for discussion." I lift a hand, silencing her just as she opens her mouth. "I'm serious. Donovan Lore will never be discussed inside these walls again."

"Okay." She shrugs and flashes an impish grin. "Want to do dinner tonight?"

A laugh falls from my lips before I can stop it. "No—now get to work."

She huffs but does what she's told.

I return to my office but I can't concentrate.

In truth, it'd be the easiest thing in the world to swallow my pride and contact Lore Enterprises. In addition to being the premier commercial building developer in Grand Rapids, they donate millions of dollars every year toward charities, nonprofits, and helping small businesses succeed.

They are the perfect company to reach out to for funding.

But I'll never do it.

I wasn't lying to Marisa, either, because I don't know Donovan.

It took me weeks to realize after he left school without a word to me that I might have fallen in love with an apparition and not a real man.

It didn't matter that even after I found out his dad had died, and that was most likely the reason for him leaving my bed in the middle of the night, he still never returned my phone calls.

A year later, when he married Cassandra Kyle—the girl who made my life hell on campus while Donovan and I dated—I faced the horrible truth that Donovan was most definitely not the man I thought I had known.

I'd been young, blinded by his looks and his money and his manipulative words.

I was the poor girl, a mechanic's daughter, fighting tooth and nail to keep my academic scholarships so I could stay on campus, praying every semester that the money would come in.

He was the golden boy.

We were never meant to be together, but I'd thrown on my rose-colored glasses and ignored all the odds stacked against us and fallen in love with him anyway, despite the risks.

In the end, I'd been the only one to end up looking like a fool.

* * * * *

"Are you sure you don't need me to come out and see you?" Laurie asks, the concern evident in her voice.

"No." I rub my fingers across my forehead to soothe the tension that's been building all week. I still can't get Donovan out of my head. "I'll be fine, babe. It was just that one run-in."

"Has Jeremiah been back?"

"No."

Which sucks. I want to see him. For the first time, even through his scowls and sighs and teenage angst, I almost felt like he was finally going to begin opening up to me.

"That's too bad," Laurie says, her voice softer. "I can come this weekend, though—take you out and get you drunk so we can forget all about Donovan."

Ugh. That name. My body betrays me, and warms and pulses with indistinguishable lust like it's been doing all week long. I press my thighs together to soothe the slow burn that just thinking of his name causes inside me. Or thinking about the way he looked. Damn.

"How are you and James?" I ask, changing the subject.

Laurie and her husband have had a horrible year. As much as I don't fully believe in everlasting love, they seem to be working on their issues, and the last time I saw them, they looked and acted happy. Every time I talk to Laurie, she says things are continually getting better—although they're still seeing a weekly marriage therapist. They moved back to their hometown of Ann Arbor just over a month ago. I hate not seeing her all the time.

"We're good, I think," she says, her voice taking on a wistful tone.

I laugh. "You're looking at him right now, aren't you?"

"Yeah, we're cooking dinner."

I laugh harder. "You're such a girl, drooling over your husband when he's in the same room."

"I know," she says, and I can practically see her grin widen as she runs her hands through her hair nervously, all while unabashedly staring at James.

"You're a dork. I'll let you go."

A muffled deep voice comes through the background and Laurie comes back on. "Okay, sounds good. But let me know if you need anything, and James said that if you see Donovan again, to let him know and he'll come out and kick his ass."

"Right." Because that'd happen. James is too much of a gentleman—despite his one-night stand with his assistant, who also happened to be a friend of mine and Laurie's—to get in a fistfight. "Tell him thanks, and I'll talk to you later."

After our final goodbyes, I hang up the phone and then collapse onto my couch.

It's old and worn and completely comfortable.

Closing my eyes, I have to fight the vision of Donovan standing at the center. That suit. Those penetrating eyes. The slightly crooked nose and strong jaw. The hint of scruff on his jaw that said he'd shaved that morning and would need to do it again the next day.

"Shit," I whisper, aware my hands have taken on a mind of their own and I'm squeezing my full breasts while I picture him.

One hand trails slowly down my stomach. I squirm from my own ticklish touch.

I shouldn't be doing this, but it wouldn't be the first time. I've masturbated to thoughts of Donovan Lore all week.

Damn him and his sexiness.

As my hand slides lower, beneath the waistband of my tight

yoga shorts, the fingers of my other hand begin teasing my nipple beneath my lace bra.

"Oh," I groan as my fingers find my warm, wet center. My finger slides easily through my folds, and my hips arch into the arousing touch.

Donovan. His voice. His strong hands. The way the suit fit him like it'd been made for him.

I almost laugh. With the amount of money he has, it probably was.

My fingers keep moving, teasing my nipples with one hand, alternating breasts, and I slide two fingers of my other hand inside my swollen, sensitive flesh.

I rock my hips, press my thumb against my clit, and it doesn't take long—moments—until I'm making myself whimper, my body shivers, and I come…thinking of Donovan and what it would feel like if it were his hands…his cock…his tongue doing all the work instead.

I squeeze my eyes closed as the tremors leave my body and my chin drops to my chest.

I'm sick of this.

I need to get laid. Find someone else to take my mind off the damn man.

Donovan Lore will never be an option for me again. Hell, besides the fact that he's married, he'd never want someone like me. He made that clear eight years go.

Pushing off the couch, I head to the restroom to clean up.

My cheeks are flushed, and I take a few minutes after I wash my hands to splash cold water on my face and fix my ponytail, redoing it so it sits at the base of my neck. The few strands that escaped earlier are slicked back into place.

I'm drying my hands in my small hall bathroom when the buzz of my doorbell echoes in my quiet house.

I frown into the bathroom mirror, my heart skipping a beat.

Wondering who it could be, I quickly hurry to the front door.

I live in an older neighborhood in Denton. The houses are small, and most are showing signs of their age at over fifty years old. A lot of my neighbors are either retired or getting close to that age, but I like that it's quiet and safe.

But it also means that sometimes the older ladies like to stop by and keep a young, single woman company. Usually that makes me laugh. They're so certain I'm lonely, living all alone without a man to take care of me. Since my dad's stroke, visitors have come more frequently, and while unnecessary, I actually appreciate the company.

Especially Mrs. Bartol. She's seventy-two and seems to have an uncanny ability to know when I need a glass—or a bottle—of wine. At least once a month she shows up on a late Saturday morning with mimosa fixings in her hands, and we spend the day talking and drinking.

I pretty much want to be her when I grow up.

Lost in thoughts of Mrs. Bartol and our last mimosa-drinking day, where she waxed poetic about the pros and cons of her husband's little blue pills—something I didn't need to know—I forget to check the window next to my door to see who my visitor could be.

When I open it, I'm shocked to see Marisa standing on my front porch step.

"Hey," I say, my voice showing my surprise. "What are you doing here?"

I push open the storm door and wave her in.

The fall breeze is kicking up and it's chilly outside. I quickly shut the doors, shivering from the cold wind.

"I had to talk to you," she says, unwrapping her gray-and-white checkered scarf from around her neck.

Her fingers are shaking as she does it, and by the tone in her voice, I don't think she's just cold.

"What is it?" I back up to give her more room...

She digs through her purse and whips out a folded sheet of paper.

"This." She shoves it into my hands. "Why didn't you tell me we've found funding?"

My head jerks back and the paper in my hand crinkles. "What?"

She points to the paper in my hand. "That. I was running the bank statements before I left work and that…" she waves her index finger back and forth, "came in right before closing time today."

"I have no idea what you're talking about," I mutter, and unfold the paper.

I hear Marisa following me as I head to the kitchen to get us a drink.

My eyes scan the top of the statement from our bank account, glancing over today's date.

"Holy shit," I mutter as my own fingers begin trembling.

With widened eyes, I snap my gaze to Marisa. Her expression is a mixture of excited and wary.

"What the hell?" I ask, as if she knows.

"I know. One million dollars."

I shake my head and glare at the paper, as if inspecting all the zeros on my bank statement will give me answers.

"Who did this?" I ask, and thrust it in her direction.

"I thought you would know."

I don't. I have no idea. In fact, before I left the center early this afternoon, I had just been declined funding from the last foundation I could think of to contact.

I came home with no hope of the center remaining open after next month.

ENFLAME 21

I'd almost drowned my sorrows and self-pity in a vat of wine, but thankfully I had held off.

If I was drunk right now, I'd be certain I was hallucinating Marisa's visit. As it is, I want to pinch myself to see if I'm still awake.

"Wow." I shake my head, completely stunned. "Did you call the bank?"

"It was an anonymous wire transfer."

It doesn't make sense. I arch a brow in question. "Can people really do that?"

"I guess." Her slow shoulder shrug speaks volumes.

Neither of us know what in the hell is going on, but I can't take the money without knowing who it's from.

It's my experience that nothing comes without a price.

"Hmm." I run my finger along the large sum in the deposit column.

This potentially changes everything for me. For my dad. For the kids.

Accepting it's Friday night and I won't find answers anytime soon, I set the statement on the counter, smoothing out the wrinkles.

"We'll figure this out next week," I say, looking at Marisa. Her eyes dart from the paper to meet my gaze, my lips slowly stretching into a small grin. "Until then, I say we celebrate."

Chapter Three

I sway slightly on my feet and wave goodbye to Mrs. Bartol. I can't help but grin as I watch her slowly shuffle down my driveway. My smile is slow and I'm a little bit drunk.

We spent the morning gorging ourselves on mimosas and a breakfast that tasted like heaven. Or bacon-wrapped tater tots.

Amazing.

My stomach is full and warm and slightly bloated, but I don't care.

Between Marisa's visit Friday night, nursing my hangover yesterday, and my morning today spent with Mrs. Bartol discussing the benefits of penile implants, I have heard more than I needed to, and drunk way more than my limit.

I also feel more relaxed than I have in months—the bank statement that's now posted on my fridge helps ease the burden and weight I've been carrying on my shoulders.

"Don't forget!" Mrs. Bartol turns around and shouts as she reaches the end of my driveway, her finger waggling in my direction. "You need to use what the Good Lord gave ya before you get all rusted and forget how everything works. No man likes a woman's girly parts to be filled with cobwebs."

"Right." I nod, equally mortified and amused that she's shouting this while Mr. Enoch next door is pulling weeds from a flower bed. He raises his bald head in my direction, looks at Mrs. Bartol over his shoulder, and then shakes his head, returning to the task at hand. Apparently everyone in the neighborhood is accustomed to Mrs. Bartol and her sex talks.

I smile, because the woman can talk about Viagra, blowjobs, and penile implants, but she can't say "vagina" or "pussy."

I wave her off, ensuring her I'll go out and practice soon, when my eyebrows dart up my forehead.

A black car with the telltale Bentley insignia slows down and waits for Mrs. Bartol to cross the street. As soon as she does, and I'm about to shut the door, I pause as it slowly pulls into my driveway.

My heart stutters in my chest as the car stops. I take in the darkened windows that don't allow me to see anything except a glimpse of the driver.

My brow knits together and a feeling of unease rolls through me when the car turns off and the back door opens.

My fingers dig into the wood door and I fling my other hand to the doorframe, bracing myself.

I watch as Donovan Lore steps out of the backseat.

I have a split second to realize I'm slightly drunk at eleven o'clock in the morning. My hair is pulled into a messy, knotted bun on the top of my head. I have no makeup on, and my clothes—which are completely not presentable for public viewing—are in direct contrast to the suit Donovan is wearing.

He saunters up to me, his lips pulling to the side, and I watch as his eyes drop to my pink-painted toes and then slowly rise, taking in every inch of me.

Nervous bumps flare all over my skin as his eyes rake up my body, and when he meets my own eyes, which are narrowed on him, he gives a slight nod, seemingly enjoying what he sees.

"Good morning, Talia."

His voice. It instantly reminds me of my fantasies I've had of him—the way I pleasured myself, thinking of my name rolling off his luscious pink lips. My cheeks warm, the light fall breeze unable to soothe my rapidly heating skin.

Damn it.

Barely finding my voice, I ask, "What the hell are you doing here? And how in the hell do you know where I live?"

He smirks, his lips twisting, and oh, my God…

As he stares at me, taking in my flushed cheeks, all I can think of is… Can he tell what I'm remembering?

No.

There's no way.

His eyes narrow and his lips spread into an arrogant smile.

Asshole.

"Google."

"What?" My hand tightens on my door. I lean against it slowly, needing it to help hold me up. My legs are suddenly trembling and my heart begins a staccato beat against my ribs.

"I looked you up online," he says.

Oh. He's answering my question.

What question was that? I must be drunker than I thought or… shit. The man is making me stupid.

"Can I come in?"

He's already taken over my office, because I haven't been able to work or think clearly all week long while I was at the center.

No way in hell am I letting him in here.

"No," I snap, knowing I sound pissy. I don't care. "I want you to go."

His expression doesn't change. There's still a cocky grin on his face and his eyes sparkle with interest.

"I have a proposition for you."

My stomach flips, butterflies taking root. A throb starts pulsing at the apex of my thighs.

"What?" I ask, and my voice breaks. My knuckles ache from clenching the door so tightly.

He swallows and I watch the slow, delicious journey of his Adam's apple. God, he's so damn sexy.

Sexier than he was in college, for sure.

I've never met a man I could compare to the asshole in front of me.

Yet he's different now, too—harder, maybe. More serious. The Donovan I remember used to laugh frequently and smile easily. This version of him seems way too uptight.

"Let me in, Talia. And I'll tell you how I plan on saving your business."

"What?" My head snaps back. "How did you...what are you...?"

I'm saved from my stuttering when he simply smirks.

I want to slap his cocky expression off his face. But then his gaze drops, his eyes narrow, and any appreciation he might have had toward me disappears.

Just like my resolve when he mentions saving my business.

Because I suddenly know, without him having to say it, that he's the one who deposited that asinine amount of money into my bank account.

And I know, as I pull the door open, lifting my hand and allowing him to enter...

I was right.

Nothing is given for free.

* * * * *

Trailing behind Donovan as he enters my house, I watch him out of the corner my eye as he silently peruses the small space. At the same time, his presence seems to suck all the oxygen out of the room and replace it with strong pheromones that seem to scream sex. I can suddenly taste it in the air. Feel it against my skin.

Hear it thrum in my ears.

Sex. Sex. Sex. Naughty, angry, passionate sex. Revenge sex. Hot sex.

It's all I can think about as I leave Donovan in the living room where his gaze roams over every surface, seeming to take in my old furniture, shelves of books, paintings and decorations that line the space.

I like clutter.

It makes me feel like I have company.

I've always loved my house, but seeing Donovan in it makes me feel something different—defensive, maybe. Or protective.

I grew up with a mom and dad who lived paycheck to paycheck my entire life. When my mom died when I was only twelve, it was just my dad, and he somehow made those paychecks continue to stretch even without my mom's nursing income.

Donovan grew up in the land of nannies, housekeepers, chauffeurs, and trust funds.

He's never had to worry about money a day in his life, where I've never gone a day without.

"Want anything to drink?" I call from the kitchen. I can no longer see him, but I can still feel his presence hanging in my house like a thick, lust-filled cloud. "I've got whiskey, beer, water—"

"Water," he says, appearing in the doorway to my small galley kitchen and cutting me off. "Just water."

I notice my fingers trembling while I grab two glasses, fill them with ice cubes, and pour water from the filtered pitcher in my refrigerator.

He takes the glass I hand him, and my breath hitches as his fingers dance over mine—just a whisper of a touch—and my lips part. The zing of electricity spreads up my arm and slams into my chest.

Damn it. He still affects me just as much as he did when I was twenty.

"Living room?" I ask, pressing the cooling glass to my lips.

Hopefully the cold water will calm my racing heart.

"After you," he says. With a lift of his arm, he gestures for me to take the lead and I do, walking down the small hall into the living room. I stare at the couch, the place where just the other night, I got off thinking about him. I quickly slide into an oversized chair that faces the couch.

No way can I sit there.

Setting down his glass on a coaster on my coffee table, I see one side of his lips twitch, like he knows what I've done.

"Why are you here?" I ask.

He leans back on the couch, casually drapes one foot over his other knee, and spreads his arms wide on the back of my couch.

I arch a brow. "Settling in for the day?"

"I think this conversation might take a while. Might as well make myself comfortable."

I take another gulp from my water. The ice isn't helping. The fact that he's wearing an obviously tailor-made suit, and then runs his hand through his wheat-colored hair before dropping it back to the couch, makes everything worse.

Spread out on my furniture, he looks like a formidable opponent. A god.

Trouble.

"Suit yourself. Want to start talking so we can get this over with?"

He ignores me, his gaze roaming the knick-knacks that cover my fireplace mantle. They're nothing special, most of them artwork and silly creations some of my kids have made for me at the center during arts-and-crafts time. Some of them are brought from school projects.

I love them.

"This is a nice place you have here."

I scoff and roll my eyes. "Please. Your guesthouse is probably bigger than my house."

My sarcastic comment earns me a wicked smile. "Doing drive-bys on my house?"

"You wish," I mutter, and clamp my lips shut.

I don't want flirty, sassy banter with Donovan. I want him to tell me why he's here so he can get the hell out.

We're silent for several moments, him staring at me, daring me to ask...when I finally cave.

With a frustrated sigh, I lean back in the chair. "How did you know about my business?"

One side of his nose twitches and he leans forward, resting his elbows on his knees, hands clasped casually together. "I told you: Google."

"Google knows the financial status of my nonprofit organization?"

His lips press into a line, and he shoots me a look that tells me precisely what he thinks of my sarcasm. "Google told me that you own the center and I looked into it, for Jeremiah's sake."

Hearing the boy's name causes my heart to stir. I shouldn't have favorites, but damn it, I do. And he's one of them.

I arch a brow. "What difference does it make? Didn't you tell him he can't come back?"

With one hand, he scrubs his chin and his cheek. I hear the quiet scratch of his stubble against his skin and my body tingles. I wonder if his scruff would be scratchy or erotic if he were to run his jaw along my inner thighs.

Stupid body.

"I want to save your center," he says, his green eyes on me once again.

"Why?"

"Because I looked into your history and you do good work. And apparently Jeremiah feels safe going there, talking to you. Not that I'm surprised," he says, his eyes softening and his smile turning wistful. "You were always a pleasure to be around."

I focus on keeping my breathing calm, collected.

The man undoes me. Reminders of our past aren't helping.

Donovan used to say that I was the only person who got him—truly understood him. With me, he was free to be himself instead of living up to the expectations his parents—mostly his mother—placed on him.

His father may have been CEO, but his mother was the boss.

"Don't do that," I whisper harshly. Embarrassment floods my blood that I'm becoming emotional, but I look away from him.

"Don't do what, T? Remind you of how good we were? I miss you."

I flinch at the nickname he used to call me. His admission shocks me to my core. Heat bursts on my skin, and I close my eyes before opening them slowly, erasing any emotion, any painful memory his words incite.

With my heartbeat thundering against my ribcage, I hope my words are professional and cool when I turn back to him. "What do you want in exchange for saving my center?"

Because nothing is free. Not in the Lores' world.

I prepare myself for the answer, my fingers gripping my glass until my knuckles ache.

"You," he says, and even though it was what I assumed he would say, I'm still shocked. "For thirty days."

Disgust at his words makes my lip curl.

"I may be the poor girl you went slumming with," I say, leaning forward. Screw professional and calm: this man hurt me more than anyone else in my life. "But I am not, and have never been, a whore."

"You weren't someone I went slumming with." The words roll off his tongue as if he's enraged. His jaw is tight and his teeth clench together. His hands ball into fists. "And while I plan to have you again, and I don't plan on waiting long for that to happen, I need help with Jeremiah, and you seem to be the only person he trusts."

My mind swirls, and the room shifts and spins.

I push to my feet quickly, intent on getting some space. Getting away from him.

I can help Jeremiah. I can't even begin to fathom the rest of what Donovan just spoke so confidently.

"No," I say, raising a hand to stop him from moving when he stands from the couch and matches my stance. "Just…give me a minute."

My voice drops and shakes. I hate it.

I hate that even though what he's said should repulse me, I know if I were to close my eyes and imagine…I want that, too.

Maybe what he's offering isn't such a bad thing.

I can take thirty days. Save my company. Help Jeremiah. And screw Donovan out of my system.

This time for good.

As the thoughts roll through my mind, I quickly weigh the pros and cons.

The con being my heart will most likely end up shattered at the end, despite my barely there confidence that I can do this. My body shouts Yes! Heavens to Betsy! Sleep with this man again!

And just like that…my pulse speeds. My nipples harden and tingle with anticipation.

I walk toward my fireplace, needing space from Donovan although I can feel his stare at my back.

Running my fingers over ugly ceramic bowls that were carved by small hands and aren't large enough to hold anything other than a few pennies, I think of the smiles on my kids' faces when they bring me a gift. When they ace a test I helped them study for.

When they come in, tears in their eyes, and just need a hug and some quiet time. I think of the kids who we've gotten off the streets, into loving foster homes, and away from homes filled with physical and emotional abuse—not to mention drugs and alcohol.

I can't lose what I've worked so hard for.

And with my father's health, the cost of his nursing facility, and a large bill looming, weighing down my shoulders—

I have no choice but to accept his offer.

"What did you have in mind?" I ask, turning to him and crossing my arms over my chest.

Tears burn in the backs of my eyes because even though I haven't admitted it, I've just essentially agreed to sell my body.

And yet there's no other choice.

I'm also not nearly as disgusted with the idea as I let on.

I want him—at least for sex.

Donovan licks his lips and his shoulders drop marginally, relaxing. As if maybe he thought I'd say no. "Do you remember my sister?"

I shake my head. "No, I never had the pleasure."

My words are clipped and I don't feel guilty. Donovan never took me home to meet his family, always saying he was protecting me from them, not the other way around. But I felt hidden and I hated it. At least until the day his mom walked in on us at his off-campus apartment early one Sunday morning.

We hadn't even had sex yet, but the assumption on her face was clear.

I can still vividly remember the proverbial steam flying from her ears when she caught sight of him with someone "like me."

He slowly pushes his hands onto his hips, rocks on his heels. He looks away from me for a moment before meeting my gaze again. "She died three years ago. Car accident. Took her, her husband, and their youngest child. Jeremiah was the only one to survive."

My fingers fly to my mouth and I gasp. "That's...I'm sorry. I never heard."

"You wouldn't. Emily's husband was drunk as a skunk, two times over the legal limit, and it happened near Lansing. My mother paid a hefty penny to keep that suppressed from local news."

It doesn't surprise me. But still...Jeremiah. "Was he in the car?"

Donovan nods slowly. "He suffered a concussion, but the rest weren't so fortunate."

"I'm so sorry," I say again, because what else can you say to that? I know Donovan really loved and admired his older sister.

"Yes, well," he pauses and blinks, as if erasing a memory, "Jeremiah's a wreck, and even though I've tried to reach him, it doesn't seem to help. He's constantly in trouble at school, ditching curfew, and is essentially a pain in my ass. I need help, and I've exhausted every possible option. Which is where you come in."

"What do you want from me?"

Donovan smirks. My cheeks flush as I realize the double entendre in my words.

"With Jeremiah," I clarify quickly.

"Of course," he murmurs, but his eyes darken and he takes a step toward me. "I want you to stay with me. Move into my house for thirty days and be there for Jeremiah. He can come to the center after school and hang out with you, and then his driver will bring you home at night. He'll also be taking you to work in the morning so I know you're both safe."

By the time he's done talking, he's standing directly in front of me.

I have to tilt my head back to maintain eye contact. He's so close...smells so good...looks so...perfect.

My heart dips, my brain turns to mush, and my hormones go berserk.

I want him.

I always have.

There was probably a reason why no other man I've been with has been able to erase Donovan's memory from my mind.

They simply don't measure up.

"You're awfully bossy," I mutter, trying to lighten the sexual tension sparking between us. I can feel it. I can practically taste it when he licks his lips and they spread into a wide grin.

"I like being in control."

Wetness seeps into my panties and I resist the urge to press my thighs together. There's an ache building that I can't deny.

"What about your wife?" I flinch at the question, the words falling from my throat. A cheese grater on my skin would be more comfortable than asking this question, but I need to know. I may be agreeing to whore myself out, but I'm not a mistress.

He grimaces and runs his hand through his short hair. He grimaces. "Cassandra is…Cassandra."

I take a step back. "That doesn't answer my question."

"It's complicated."

"Are you still married?" I ask, my lips twisting into a sneer.

"Separated, papers filed. Divorce is inevitable."

I don't apologize. He wouldn't believe me if I did.

He appears to be honest. I hate that we're even discussing this. Discussing her.

"Cassandra didn't take well to the fact that I was given custody of Jeremiah. Let's just say she didn't make the adjustment easier for either of us, and after a while I finally realized that she always has been, and always will be, a bigger hassle than she's worth."

I frown, not understanding.

I try not to care and change the subject.

"So thirty days of being with Jeremiah and you save my center. Is that it?" I tilt my head to the side.

Donovan chuckles. That deep, quiet rumble that leaves his lips and hits me straight in my gut. God, he's sexy.

I hate that my body responds so easily to him.

"No," he says, and raises his hand. His thumb brushes across my cheek to my chin, which he grips lightly but firmly between his thumb and forefinger. "That's not all I want." His eyes seem to assess me and his pupils dilate. His own cheeks show a hint of pink.

I swallow thickly. "What else?"

He leans in and brushes his lips against the very corner of my lips, and his tongue comes out, tasting my skin before he pulls back. With his large, warm frame in front of me, his gaze holding mine captive, and his fingers still on my chin, I'm unable to move away from him.

I don't know if I want to.

"We'll save that for another time," he whispers and drops his hand.

Goose bumps flare on my skin, which is instantly cooling from the loss of contact.

"So what now?" I ask as he takes a few steps away and I regain the ability to speak.

"Yesterday, one million dollars were wired to your bank account. You will receive another million at the end of the thirty days."

My eyes fly open. "That's way more than I've been trying to fundraise. I don't need that much."

I should be angry. He essentially bought and paid for me without discussing this with me, and his proposition is insane. Yet there are benefits to it, and I'll do almost anything to save my dad and the center.

Two million dollars is way too much money. It's enough to keep the center running for at least five years with no further outside funding. I shake my head. I can't believe this.

"You will move into my house. My driver, Bentley, will arrive tomorrow morning, so have everything you need packed and ready to go because you won't be returning. For the next thirty days, you'll essentially be Jeremiah's in-house therapist and nanny, but for crying out loud, don't tell him I just called you that. He'd be pissed." A slight smile forms on his lips.

"You like him."

"I love him," he states, and his words are crisp and clear. "It's my job to take care of him. It's what Emily wanted, and unfortunately I've been fucking it up left and right. But I have a feeling you can help us with that."

His slight smirk makes me smile. I like seeing this side of Donovan—so determined to win Jeremiah's approval.

"What's really been wrong with him? Is there anything I need to know specifically?"

He shoots me a look that tells me pretty much everything is wrong before he sighs.

"He likes you, if he keeps returning to your center—that's all I know. And I'm willing to do anything, use any resource at my disposal, to ensure he stays out of trouble." He pauses, chews on his bottom lip, and continues. "I think with your past experience with your mom, you have the ability to understand him more than anyone else."

My eyes widen for a brief moment. I'm surprised he remembers how my mom died.

The memory of her funeral, of life without her at such a young age, and memories of seeing Jeremiah in my office bloody and broken send a pang to my chest that I can't ignore.

I nod my acceptance. "Okay, then. I'll do it. For Jeremiah's sake and the center."

"And me?" he asks. His voice rolls over my skin even though he's several feet away. "I really did miss you. I've thought about you often over the years, wishing things would have been different. And I haven't been able to stop thinking about you all week."

"Stop," I whisper, shaking my head. His honesty is too much. Makes me feel too much. If I'm going to have any chance of getting through thirty days with Donovan, my heart needs to remain unattached.

Before I can step away, he closes the distance and his hand is at the nape of my neck, his fingers in my hair. He leans down and brushes his lips down my jaw—not kissing me, just...grazing my skin.

I sigh and lean into his touch.

"I'll have you again, Talia. And I won't wait long."

With that, his hand drops and he takes several steps away, toward the front door.

"There's one thing," I say, as he's walking away.

He stops and looks at me over his shoulder, arching a brow.

"You mentioned your driver taking me to and from work, but I need access to my car during the day.

"Bentley will take you wherever you need to go."

There are things I need to do—mostly visiting my dad—that I don't need him knowing about.

"I will only agree to this if I can have access to my car whenever I need it. Bentley can take me home from work with Jeremiah, but he can follow me in my own car. I won't give up my independence and my responsibilities for the next thirty days."

I watch as he figures out a way to get what he wants. His eyes question me, studying me, before he finally nods. "Fine. We'll figure something out."

I follow him to the door, feeling oddly misplaced in my own

home.

Everything has changed in the span of an hour.

It's obvious he wants me. He's made that clear.

So when we get to the door, him casually standing on the threshold with his hands shoved into the front pockets of his pants, I can't figure out why he's not trying…why he's not taking me now.

I'm not even sure I want him to try.

But then he leans in, his lips at my ear. "Do not mistake my patience tonight for lack of interest. But the next time I have you, it will be the way I want it…where and when."

He pulls back and our gazes meet. My lips part and my skin flushes.

He simply smiles and taps my nose with his finger. "Tomorrow. Be ready."

Tomorrow, I mouth, right before he turns to walk away. Because somehow, my speech has evaporated along with my common sense.

I just sold my time and my body for two million dollars.

It changes everything for me professionally.

It changes everything for my dad.

And as I walk through my house, putting the glasses in my sink and slowly slinking into my bed for a sudden but much-needed nap, I have no doubt that the next thirty days will change my entire life.

I just hope it doesn't end up ruined, with my heart in shattered pieces like eight years ago, when my time with Donovan came to an end.

Chapter Four

I have been on pins and needles all day, unable to focus on work or my time with my father, dreading and preparing for this very moment. I wanted to be angry with Donovan for practically forcing me into this position. But in reality, my lack of options to save my company and keep my father in a just-barely-adequate nursing care facility wasn't his problem.

He has only offered me the solution.

Now, a thrill of nervous anticipation trickles down my spine as I follow Bentley up a secluded and curved driveway.

Ironically, Bentley is driving a car bearing his same name. I had snorted when I walked outside my office after work to see a sixty-year-old man wearing simply khaki pants and a pressed white shirt, standing next to the same vehicle that had appeared in my driveway yesterday.

As I pull my car to a stop behind the black car and watch as he exits it to walk toward mine, I am suddenly terrified by the solution that Donovan has provided for me.

Yet my body feels primed, looking forward to my first interaction with him.

I'd be lying if I said I hadn't dreamed of him last night, wondering how far his control—that he'd insinuated he had—extended.

In the bedroom? Or just the boardroom?

"Knock it off, moron," I scold myself as Bentley gently opens my door. I smile up at him and swing my legs to the pavement. My ankles teeter on my heels and I slowly inhale a calming breath through my nose. "Thank you."

"Anytime, Miss Merchant."

"Talia, please," I say with a smile.

Bentley nods. Somehow, I have a feeling I will be hearing Miss Merchant frequently in his presence.

As I exit my car, Bentley waves toward the front of Donovan's house. "Mr. Lore is expecting you."

I spin on my heels, thankful my legs aren't trembling like my heart seems to be with its wild fluttering.

Donovan stands at the top of a small brick staircase wearing another black suit that was made for his body.

With another fortifying breath, I calmly walk across the driveway, my gaze wandering as I finally take a minute to survey my home for the next thirty days. The yard is lush and green, and gorgeous landscaping frames the front of the house, with plants and shrubbery in vibrant colors.

A small part of me is impressed as I take in the house and the attached four-car garage. While the home seems large, it isn't overly intimidating—not like the mansion I know Donovan grew up in. He used to tell me that even he could get lost inside his own house as a child. He said it would take his nanny hours to find him, especially when he began using the secret passageways and hidden doorways. I always assumed he grew up in something akin to a castle. While there is no mistaking that this home in front of me, with large peaked gables and a combination of brick and rock on the front, is way outside my price range even in my wildest dreams, it doesn't seem as extravagant as I expected.

"Does it meet your approval?" Donovan asks as I near him, one eyebrow raised in amusement.

His calmness and playful tone help slow my racing pulse.

My lips twist and I look up at the enormous window over the front door. I drop my gaze and meet his sparkling green eyes as I shrug, looking unimpressed. "It'll do, I suppose. No guesthouse, though."

He laughs softly and shakes his head. "No, no guest house." Turning, he opens his front door and gestures for me to enter. "Welcome to my home."

His lips are still tilted up in amusement and I wonder if I'm missing a hidden joke, but I follow him, my hands clasped together in front of me, and look around the warm house.

It feels cozy despite its size, and when I see the windows on the far side of the house, my breath stills in my chest.

I can see nothing except Lake Michigan, and the view is spectacular. The early fall's setting sun casts a colorful hue over the massive lake. Sailboats and barges sprinkle the water's surface, and the sky is alight with shades of oranges and purples as it spreads across the horizon and peeks through the clouds.

"Wow, this is beautiful." My feet move forward of their own accord. Behind me, I hear the gentle click of the door shutting and a string of beeps that I assume is a security system. There is no other noise in the vast space besides my pulse thrumming in my ears.

"We have a private beach below," he says, his voice quiet. I catch his reflection in the window as he walks up behind me. His hands hang loosely at his sides and his eyes crinkle with something I can't place.

"Did you build this house?" I ask, still stunned by the gorgeous view. It's so peaceful, and I can tell the water is far below us. In fact, just past the edge of the deck outside, all I see are the tops of trees until the water, and just the very edge of a dock.

The house is high and must be built on a bluff.

"No. Fortunately it came on the market at the right time."

"Well." I slowly turn around to take in the rest of the space. I immediately notice the walls are warm browns, and there's a chocolate brown leather sectional that can probably seat twelve, that sits in the center of the room, taking up almost the entire, vast space. There's artwork and potted plants in the corner, and built-in shelves with books, but what I notice as I see the living room and the formal dining area is a complete lack of any personal effects.

Everything seems staged by a designer, and even though the space feels warm and homey, it doesn't reflect Donovan at all.

At least not how I remember Donovan being from when we were younger.

"Where's Jeremiah?"

He didn't stop by the center today and I had been expecting him. The fact that he's not here, either, concerns me.

Donovan doesn't seem as affected.

His hands slide into his front pockets. "He's in the game room. I can take you to him, unless there's something else you want to do first."

I understand the implication in his husky tone.

My body responds with a flutter low in my stomach.

"I'd like to see the game room," I say, my voice breathy, as if I've just finished a kickboxing workout. I can't pull my gaze away from Donovan as he walks closer to me. He reaches out his hand and his knuckles brush along my jaw.

Hairs spike at the back of my neck and I suck my lip in between my teeth.

"It's nice to know," he says, and brushes his lips against my ear, "that you're more affected by me than you let on."

My lip curls into a sneer. "I promised to help with Jeremiah, and that's all."

We both know I'm lying. It's clear in the way I find myself leaning into him. My hand lands just above his hip and my fingers dig into his suit coat, holding me up.

"I know. You're not being paid for your time with me. That will happen naturally."

I scowl, hating that I know it will. But I'm committed to doing everything necessary to not only get Donovan out of my system once and for all, but save my dad and my business. "We'll discuss this later."

His mouth drags down my jaw, following the line his knuckles did moments ago. I can't hide the shiver that courses through me, and I inhale a quick, needy breath of air.

"We'll be doing more than discussing later," he assures me.

I close my eyes and swallow thickly. I can only nod as Donovan moves away, his hands and lips drifting away from my skin.

I look up at him through lust-filled, half-lidded eyes. I don't say anything as he turns and gestures for me to walk with him.

I follow as he gives me a tour of his house, where I see five different bedrooms, an indoor two-lane gun range, two different kitchens, three laundry rooms, and a bar that rivals anything I've seen on Beacon Street in downtown Denton.

I wasn't told which bedroom would be mine as we walked through the upstairs hallway, but I definitely noticed that while Jeremiah's room is on one end of the massive hallway with four other bedrooms close to his, Donovan's is clear down at the end of the hallway and around a corner.

The gorgeous lake views can be seen from almost every room in the house, through floor-to-ceiling windows.

It's too big for one or two people, yet it's not pretentious at all. Whoever Donovan hired to decorate it made it completely feel like a family home. But what makes me sad as we walk through the house is the complete lack of anything personal.

There still isn't a single picture in sight.

By the time we reach the game room, from which I hear the distinctive sounds of zombies moaning, I'm entirely enamored with this place.

"Jeremiah," Donovan calls, and raps his knuckles twice on the door as we enter. "Miss Merchant is here."

Jeremiah doesn't show any hint that he's going to acknowledge Donovan's statement. I don't let it stop me from entering the room and taking a spot in the gaming chair next to him. There are three rows of leather chairs, each row with five seats. An armrest with cupholders separates the black leather chairs.

Focusing on the real reason I'm here, I ignore the way I can feel Donovan's stare burning a hole into the back of my head as he watches me walk away and slide into a chair next to Jeremiah.

Tugging on my feet, I curl them under me and rest an elbow on the armrest.

"Controller?" I ask, after Jeremiah's shot and stabbed a small horde of six zombies.

Without saying a word, he reaches over, lifts something on his armrest, snaps it closed, and hands me the Xbox controller.

He pauses the game and gives me just enough time to join in.

After we kill another group of the moaning, slow-walking beasts, and do this while we both somehow step on a trap and end up hanging upside down from ropes tied around our ankles, Jeremiah raises his right fist and puts it close to me.

I take the silent signal and return the fist-bump. Out of the corner of my eye, I see the outer edges of his eyes crinkle, his lips pressed together as he fights back a smile.

And suddenly, I can see an uncanny resemblance to Donovan. How I didn't recognize it earlier, I have no idea. Perhaps because I never would have thought that for the last couple of years, the wealthy young boy that showed up at my center was in any way connected to someone from my past.

Looking in the other direction over my shoulder, I catch Donovan still standing in the doorway, his arms crossed over his chest, a visible line between his brow.

I raise my controller. "Wanna play with us?"

His nose twitches. Next to me, Jeremiah scoffs.

"I'll go prepare dinner. It will be ready in thirty minutes." Donovan's chin dips and his gaze pierces me with an intensity I don't understand. "Don't be late," he clips, and turns on his heel, leaving the room and disappearing from sight.

"Well, he got grumpy," I mutter when I'm facing the large screen again.

"Uncle D is always grumpy. And he thinks video games are a waste of perfectly usable brain cells."

Hm. As I listen to Jeremiah's voice, I catch the sad tone. But there's more to it than that. He sounds lonely and frustrated.

I can't push him tonight, but the small hints into what he's struggling with help me mentally create a plan of attack for the next thirty days. I can't imagine what it's like to not only lose your family, but to be with them when it happened.

I also can't imagine what it's like to suddenly wake up and have to live with Donovan. But if he's correct and Cassandra never changed or grew up, I can imagine how wretchedly horrible she was to Jeremiah.

She was always a selfish bitch, wanting all attention on her at all times.

If Jeremiah came along and disrupted that, then there would have been hell to pay.

Forcing myself back into the game, Jeremiah and I spend the next twenty minutes killing zombies and trying to save the world from a complete zombie apocalypse.

I might not be able to do that in real life, but while we don't talk at all while we play, I do have a better idea of how to save Jeremiah.

* * * * *

I have never sat through a more uncomfortable dinner. There was tenseness through the entire meal that I have never experienced in my life.

Between Jeremiah's obvious scowls and displeasured snorts when asked a direct question by Donovan, and Donovan's tight jaw and white-knuckled grip on his silverware in response, even I was on edge by the time the meal was done and Jeremiah was excused to his bedroom for his homework.

I did learn, however, that he's on thin ice with his private school for getting in too many fights—although the cause of those fights wasn't discussed.

It seems as if Donovan is trying to build a relationship with his nephew, and Jeremiah is fighting it. It saddens me to think that this has been their life for the last three years, and my compassion for both of them grows with each passing cold and tense minute.

It's after Jeremiah is done with his homework—which I check for him and almost give myself a migraine with his algebra homework—that I leave him alone when he tells me he's going to read before he has to go to bed.

At first I thought he was lying, or that reading was code for video games, but my smile grew when he held up The Scorch Trials, the second book in a popular teenage dystopian series.

Now I'm in the living room, my feet curled under me on the large and comfortable couch, sipping a glass of red wine and watching the flames flicker in the fireplace. It's not a cold night, but with the large room and the vaulted ceiling that opens above to a walkway separating the bedrooms upstairs, the room is a bit chilly. I was thankful when Donovan started a fire before excusing himself to get some work done.

I've been trying to read my own book, a paranormal romance involving a vampire hunter, but failing to focus for the last thirty minutes.

My heart hurts for Jeremiah. I don't make it a secret to any child who comes into my center that I've suffered my own loss.

My mom was a neonatal nurse and worked three twelve-hour overnight shifts a week so she could be home with me during the day and after school. I remember how she would drag herself in through the front door as I was eating my breakfast in the morning with dark circles under her eyes and her hair disheveled.

She would kiss my father goodbye as he left for work, and then turn her smile toward me.

She always smiled, even when exhausted from long shifts. I will never be able to forget how much she loved me as well as the world around her.

She used to say that helping other people bring babies into the world was her honor—to have been given the gift of seeing miracles happen every single day.

I blink away the tears that fill my eyes, and open them only to jerk back in surprise when I see Donovan at the bottom of the stairs. His hand is on the railing and his eyes are on me.

He has changed from his suit into a simple, light blue T-shirt and a pair of navy athletic pants that have two lime green stripes down the sides.

Seeing the bright colors on him almost makes me smile.

The intense and serious expression in his eyes and his tightened lips make the smile disappear before it can form.

"Hey," I say lamely and sniff, hoping the tears dry before he notices. "Done with work?"

His penetrating gaze seems to see right through me. If he notices that I've become sad, he doesn't say anything as he pushes off the railing and walks toward me. Taking a seat on the other end of the couch, he leans back and drops his head.

"The kid is a mess," he says, but it's more like a groan.

That familiar pinch in my heart returns. "He's struggling with his mother's death, another woman who—I'm assuming here, but I'm guessing Cassandra made it clear she didn't want him, and an uncle who's been forced to take him in. I'm not sure how happy and well-adjusted you expect him to be."

By the fire shooting from Donovan's eyes, I assume I've gone too far, been too blunt. I look away, back to the flickering flames, and take a sip of wine before I apologize.

I haven't said anything that isn't true.

"I wasn't forced to take him in. Even if Emily and Sean hadn't named me as guardian in their will, I would have done so."

I shrug, avoiding eye contact. His green eyes are dangerous to my sensibilities. "Regardless, it took me years to get over losing my mom, and I had my dad with me."

And I wasn't there to see her die, either. I cringe at the thought.

"Has he had counseling?" I ask, turning to Donovan but looking at his shoulder and not his eyes.

"That's what you're here for." He scowls.

I don't bother to mention that three years afterward is three years too late. Besides Emily's car accident being hidden by the press, I have a feeling there are a lot of secrets the Lore family keeps protected. It only begs the question of what Donovan is hiding.

More silence fills the room as Donovan pushes himself off the couch and walks out. I unwrap my legs from under me, intent on going to bed when he doesn't immediately return.

It's been a long, mind-bending day, and the half glass of wine I've had is making me sleepy.

As if on cue, and my body is telling me I really do need to get to sleep, I yawn loudly, my hand covering my mouth when Donovan walks back into his living room.

In one hand, he's holding a tumbler filled with amber liquid and ice.

I shake off the yawn and smile sheepishly. "I'm exhausted," I say, and point toward the stairs. "So I'm just going to go up to bed."

Donovan walks closer, reaching me in three quick strides. "Thank you."

His simply spoken gratitude makes me blink.

The Lores are not generally thankful people. They take and expect people to give them what they want.

The very fact that I'm here, not giving up much of a fight, is proof of it.

"Right." I nod, another yawn stretching my lips wide.

He grins down on me, his green eyes twinkly with amusement. "Tomorrow," he says, and even in my tired state his voice affects me, "we'll discuss the rest of why you're here."

Reaching out, he runs the backs of his knuckles down my jaw.

My breath stalls in my chest and my lips part.

I'm shocked by the fact that he's touching me. My body responding immediately is becoming less of a shock. I'm beginning to crave that brief contact of his skin against mine.

I nod, unable to speak, when he leans down and his lips brush against my ear. "Sleep well, T. You're going to need it."

I pull back quickly, puzzled at the warmth flooding my stomach and the instant buzzing in my veins.

Finding my breath and my voice, I whisper, "Okay," and turn away as my cheeks heat.

Then I turn toward the stairs and hurry my little fanny to the room he prepared for me.

Yet I can feel Donovan's eyes on me as I walk away from him.

And I know that just like he's already promised me, it won't be long before I give in to my body's attraction to him.

ENFLAME

I just have to figure out a way to bubble wrap my heart, encase it in stone, lock it in a safe, and throw away the key before I do so.

Because even being around Donovan again for only a few hours, and even though he's more serious and more distant than the boy I remember falling in love with—he's still there, somewhere. I can see him dying to break through.

Fighting to be free.

From what he's trying to escape, I haven't figured out yet.

As I crawl into the largest bed I've ever seen in my life and cover myself in the most comfortable and satiny sheets I've ever felt, I know that the young girl who fell in love with him wants to not only help Jeremiah, but Donovan, too.

And that's dangerous.

He can have my mind and my body, but there's simply no way I can afford to give him my heart.

Chapter Five

"How's your dad doing?" Marisa asks, her eyes lined with concern.

"The same."

Taking off my jacket, I quickly hang it in the coat closet and walk around her desk.

Propping my denim-clad hip on the side, I swing my gray riding boot back and forth. I hate it. I hate seeing his unfocused eyes. I hate that he can't squeeze my hand with any noticeable pressure.

And I mostly hate the way the horrible administrator, Ms. Zelder, eyed me with suspicion when I paid cash for his stay. The fact that I paid for three months in cash probably has her thinking I robbed a bank over the weekend.

Marisa rests her hand on my thigh and squeezes. "He'll get better, sweetie. You just have to keep the faith."

I wrinkle my nose and look toward my office. I'm not sure how much faith I have anymore.

Too many people lose their loved ones, and while I'm not ready to say goodbye to my dad, he doesn't seem to be improving at all.

I take small comfort in the fact that he's not getting worse.

"How's the afternoon been here?" I ask, shaking off my visit with my dad. Nothing good comes from dwelling on things I can't change.

"Slow." She looks down at her paperwork before nodding toward the television room. "Kaleb is back, Joseph just got out on bail from selling pot to a classmate, and Ben has been spotted outside the food shelf."

"And that's slow?" I tease.

Marisa shrugs and smiles. "Cops haven't shown up yet today."

I laugh softly. They're not altogether uncommon visitors at our place.

"Okay then." I push off the desk and straighten my striped cotton hoodie.

I make my way into the television room to see Kaleb. He's fourteen and has been in foster care since he was four. He doesn't make it easy for his foster parents to care for him, though, and he's been in several different homes. However, I know that his two current foster parents truly want to love him. They have been foster parents for almost twenty years, since the wife found out she'd never be able to have kids of their own. I know the Samuels well, seeing as how several of my older kids have been placed in their home over the years.

"Hey, Kaleb," I say, and take a seat next to him.

He glances at me and returns to a Lord of The Rings marathon that's been playing all day long. He offers me no expression as I relax next to him.

"What happened?"

"Stupid Mr. Samuel tried fucking grounding me."

"Manners," I say, scolding him.

He grunts.

"What for?"

He shrugs before he finally says, "Stayed out too late over the weekend."

I almost want to smile. Some of these kids who have come from tough backgrounds don't realize how good they have it when an adult actually wants to discipline them and teach them. Kaleb comes from a family where both parents were drug dealers. After his mom was picked up prostituting herself on a corner, DHS looked into his housing situation and discovered that the small child knew how to efficiently tie a tourniquet around his father's upper arm before the man injected himself with heroin. Needles, pipes, lighters, and all forms of drugs were found in his house before he was removed.

"It's only because they care, Kaleb. You probably worried them."

He grunts again, disbelieving.

"Stay here this afternoon, but then you have to go home," I tell him, standing up when the door opens.

Jeremiah walks in, his eyes wide and his cheeks flushed.

Looking down at Kaleb, I point my finger at him. "They care, kiddo, and if you want me to help smooth things over, I'll tell them you're here. But you have to help me out here. The Samuels are great people."

He rolls his eyes. "Whatever."

I take that as my cue to leave, and follow the angry trail Jeremiah left in his wake as he rushed to my office.

I raise my brow toward Marisa, who returns my look and shrugs as I walk by.

"What's going on?" I ask as soon as I enter my office.

Yesterday Jeremiah showed up after school, sat quietly in my office, refusing to hang out with the other kids in the television room or game room, and worked on his history paper.

He was quiet and morose, but the emotions rolling off him today are completely different.

"Adults are a bunch of a—" He looks up, cutting himself off, and shrugs. "Sorry."

I give him a small smile. "No worries, you caught yourself."

I take a seat in the chair next to him. Holding onto the chair's arms, I lift myself up until my boots are under me and I'm sitting crisscross in the chair. I rest my elbows on my knees and tilt my head to the side. "What's going on?"

He doesn't say anything as his eyes scan my wall of quotes. I'm about to ask him another question when he turns to me and asks, "How do you know my uncle?"

I'm surprised Donovan hasn't already told him, or that he hasn't asked before now.

"We knew each other in college."

"So you know Cassandra?"

"I do." I don't know what look I give him, but it's clearly one he agrees with because I get a hint of a smile before it quickly disappears. "Is that why you're mad? Did you see her today?"

He shakes his head. "No way. Like she'd have anything to do with me."

I sigh, fighting the urge to reach out and hold him. I hate that he thinks someone doesn't want anything to do with him. Other than carrying around way too much anger, Jeremiah's a great kid.

I keep my mouth shut, letting him wait to give me the real reason why he's mad. I don't want him to feel pitied.

"My grandma showed up at school today, though, and was a bitch."

I flash him a well-known look of disgust. I don't even bother correcting the name-calling…if the shoe fits and all that.

"You've met her?" he asks, his eyebrows arching.

"Once or twice."

Immediately the memory of that morning in bed with Donovan flashes through my mind. The way Claire Lore showed up, angry but dressed in a pale blue suit as if she were going to church or an office instead of simply making her way to her son's apartment, her gorgeous and most likely incredibly expensive blond hairstyle swaying and swishing as she barged into his room.

The look she gave me said I would do better serving her by cleaning her toilets or taking out her trash than sleeping in a bed with her son.

"She wants me to be just like him."

I frown, not understanding. "Your grandpa?"

"No," he scoffs. "My uncle. And I hate him."

"Donovan?" I ask, although I should already know this. But from what I've at least seen between the two of them, Donovan is trying.

Jeremiah shoots me a look, lips pressed firmly together, and looks away.

I don't fully understand, but when he reaches down and pulls out a notebook and begins scribbling in it, I sense the conversation is over.

I press forward, though. This is the most he's ever given me. "Did Donovan tell you about my mom dying?"

His hand stills on the paper, the ink making a slight scratch. "She did?" he asks, keeping his head bowed down.

I shake my head, befuddled. Why is Donovan doing this if he's not telling either of us what we need to know?

"Yeah." I clasp my hands together and prop my chin on them. "She was coming home from work one morning and a truck driver fell asleep at the wheel of his semi. Ran her right off the road, over a bridge, and onto a highway below."

"Damn," he says, drawing out the word.

He raises his head and our eyes meet.

I smile, a wistful smile, one I usually wear when I talk about my mom. She might have died sixteen years ago, but sometimes if I think hard enough, I can still remember how good she smelled. Like peonies. Bright and cheerful, just like she was.

"Yeah. She was pretty amazing."

He looks away, up to a sign that says Don't follow your dreams, chase them. "My mom was, too. She always said I could do whatever I wanted."

"You can." I nod. I firmly agree with that. Anyone can do

anything they put their mind to. Some goals just require more effort.

He snorts and starts writing away in his notebook. The scratch of ink scribbled on paper is the only sound in the room. "Not if they have their way."

I lean back in my chair and let my hands fall into my lap.

He's given me more than I expected today. While I'd like to reassure him that Donovan wants that for him, too, I hesitate to say anything.

The last few nights of awkward and tense dinners and the few interactions I've seen the two have with each other leave me feeling like maybe he wouldn't.

Uncurling my legs from the chair, I rest my hand on Jeremiah's shoulder as I stand up. "I'll always be here for you, Jeremiah."

He pauses for a moment before giving me a quick nod. Then it's back to ink on paper.

Leaving him alone in my office, I exhale heavily and rest against the hallway wall. Closing my eyes, I try to take a few calming, relaxing breaths.

I don't know why I feel so connected to Jeremiah, but there's a possessive urge growing in my chest whenever I'm around him.

I sort of want to slap anyone who has crushed this kid's dreams.

* * * * *

Jeremiah and I are in the living room when Donovan comes barreling through the door.

His eyes narrow directly onto Jeremiah, whose back goes ramrod straight.

"Hi," I say, taking note of the instant sparking tension in the room and trying to diffuse it. "How was your day?"

Donovan shoots me a look, drops his briefcase on the floor, and begins unbuttoning his suit coat.

I try to focus on the fact that he's pissed—I really do—but as his fingers deftly work the buttons and he tears his coat off, I take sight of his heaving breaths, the way his chest fills out his white dress shirt, and when his fingers begin loosening the perfectly done knot at the base of his throat and he whips off his tie…

Well…

My jaw goes slack and my body instantly begins to heat.

Because what would it feel like to have all that masculine energy directed at me? I'm not sure I've ever been with a man who can so quickly turn me on, especially when he's clearly so pissed off.

It makes no sense.

Yet I instantly find myself moving toward him. I lay a hand on his forearm, trying to stop him from whatever hell he's about to let loose.

"Calm down," I whisper, although I salute myself for saying it like I mean it.

I don't really. I like him all sexy angry.

He glares down at me, and for a moment I see his eyes soften before he barks, "Stay out of this." His eyes immediately go back to Jeremiah. "I heard you were disrespectful to your grandmother today. Would you care to explain?"

Jeremiah rolls his eyes, and I swear I hear Donovan growl. "No."

"No? That's it? How about 'thank you, Grandmother, for speaking to the headmaster so I can remain in school'? Or 'thank you, Grandmother, for sending me to the best school in the state in the first place,' or even 'thank you, Grandmother, for preparing me for a future'?"

Jeremiah climbs off the couch, his thirteen-year-old body rigid with anger. As my eyes dart back and forth between the two, I can practically envision Donovan at thirteen. Jeremiah is tall and muscular, even for his young age. He's not nearly as tall as Donovan, but I assume in a few years they'll be able to match each other almost perfectly. The only differences are where Donovan's nose is slightly crooked, Jeremiah's is straight and his jaw isn't as square.

"I never said I wanted to go to that stuck-up school! I wanted my old school and my old friends. I hate that freaking place and I'm not going to thank anyone, ever, for making me do things I don't want to do. I hate you and Grandma!"

He barrels past Donovan and me. Tears fall down his cheeks as he screams his tantrum, and his feet pound on the stairs.

I jump when I hear the door to his room slam closed. Seconds later, the light fixture in the entryway begins shaking from the vibrations of Jeremiah's loud music that filters down the hallway and downstairs.

"Fuck!" Donovan growls and throws his hands to his hair.

"Yeah," I say, taking a cautious step away from him, "you totally screwed that up."

"What?" His head jerks up and his green eyes land on me, sparking things I shouldn't be feeling in this situation. "He is totally disrespectful. He has no concept of what he's been handed, and he's taking it out on everyone. Selfish little—"

"Teenager?" I supply, and take another step back when Donovan advances on me. "You can't mean that shit, Donovan. Not now, not when he's lost his entire family."

"I know, and I'm trying. But it doesn't help when he doesn't realize the opportunities he's being given here."

His voice is cold and forceful. My head flinches back slightly. He is not the Donovan I remember.

"What in the hell happened to you?" I ask, jerking my arm back when he reaches for me.

"What do you mean?"

"God." I shake my head, my hand flying through my hair. "I can't believe you're such an asshole now. Do you really think Jeremiah gives a shit about any of that? Did you not just listen to him? It sounds like he lost his entire family and then his entire life. Sounds like he got ripped away from everything he knew and he's being forced into what…becoming the next CEO?"

Donovan looks at me, showing nothing.

My pulse flutters and I press my hand against my chest, trying to keep my heart contained inside.

"Oh my God. I'm right, aren't I? He's thirteen and you're already grooming him? Do you know how insane that sounds?" I'm shrieking by the time I'm done, and my hands fly wildly in the air.

Donovan braces his hands on his hips, his expression stern and unmoved. "If I've learned anything in life, it's that you need to be prepared. You never know what's going to happen. When I had to take over, it took me years to feel like I was on firm footing. I don't want Jeremiah to suffer that way. I'm helping him."

"By not giving a shit about what he wants? Jesus, Donovan, when did you, of all people, become a sheep for your mother to maneuver?"

"You have no idea," he leans in, hissing. "what I've been through with her, and what my father's death did to her."

"You're right, I don't. But it's not fair to project that crap onto a kid, either. And can you stand here and tell me you're thrilled with the way you've had to live?"

I rub my fingers against my forehead. This whole argument is giving me a headache. I spin on my heels, intent on giving us both space, when he reaches out and grabs my arm. He pulls, spinning me back to him. I stumble on my feet, almost into his chest.

My hands fly out and I brace myself against his body so I don't face-plant.

I stare at my fingers, watching as they dig into his chest a little bit. Damn...he's so firm. Tight. Muscled.

"I don't want to fight with you," he murmurs, and I feel his lips on the top of my head. "I'm losing him, I know it. And I do care about him, but he has to start realizing what his future is going to look like, too. My sister didn't do that for him."

"Your sister wanted him to be happy," I whisper, nervous because his other hand is running slowly down my back.

His hand on my arm slides up to my shoulder and then around to the nape of my neck. "He has responsibilities to learn, that someday will become his."

"And you? Are you glad you followed your responsibilities?" I ask the question I asked earlier that he didn't answer, and pull back, tilting my chin up to look at him.

I see so much now and understand more. I have a feeling I know exactly why I never heard from him again, why he married Cassandra...that's what was always expected. He ran from it in college, but his father's death changed things for him.

His dark green orbs swirl with conflict. "No," he softly says, his voice barely audible. "I'm not always glad."

My lips part, and before I can speak or move away, he dips his head, tilting it to the side and his lips press against mine.

His kiss is demanding from the moment he touches me, and his hand at my neck tightens.

When his tongue slides against my bottom lip, teasing me into submission, I relax into his hold.

It's everything I knew it would be, and as his tongue slides into my mouth, I taste a faint hint of mint as electric heat flies straight to my chest.

I whimper, falling into him, and my hands drop from his chest to his hips. I squeeze tight, holding him against me. My knees begin to tremble as I feel his hard erection through his pants and my jeans.

The hard, rigid line against my sex snaps me out of the moment.

"Holy shit," I gasp, pulling out of the kiss.

"That was as amazing as I remember," Donovan whispers, pulling me back to him. "But I'm going to need another taste to be certain."

I chuckle softly, my eyes wide in shock and with lust as he brushes his lips against mine.

"Dreamed of this, Talia. For years I've dreamed of that night we spent together."

I can't think about that. Not now. Pushing away the ache in my chest caused by his words, I press my mouth against his and kiss him deeply. He takes control almost immediately, his fingers tangling in my hair.

He angles me back and takes the kiss deeper. If I could orgasm from a kiss alone, I would be quaking in front of him right this very moment.

It's hot and needy and there's still a hint of residual anger as he completely takes over.

His body pushes me backward as we swallow each other's whimpers and pleasured groans. I feel the couch at the backs of my legs and then I'm tumbling backward, Donovan directly on top of me.

This is what I want.

Him.

His body and his touches.

I don't want to hear his words.

His hand begins trailing down my shirt, brushing over my

breast, and my nipple hardens in response. I almost explode when his hand reaches underneath the hem and I feel his skin on me for the first time in eight years.

He's larger than he used to be, stronger. The way he controls my body with just a touch and a small taste is heady, igniting flames throughout my body. He's just like he used to be when he touched me, except more...better.

"Donovan," I gasp. My hips arch into his and my legs open further, making room for him to settle in between them.

My chest pushes against his, needing more contact.

"So good," he murmurs. His lips leave mine and begin trailing along my jaw, back to my ear and down the column of my throat. He bites and sucks, teasing me with playful nips until I'm grinding my hips against him.

I need relief quickly.

My hands grip his shoulders and my nails dig in as his hands move up my shirt, cupping my breasts over my bra. A groan is torn from my throat, loudly, as he pinches my covered nipple through its lace.

I don't know what happens, but Donovan's head snaps up, our eyes meet, and then he jack-knifes off the couch and slams his hands to the back of his neck.

I'm sprawled out on the couch, shocked from the suddenness of his move, and am just pushing down my shirt when he spins around and faces me.

"What in the hell are you doing to me?"

My head jerks back into the pillow it's resting on. "What?"

"Damn it, Talia. I've got a kid upstairs and I'm molesting you like some randy teenager."

My cheeks flush and I push myself into a sitting position. "Oh."

He sounds pissed that he let himself get carried away, but he does have a point. How could I have forgotten?

"I haven't been able to stop thinking about you ever since I walked into your office last week. You're distracting me with everything."

My eyebrows knit together and I frown. He sounds like this isn't a good thing.

"Shit," he groans, pressing the heels of his palms against his eyes. "I don't have the option to not be focused right now, and all I want to do is stay home and bury myself inside you, remind you how good we used to be…how good we could still be."

Chapter Six

I jump from the couch.

He's giving me whiplash, and I'm not sure my heart or my body can handle his sudden mood swings.

"What are you saying?" I ask, walking around to the back of the couch. I need distance between us.

His lips twist into a grin.

I know that look. He's just found a new challenge. A new game. He's found something new to be conquered. If his predatory look, fixed directly on me, is any indication...I've become the prey...the thing to conquer.

"I'm saying that for eight long years, I've only had my memory of the night you gave yourself to me. It's kept me warm in my cold bed. It's gotten me through showers that would have been much more lonely had I not had the vision of you sprawled out beneath me, having an orgasm—one given by a man for the first time ever—ingrained so deeply in my brain, that it makes me hard, just thinking and talking about it now."

"You said you wanted my body." I choke out the words and back up further as he continues stalking toward me. "That's what we agreed."

"I want more."

I shake my head. "You can't have it."

He reaches for me, but I jump back, darting out of the way. I grin.

"I'll take it, anyway."

My feet stumble over a rug, but I right myself before he can make another grab for me. This is foolish. Ridiculous.

But I watch Donovan's eyes light up as I continue to thwart his advances. Most likely, this is the most playful he's been in a long time.

I nod toward the stairway, but he doesn't look. "Jeremiah's awake."

"I know." He takes one long stride, and before I can move, his hands are on my hips and he's lifting me to him. One hand leaves my hip and goes to my neck. His lips press against mine quickly but firmly before he pulls back. "We also haven't eaten dinner."

Knowing he's caught me, he smiles, lighting up the room.

I want to do anything to continue seeing it. Maybe if he can lighten up a little bit, it will make it easier for Jeremiah to be around him.

It will spear my heart when I have to leave him, but if Jeremiah's okay, I can always go back to pretending I am, too.

I've had eight years' practice.

I wrap my arms around his neck as he begins walking toward the kitchen. "Are you going to put me down?"

His lips drop to my neck, his hand goes back to my ass, and he adjusts his hold on me, bouncing my breasts against his chest in a deliciously playful friction.

"Nope."

"Hmm." I feign offense and fight a smile.

He smells good, he looks fantastic, and his rock-hard abs and muscled arms wrapped around me feel too good to argue.

Sliding me onto the counter, he flashes me a mock scowl. "Stay here and don't move."

His voice is playful but firm, so I grip the edge of the counter and nod. "Got it, boss."

I watch in awe as he begins cooking the meat, dicing a variety of vegetables and mixing a stir-fry sauce along with rice.

The entire time, we speak of nothing serious, but important nonetheless. I take small sips of the wine he pours for me, and call

Jeremiah down for dinner when it's time.

And while the meal is just as tense as it was the previous nights, with little being spoken and nothing real being said, I can't stop the expectant arousal that warms my blood and causes the area between my thighs to pulse with need and want.

The rest of the evening slides by slowly, in an almost physically painful manner. Donovan brings his laptop into the living room, where he clicks away, sometimes seemingly furious at the keyboard.

Jeremiah watches reality television that I believe he's too young for, but I don't say anything.

And I pretend, like the night before, to be completely engrossed in a book.

But it's when Jeremiah has been in his bedroom for over an hour, and my eyes are burning from staring at the lighted screen for hours on end and only getting through a couple chapters, that something in the air sparks and crackles.

I slowly lift my head, that familiar pulse in my groin already telling me what's about to happen, and meet Donovan's heady, intense gaze.

The slight click of the laptop closing echoes in the vast space, thundering in my ears.

My throat goes dry, and I swallow thickly.

"I want you in my bed. Now." He nods in the direction of the stairs.

Before I can argue, Donovan rises from his chair, takes my hand in his, and pulls me to my feet. His lips press against mine and his tongue slides inside, taking what he wants before I know what's happening.

My body relaxes into his body, submitting to what I know is about to happen, when he pulls back.

"I'm going to lock up down here. Go to my room and I'll meet you there in a minute."

He pushes me gently toward the stairs and I move, wanting this more than anything…and equally terrified at the same time.

*****

My body is primed by the time I reach Donovan's room.

I don't know what it was exactly—maybe the tone in his voice. Maybe it was the heated stare that left no room for arguing when he looked at me in the living room that had me moving and heading up the stairs without even thinking about denying him.

The kiss earlier, the feel of his body against mine on the couch, has left little room for doubt as to what will occur in his room.

I brush my hands down my thighs as I stand in his doorway, hesitant to enter despite the pleasure I know awaits.

Donovan was my first.

He is the man I've compared every man to since then, and I know this, even if I haven't admitted it to anyone. And probably never will.

I hear his footsteps behind me.

Feel him moving closer.

Sigh as his hands press against my hips, and he pushes me into his room.

He doesn't speak, but I follow his silent commands. He slowly turns me around, drops his hands, and takes a step back.

His arms cross over his chest.

My pulse thrums along my skin, igniting it, and I lick my dry lips.

"Take off your clothes."

My gaze meets his and my lips part.

His seductive voice excites me.

"What about you?" I ask, as my fingers find their way to the hem of my shirt at my waist.

Slowly, I cross my arms, grip the shirt, and pull it over my head, dropping it to the floor.

I watch as his eyes drop to the swell of my already needy, heavy breasts before he returns to meet my nervous gaze.

"I have wanted this moment, wanted to see you naked again, since the moment I climbed out of your bed eight years ago, and I want to enjoy it. Can you say the same?"

I could. If I were going to be completely honest, I'd tell him that I've fantasized about him frequently over the years. He might have played a larger, more consistent role in the last week's visions, but he has never been far from my mind.

Instead, I stay silent. My hands go to the waistband of the black yoga pants I threw on when I got back from work, and I push them down until they pool at my ankles.

Stepping out of them, I watch his eyes roam my body slowly, reverently, as if he's savoring every inch of my skin.

My hands fall lamely to my sides, my fingers tapping an erratic beat against my thighs.

Donovan arches one brow, holding his stare on my breasts. "You're not naked yet."

I swallow, uncertainty and lust filling me equally. I raise my hands and stretch them around to my back, unclasping my bra. The straps fall from my shoulders before I bring everything around to the front. It hangs from a fingertip and I return his arched brow look, teasing him before I let it fall to the floor along with my clothes and my hesitancy.

He's looking at me like he wants to eat me alive.

And in this moment, there would be no other death that could be as sweet.

Without needing further instruction, I hook my thumbs into the waistband of my lacy pink thong, push it down my thighs, and resist the urge to shiver as the soft fabric slides down my heated skin.

This is insane.

Overwhelming.

More powerful than anything I've ever experienced, because as Donovan stands mere feet from me, assessing every inch of my body and finding me more than satisfactory, I have never felt more like a woman than I do in this moment.

No one has ever looked at me with such ferocious desire.

I know before he ever steps forward to touch me, before his hand rests on my hip and he pushes me firmly back toward the edge of his bed, that there will never be another man for me.

Because I gave Donovan Lore my heart and my soul almost a decade ago.

And he still owns it.

* * * * *

"You are more beautiful than my memories."

I flush under his praise whispered in a deep, husky tone.

He braces himself above me, his legs between mine that are spread for him. My hand trails down his arm, feeling his corded muscles beneath his shirt.

"You're still dressed," I tell him, tugging on his shirt.

He nods, not looking at me. He seems so far away as his gaze continues roaming my body. Without a word, he removes his dress shirt and my heart flutters when I see him. Finally.

His abs are rippled, his pecs curved and tight. My mouth goes dry at seeing him so perfectly strong. As his hands go to his belt buckle, I watch as he quickly flicks it open, snaps it away, and then unbuttons his pants.

I watch every moment as if it could be the last time I see him naked. My entire body is enflamed, feels as if I'm lying over an open fire. But I want more.

I push up to my elbows to see him, when Donovan's eyes meet mine.

"I think I'll leave these on for now," he says, and drops to his knees.

My breath catches in my throat when he pulls my legs over his shoulder. His lips brush the sensitive skin of my inner thighs and I tremble.

"I have been dying for this, to know what you taste like here."

With one finger, he slides through my wet folds and I quiver.

"Donovan."

"Shh," he whispers. His lips press again my skin and I squirm beneath the delicious sensation. "I didn't get to do this before."

I swallow again, losing the words. And then, as his tongue slides through my sex, my hands fly to his hair.

I cry out when he stops and stands up.

Leaning over me, his eyes narrow and with one hand, he holds onto both of my wrists, pushing them into the mattress above my head. "Leave them here."

"What?"

He nods once and firmly presses my hands further against the bed. "Take what I give you, and trust me."

I blink and lick my lips. My pussy is throbbing with need, and as Donovan continues holding onto my hands, his other hand cups the area between my thighs. "You're so hot for me. So wet."

I nod and try to shift against his touch.

He shakes his head, a wicked grin on his lips. "Don't try to take what you want, Talia. Trust me to give it to you."

I don't know if I can, and he must see my hesitation because he drops his head.

His lips brush against mine and he whispers, "Next time, I'm going to tie you up. You'll enjoy it, I promise. But for tonight, I want you to stay still. Can you do that?" He pushes back slightly so I can look into his eyes.

I have no idea what's happening. No idea why I want to trust him more than anything in the world, and even though I can't, I have no doubt that he means every word he says right now.

Donovan is in complete control.

Slowly, I nod, and receive a full smile in response.

He lets go of my hands with one more warning. "Keep them there."

I listen.

And then I feel like I've been set on fire completely when he bends back down and slides his tongue through my wet folds, returning to concentrate on drawing circles around my swollen clit.

With one hand on my hip, he begins to eat me like a man starving. I can't push into him and I can't widen my legs further.

"Donovan," I cry out, the torture painful and incredible.

"Taste so good," he murmurs. He slides his tongue the length of my pussy walls, back to my clit, and then he slides it inside. I cry out again, trying to be quiet, but it's hard as he fucks me with his tongue until my inner walls are clamping around him.

His thumb brushes against my clit. He pushes it and flicks it, and it's moments before my orgasm ignites in my core and spreads to my limbs.

I fall over the cliff, biting my lip to keep from shouting his name as Donovan continues licking and tasting me.

I'm barely able to catch my breath, my eyes only half open, when he stands up. In one fluid movement, his pants are unbuttoned and they fall down his hips.

His erection springs free, large and thick.

"I want to touch you." My fingers grip the covers of the bed and I don't move.

He wraps one hand around his thick length and strokes twice. "I want to fuck you."

I can't move my gaze away from his cock. The way his hand slides easily up and down his length, his wrist twisting at the base, and the way he pinches himself at the tip.

I want it to be my hands on him. My mouth. I lick my lips and feel my body begin to pulse all over again.

"I want you to," I tell him, my voice thick. "Please," I whimper when he slides his cock against my wet sex.

A low groan falls from his lips, and it's the most erotic sound I've ever heard.

Stepping away from me, he bends down, and when he stands back up he has a condom in his hand.

A frown lines his features.

With one hand holding the condom, his other wrapped around his cock, I watch every moment with anticipation, knowing he's going to be filling me…fucking me…just like he's promised.

"You on the pill?" he asks suddenly.

"Yes." I nod. I know what he's asking.

"I'm clean. I promise you. There's only been—"

"Okay," I cut him off. Hearing Cassandra's name would douse cold water all over me, and I don't want anything to stop me now.

I've given in so easily—so quickly—and I don't care.

With a flick of his wrist, the unopened condom flies to the floor.

"Talia," he whispers and my eyes snap to his. They're dark, and he takes my breath away. As he stands in front of me, looking so much like—but more than—the man I remember, I can't say anything.

He doesn't say anything else, either, as his hands grip my hips. He tugs me until my ass is hanging off the edge of his bed and then he pushes himself inside me, slowly, one inch at a time, until I'm stretched full of him, and I feel him everywhere.

His head falls back and he groans. "Holy fuck, you feel fantastic."

"More. Please."

He slides out slowly and I close my eyes.

"Eyes on me," he snaps.

I open them, instantly meeting his serious gaze.

"I want your eyes on me as I take you. I want you to know it's me who's fucking you."

There's no way I couldn't, but I nod.

Slowly, he begins fucking me. I feel every inch of him as he slides in and out, teasing me until my clit is throbbing when he seats himself balls-deep inside me. I clamp my walls around him as he pulls out and he groans.

"Fuck."

Then he slams inside of me. I bite my lip as his speed picks up, but I don't take my eyes off him. His jaw tightened, his fingers digging into my hips, I can't move at all as Donovan plunges inside me over and over again.

My breasts shake and my knuckles hurt from gripping the sheets.

"Donovan. Please. I want to touch you." I gasp as I feel another orgasm begin to build.

It's wild and fast and intense.

"Take it, T. Take all of me."

I whimper. I am. I'm trying.

"Please," I whisper. "Harder."

"Holy fuck," he groans as he listens to me. He shifts until he's over me, one of his hands clamps down on my wrists, and the change in position drives me wild.

His balls slap against my ass and his pelvic bone rubs against my clit.

Everything inside me ignites, and I turn my head as my orgasm takes over. I bite down on his bicep to muffle my screams.

"Fuck." His hips piston faster as he loses his own control, and then he shoves himself inside me, stopping when he's hit the end of me.

His groans fill the air as he buries his head in the crook of my neck, his own orgasm taking him over the edge.

My heart thunders against my chest, and I feel his beating wildly against mine. I wiggle my wrists and whisper. "Please let me touch you now."

He instantly lets go, his voice muffled as he says something I don't understand, but I pull my hands from his and immediately wrap them around his back.

It's slick with sweat, but I don't care as I run my hands over his muscles. He's braced himself above me on one elbow to prevent his full weight from crushing me, but I wish he wouldn't have.

I want to feel all of him.

"You are incredible," he murmurs against my skin after our heartbeats have slowed.

I close my eyes, feeling myself revel in his praise.

"You're not so bad yourself," I respond, not willing to let him know how much I loved everything we just did.

Pushing off me, he brushes his lips against mine. It's a tender kiss, and I open my lips to allow his tongue to sweep inside. I arch into him, needing more, when I feel him chuckle.

"So greedy. You want more?"

I shake my head. "I don't think I can."

He pulls back, ending our kiss. With one hand, he brushes a strand of my blond hair out of my eyes and smiles knowingly. "I think you can."

It's the promise of another round that makes my walls clamp

around him and he laughs easily.

"I need a minute to recover," he says, and pulls himself out of me. "Stay here while I get something to clean you up."

I nod and brush my lips against his before he stands up.

Lifting myself to my elbows, I watch as his naked body walks to his bathroom, and I take every moment I can to enjoy watching his beautiful ass. When he comes back, I shift so he can clean me up and cringe as he tosses the washcloth onto the floor.

"Gross."

He pulls me against his chest and settles us in the middle of the bed. "I'll clean it up tomorrow. I just want to rest with you in my arms."

"I should get to my own bed," I mutter, but I already feel sleep beginning to pull at me.

He presses his lips against the back of my shoulder. With his hand splayed on my stomach, he pulls me against him. "In a minute," he whispers. "Let me hold you."

I acquiesce, because I can barely move.

In his darkened room, with Donovan holding me in his arms, I close my eyes and fall asleep to the gentle thud of his heartbeat at my back, knowing I'm smiling, terrified and completely at peace.

Chapter Seven

I roll over, awakening from sleep, and my lips turn down when I find an empty spot in the bed next to me.

Every insecurity from our first night together flashes through my mind, returning to the forefront, and I collapse onto my back. I drop an arm over my eyes and I squeeze them closed, not allowing tears to fall.

He's left me after the most passionate night of sex I've ever imagined. It was more than I'd imagined.

My thighs already ache, a reminder of the way he used my body.

The way he gripped me and moved me.

The way he thrust himself inside me with wild abandon, as if he'd never lost such control in his life.

Neither have I.

Just as the tears begin to fill my eyes and spill down my cheeks, music floats into the room. It's coming from under the door or the air vents, and it's not the fact that I hear music playing in the middle of the night that worries me, it's the haunted melody filtering through my ears.

Slowly, I push off the bed, flinching from the dull pain in my legs, and reach for the first thing I see. Donovan's white dress shirt is still puddled on the floor next to my side of the bed, so I grab it and quickly pull it on.

I look down at the bed and frown. My side of the bed.

As if I have any ownership to anything in this house except for what I brought with me.

Buttoning the shirt so it covers my breasts, I roll up the cuffs a few times and make my way out of the bedroom.

The music dances up the stairs and I follow the sound, not surprised when I see Donovan lounging in the living room.

What does surprise me is that he's practically sitting in the dark. The glow from the moon filtering in through the windows provides the only gentle light in the large room.

He's clad in only his black boxer briefs as he sits at one corner of the couch. His head rests along the back, his eyes closed. The fingers of one hand press against his eyes, and his other hand holds a glass full of ice and clear liquid.

He doesn't move at all as I walk near him, and if it weren't for the tenseness in his body, I would think he had fallen asleep.

The slow, deep, rhythmic melody filling the large room sends shivers down my spine.

"You okay?" I whisper.

His hand falls from his eyes but nothing else changes as he raises his hand, beckoning me.

I go to him, take his hand in mine, but he pulls back until he runs his hand across the back of my hip, lower, and then cupping my ass. He pulls me toward him until I'm standing in front of him, my legs straddling one of his knees.

"I should be asking you that," he replies. His eyes are still closed and his head is still resting on the back of the couch.

I keep my eyes on his face, my breath hitching as he lifts my knee and rests it on his thigh.

"Your skin is so soft. So beautiful."

I flush under his praise, my body already awakening from the gentle brushes of his thumb against my inner thigh.

He moves higher and I gasp as he slides his thumb along my slick flesh.

Slowly, his eyes open, barely, and he looks at me through hooded eyes. "Did I hurt you earlier?"

I shrug. "A bit, but I can take it."

His thumb presses against my clit, rolls around it. My lips part, inhaling a quick breath.

"Bruised?"

I shrug again. I have no idea. I ache all over my hips and my waist from where he gripped me forcefully.

"Unbutton the shirt."

His command sends tremors straight to my swollen folds. His fingers join his thumb in his teasing assault on my aroused skin. He brushes along the outside lips, then inside, outside again… giving hints at what he wants to do to me but not following through.

It's insane how crazy he can drive me, how fast my body responds to his touch.

My fingers quickly undo the buttons on the shirt and I drop my arms to my sides, letting the shirt drape open.

Finally, he opens his eyes. They immediately roam my exposed skin.

"You in my shirt is the most tantalizing thing I've ever seen."

I flush under his compliment, dropping my chin.

His finger and thumb pinch my clit, making me yelp.

"What did I say about your eyes?" he says, soothing the ache he created.

"Keep them on you." My voice is breathy to my own ears. I can barely speak, amazed that I can even think, when he presses two fingers inside me easily.

"So wet for me already."

I nod, choking down a breathless moan. My head wants to fall back, or down, surrendering to his ministrations. My thighs begin to tremble and it takes every ounce of my focus to keep my gaze on his.

He licks his lips, wetting them. I want to bend down and taste him—lick the seam between his lips, taste his mouth. I want to lick and taste every inch of his skin, from his firm chest down to the light trail of hair that leads below his waistband.

His fingers inside me press against my rigid flesh and a groan escapes my throat.

I collapse over him, my hands gripping the back of the couch. He pulls out his fingers and I mewl from the sudden loss.

His eyes narrow. "Stand up. Concentrate on my touch."

"I am," I say, taking the moment to graze my lips across his, smiling. "It's just hard."

He glances down at his crotch, and I see his erection pressing against the confines of his boxers. "I know."

My smile grows. I like it when he jokes. It lightens the lines around his eyes that always seem too intense.

"Now stand up."

I nod, pushing myself off the couch and returning to my original position. I have one knee on his thigh and one foot on the floor, and maintaining balance is difficult when he shifts his position, sitting up more.

He dips his head, and his mouth trails along my inner thigh. My entire body shivers in response as his tongue and his lips begin tasting my flesh, moving to where his fingers just were.

His other hand curves around my ass and he holds me against him as his tongue darts out and slides along my wet pussy.

"Holy shit," I gasp, my knees shaking.

He pulls back and meets my haze-filled eyes. I can barely see straight and I'm already so close to the edge. My cunt clenches, needing something inside, filling it.

"You like this?"

I nod. "You're killing me."

"There's a reason the French call an orgasm the little death." He smirks and his head drops again. His tongue lashes out, licking the outside of my pussy before he draws circles around my clit. His hand at my backside presses me against him. My hips need to shift, take what's building, but his hands hold me captive to his assault.

It's fierce and powerful and my hands fall to his head, gripping his hair as he continues to lick and fuck me with his tongue and his fingers. He thrusts them inside me, pulling out slowly and scraping against my inner walls.

"Donovan."

I'm gasping for breath, my knees are trembling—my orgasm is so close. I can feel it building inside me, crest after crest coming closer together, building higher and higher, when he lets go and pulls me down to his lap.

I straddle him, falling into his chest.

His hand adjusts his boxers and then his erection is free, rubbing against my clit.

"I need you," I pant, unashamed of my craving for him.

"I need you more." His voice is fierce, thick with lust and arousal, and something so much more than I can understand in the moment.

His hands move to my hips, and he lifts and pulls me back down, his thick cock instantly filling and stretching me.

"Oh, my God," I moan, dropping my head back.

I forget the rules and I don't care.

"Eyes," he scolds, and his fingers pinch my nipples until my head snaps up.

Sweat beads line my temple. "I can't."

His hand curves around to my lower back, forcing me to rock against him. "You can."

I open my mouth to argue with him, but he rocks his hips into me again and his cock presses against nerves inside me that I didn't even know existed.

It's too much. The energy between us crackling, the intensity in his eyes, and the way my body falls apart for him.

Everything explodes into a brilliant sparkling light as I keep my eyes focused on his, screaming his name before he covers my mouth with his, swallowing my cries.

My entire body shakes and convulses through the power of the orgasm rushing through my veins.

He continues rocking into me until I'm the one swallowing his pleasured groans. He's frantic and wild, taking me on his couch, and time stops while I kiss him, my hands scratching at the back of his head through his short, coarse hair. He slams me down onto him, growls my name, and expels himself inside of me.

I rest against him, my face in the crook of his shoulder. I continue breathing in his scent as my racing heart calms to something that feels less like I'm having a heart attack.

The whole time, his warm hands slowly run up and down my back.

I feel his own heartbeat against my chest, thundering wildly, and at least I know I'm not alone in feeling how potent the moment we just spent together is.

It feels all-consuming.

He is all-consuming.

When I can speak without my breath wavering, giving away my vulnerability, I raise up off his lap, feeling the loss as his still half-hard cock slides out of me.

I take a moment and soak him in, peruse his body with sated eyes, and still I flush, that little flutter in my belly returning.

"Keep looking at me like that, and I'll have you on the floor."

I look away and reach for his earlier discarded dress shirt. "I think I'm good now."

His low chuckle vibrates against my hand on his chest, which I use for balance. Standing up, I begin tugging on his shirt, sliding my arms through the holes.

He doesn't say anything, but I can feel him watching me. The mood in the room plummets from ecstasy to something cooler.

"Did I hurt you?" he asks.

I almost say yes, because at one point in my life he did. Horribly.

But that's not what he's asking.

Sliding the last button through its hole, I shake my head. "Like I said, I'm good. But I should probably get to bed."

He reaches for me, his hand curving around my wrist. "I want you in my bed."

An excuse comes quick. "I don't think that's a good idea. Not with Jeremiah here. In fact," I say, waving my free hand in the air, "this was probably a really bad idea. He could have seen us. Or heard us."

"He sleeps like the dead."

I wrinkle my nose. "Still, it wasn't smart."

I meet his gaze reluctantly, too afraid of what he'll see in my eyes.

"You're running," he says simply.

I lick my lips. "I'm not."

He leans back and lets go of his hold on me. "There will come a day when you don't."

But that day isn't coming anytime soon. Not when after just one night of sex with him, I already feel the lock on my safe popping open, the door widening, and my heart jumping for joy that Donovan is back in my life.

I don't argue with him. There's no point. Donovan's always been able to read me better than a well-loved and re-read book.

"Goodnight, Donovan."

He drops his head back to the couch, closes his eyes, and doesn't say a word.

* * * * *

Sunlight peeks through the curtains the next time my eyes open. I stretch my legs in the bed, my arms toward the headboard, and let out a sleepy groan.

My body aches everywhere.

It feels wonderful. Despite myself, my lips spread into a slow, happy smile as I make my way to my attached bathroom and turn on the shower.

While I wait for the water to heat, I use the restroom and begin brushing my teeth.

My eyes widen as I examine my body in the mirror that is slowly steaming over. Two purple circles are there, faint but visible right about my hip bone. As I turn to the right and left, I notice matching circles on both sides of my butt cheeks.

Fingerprints.

He bruised me.

For some ridiculous reason, the edges of my lips lift into a smile. I like having his prints, his marking, on me.

I don't know if that makes me crazy or not, and I don't give it another thought as I open the shower door and step in. The hot water burns my skin.

"Yikes!" I gasp, jumping out of the spray. I lean around, twisting the knob to adjust the temperature before I begin washing my hair.

Before I can dwell on my night with Donovan, inspect whether or not I regret it, I finish my shower and get ready for work, hurrying downstairs.

Despite my fears and my reservations, I want to see him before he leaves for the day.

A duo of masculine voices filters through the kitchen as I get closer. The fact that they're talking at all, and not yelling at one another or ignoring each other, makes my feet slow down.

I don't mean to eavesdrop, but I can't stop myself from sliding off my shoes so the click of my heels doesn't give away my presence.

I stop just outside the doorway to the vast kitchen. It's a beautiful place, and my fingers are itching to cook up a meal in there sometime. I've been surprised that Donovan does all the cooking. I would think he'd have a housekeeper of some sort, or personal chef, but not only has he cooked dinner the last few nights, he seems to enjoy it.

It softens him somehow, seeing him domesticated and comfortable in a kitchen.

"So what is it you want, Jeremiah?" Donovan asks, his voice growing tighter.

I can practically see him bent over the kitchen counter, hands gripping the edges of the gray marble, trying to not become angry.

"I hate that school, and those kids. I just want people like my old friends, who don't give a crap what kind of house I live in or who my parents are."

Silence fills the kitchen, and I can practically see both of their looks. Jeremiah, all angsty-scowling teenager. Donovan, controlled, narrowed eyes, debating.

He huffs and finally says, "I'll see what I can do. But in the meantime, stop beating the crap out of everyone who pisses you off. Deal?"

Jeremiah mutters something indecipherable and I take that as his agreement.

Slipping my heels back on my feet, I use the quiet moment to make my presence known.

"All right," Donovan says as I enter the kitchen. "Get your school stuff and we'll be on our way."

I see him smile at Jeremiah, who nods in my direction, muttering a "good morning" as he walks to me.

I run my hand down his shoulder and give him a wink.

He rolls his eyes, but I see his lips twitching, fighting a smile.

"That was really nice of you," I tell Donovan when we're alone.

He runs his hand over his mouth. "Some shit just needs to change around here."

I purse my lips, not understanding. When he turns his eyes on me, they soften.

That light green sparkles when he meets my gaze. He reaches out, cups me around the back of my neck with his palm, and pulls me toward him. My forehead collapses against his chest, and his other hand wraps around my waist.

Shivers dance on my skin when his lips brush against my ear. "How are you this morning? I woke up in my bed, alone, wanting you. You have no idea the restraint it took to not sneak into your room."

"Hmm," I murmur, my cheeks flushing at the thought of what it would be like to have his body on top of mine be the first thing I see and feel when I open my eyes.

"You like that idea."

I nod, running my hands up his arms, feeling the soft fabric under my fingertips. I wrap my hands around his biceps and look up.

My sudden arousal is obvious on my face when our eyes meet. Lips parted, cheeks flushed, eyes filled with want…I know exactly what he sees when his gaze roams over my face, and I lean into him.

"Donovan," I whisper, licking my dry lips. "I do want that."

His eyes narrow and his chin dips. He brushes his lips against mine—softly, just once—and I inhale a sharp breath.

"Beautiful," he murmurs as he pulls back, his eyes hazy. "Better than I remember."

I'm stunned speechless as his fingers tangle in my hair, messing up my low ponytail.

I don't care, because when he looks at me like he is, I never want to be anywhere else.

I'm sucked into his eyes and touch and the feel of him against my skin, his taste that hints of coffee and vanilla creamer.

"I have to go to work," I whisper, still feeling the burn of his lips against mine.

His breath warms my skin as it drifts along my jaw. His teeth nip at my earlobe, and his tongue soothes the slight sting of pain. "I'll see you later."

My safely encased heart warms and breaks free. I remember his promises from years past, flashing in my memory like the blink of an eye, and suddenly I want so badly for them to be true again. To have the night we spent together mean as much to him as it meant to me.

In Donovan's arms, I suddenly want everything he once promised we could have.

He drags his hands down my back, slowly letting go of his hold on me.

I sway on my feet, regaining my balance without his body steadying me.

"Have a good day." I grin shyly. Although I don't know why.

Maybe it's because I have finally admitted to myself what I've spent the last eight years denying.

Chapter Eight

It's amazing how being given a million dollars can instantly ease most of the stress in someone's life.

Or it could be the scorching sex that Donovan and I are having late at night, after we're sure Jeremiah is in bed and fast asleep.

My body has never been so satisfied yet still desiring so much more.

I want him. All the time.

Even when I'm at work, or visiting my dad, he's always forefront in my mind.

Electricity seems to buzz in my veins at a constant pace, my body primed for him whether I'm near him or not.

It's why, even though I'm sitting at my dad's bedside, I'm still thinking of Donovan.

His hands and the way they light up my skin.

His eyes and the way they seem to look directly into my soul.

I want so much for his whispered words to be true.

The ones he whispers when his mouth brushes up my thighs, when his fingers press into me, his tongue tasting me.

And when he thrusts into me, my arms restrained above my head, allowing me no purchase to seek my own pleasure, but only to receive whatever he wants to give me, I want nothing more than to get lost in him.

"Miss Merchant."

A warm, masculine voice snaps me out of my revere and I turn to the doorway, looking over my shoulder.

"Yes?"

My dad's occupational therapist, Dr. Getting, is a man not much older than I am, with a kind smile. "Your father is not

ENFLAME

improving much."

I already know this. I can see it in his cloudy eyes and the way the left side of his face still droops. While his right hand occasionally twitches, he lacks any muscle memory to grip my hand with either one of his.

There is nothing more devastating to me than to see my dad in his bed, unable to communicate. Unable to wrap his arms around me or press his comforting lips to my forehead like he's done every day since I was born.

Tears swell in the backs of my eyes, but I fight them back.

"What else can be done?" I ask, my hands growing cold. "Is there any other medication we can try?"

I'll do anything. Try anything. And now I have the funds to make it happen.

As if he's afraid of making me cry, he hesitates before shaking his head. "Unfortunately, no. We can continue his therapy, trying to help his muscles remember how to move, but at this point, it's very much a waiting game. I don't want you to become disheartened, though. Many patients who have suffered a massive stroke like you're father don't begin to improve for a few months."

I sniff and nod twice. "Thank you for the update."

His hand taps the doorframe twice. "Let me know if you have any questions."

"I will. Thank you."

Once he's gone, I squeeze my father's limp, cool hand with both of mine. I lean forward, resting my forehead on top of my hands, and begin praying.

I've never prayed harder for a man to regain his health, or for a miracle, than I do for my dad.

Tears line my cheeks, running onto my hands, falling to his, before seeping into the sheet beneath him.

My dad is the best. Even during his overwhelming grief after my mother's death, a grief that lasted years, he still woke up every morning, hugged and kissed me like he always did, and immediately took to caring for me as if I hadn't lost anything.

His strength is incredible. His caring heart even larger.

It was because of him—and the fact that I was stuck at his automotive repair shop for hours after school when I was too young to be left alone—that I first started sanding wood from scraps found behind his lot.

One of his part-time workers, Enrique, who was a teenager at the time but learning to work on cars because his family of eight needed his income and my dad was too kind to turn him away, taught me what could come from another person's junk.

It's a craft and a hobby that helps ease my mind, helps clear my thoughts from everything else going on in the world. When I'm working on my quotes, which may be cheesy to some, I focus on nothing besides the words I'm carving and painting into wood. I concentrate and see nothing besides the grooves in the boards, losing myself in the entire process.

I have my father and Enrique to thank for that. I have them to thank for almost everything good in my life.

"I miss you," I sob over tears and squeeze his hands. Sitting up, I swipe tears off my cheeks and rub them into his hand. "I need you back."

Like always, I receive no response from him—no recognition in his eyes and no movement, even an involuntary twitch in his right hand, that tells me he sees me or hears me.

I leave his room, trying to find strength and hope in Dr. Getting's words, but it all feels out of my reach.

Money may have been able to secure his stay, but nothing can fix him besides a miracle.

* * * * *

"You're quiet tonight," Donovan says as I clear the dishes.

I haven't been able to stop thinking about my dad, and I know both Donovan and Jeremiah have noticed.

There was no satisfaction to be found while I blasted zombies with machine guns and sliced through their brains with a machete when playing with Jeremiah earlier.

He even stopped trying to give me the occasional fist-bump when mine were returned lamely and without a smile.

Eventually he simply dropped his controller, huffed something about it being a stupid game anyway, and left the room.

I have never felt like I've disappointed him, but seeing the frustration of a thirteen-year-old boy, who I can tell just needs a friend, has left me more down.

"Just stuff on my mind," I reply, turning my back to him.

I don't know why I haven't been able to tell Donovan about my dad, but some things are just too personal.

Opening up about my dad will make me more vulnerable, and while I've admitted to myself that I've given Donovan my heart, I still don't know if I've fully given him my trust.

"Something happen at work? Or with J?"

I shake my head, rinse off the dishes, and load them into the dishwasher.

Behind me, I can feel him turning into a wall of restrained frustration.

The air crackles, sparking tension so thick I can feel it rolling down the exposed skin on my arms. I close the dishwasher and start it.

Turning to him, I cross my arms over my chest.

I almost smile when I see him in the same position, glaring at me. "Tell me."

"No. And I'm too tired to argue about it."

With one hand I rub my forehead and try pointlessly to soothe the stress and sadness giving me a headache.

He opens his mouth to say something or argue or manipulate me into giving him what he wants to hear, but I shake my head and sigh.

"I really just want a warm bath, a bed, and to sleep tonight."

"I'll find out what's bothering you one way or another," he says, his voice carrying an ominous tone.

I remember how he found out about my center's financial situation and shrug.

If he wants to figure it out, more power to him; I just don't have the energy to explain anything.

As much as I hate breaking down in front of my dad, it's more dangerous to break down in front of Donovan.

He sees too much of me as it is.

* * * * *

His tongue teases my slick flesh, and my inner walls clench ferociously together, needing something more.

I push my head back into the pillow, my chin tilted up, my panting breathy and needy.

"More," I demand on a raspy breath.

I can't handle his touch, the way he tastes me as if I'm the most decadent dessert he's ever had placed in front of him. It enflames my body, from my toes to my scalp.

His palms press into my thighs, spreading me wide open for him. With my hands restrained and Donovan pushing my hips into the mattress, I can't move.

I can only take.

The thought, the knowledge that I'm under his complete control, sends a pleasured spasm straight to my core.

He presses two fingers into me. "That's it, T. Give it to me."

"Too much." I strain against the leather wraps around my wrists and my back arches.

His tongue replaces his fingers and he delves inside. His fingers move to my clit, his thumb presses.

"Donovan." My voice is a whimper, barely audible as my orgasm coils inside me so tightly I feel like I might explode.

Sharp pain on my clit, as he pinches and flicks it once, unleashes the burning fire and I crumble, shattering beneath his unyielding touch.

"Yes," he murmurs. His gaze meets mine, sharp with need and satisfaction. "I love watching you like this."

The chilling click of a lock snaps my eyes open and I instantly gasp at the feel of cold metal and warm hands on my ankles.

"What the hell?" My eyes widen and I jump when I make out a shadow at the foot of my bed. I try to move, only to find my arms secured to my headboard, my ankles hooked to something that doesn't allow me to push them together.

I blink rapidly, quickly adjusting to the darkness, and see Donovan at the foot of my bed, his arms crossed over his naked chest.

The dim moonlight filtering through the cracks in my curtains is the only light in the room.

"What are you doing here?" I ask, my voice ragged from sleep and from my dream.

Was it a dream? Or did he just bring me to an earth-shattering orgasm while I slept?

My chest heaves from the memory, trying to figure it out.

I stop trying when he says, "Were you dreaming about me—when you just came in your sleep? I barely touched you and you shattered."

My cheeks burn hot and I'm thankful for the darkness in the

room so he can't see me.

I can't think quickly enough to come up with an answer—most likely a lie—when he gestures toward my lingerie.

"Did you wear that to bed, hoping I would make good on my earlier threat?"

If I wanted to be honest, I'd tell him that yes, I did. My babydoll is black lace, opening in the front, only secured between my breasts with a thin black ribbon that's tied into a bow.

My matching black thong has disappeared.

I can feel my bareness against the satin sheets.

But I'm too thrown by his presence and the fact that he's somehow manacled me to the bed while I was sleeping—dreaming of him pleasuring me with his tongue—to answer.

I force out the words lodged deep in my throat and repeat my question: "What are you doing here?"

"You wouldn't talk to me earlier, and for some reason, I hate it that you won't. I hate it more that I haven't earned that trust yet."

"I'm not sure locking me to the bed is the right way to earn that trust."

He chuckles softly. The heat swirling low in my belly belies my words. I'd do anything for him right now because somehow, as soon as Donovan cuffs my hands, I become completely willing—pliable and needy under his commanding touch.

He leans down, brushing his palms slowly over my ankles, up to my knees. Shivers dance along my skin, making me restless.

"I love seeing you spread for me like this," he murmurs, leaning forward and crawling onto the bed. "The fact that you can't run from me or hide anything. It's incredible, seeing how your pussy is already wet, wanting me."

"I'm not the one who ran," I say breathlessly.

His hands are doing amazing things to me, barely touching me but igniting my body all the same.

ENFLAME 93

His head dips slightly before he lifts it and meets my gaze. "Worst mistake I ever made."

I inhale a sharp breath, stunned by his admission. His mouth falls to mine before I can say anything.

He tastes like scotch and cool mint. His tongue plunders my mouth, as if he wants to commit the deepest parts of me to his memory.

I'm aroused. I was as soon as I woke up, as soon as I realized he was at the foot of my bed.

He came for me.

Seeking answers to what was bothering me earlier.

This isn't the most polite way, but any other way wouldn't be him.

With one hand bracing some of his weight off my body, his other hand slowly roams down my torso, barely touching my breasts, just teasing me at the edges.

His thumb takes one quick swipe against my nipples, already hardened into tight buds.

I mewl into his mouth, leaning forward, but my cuffs prevent me from pressing into him like my body desires.

Lust-filled anticipation pulses at the tops of my thighs and I try to spread my legs, to arch into him, to have him press against me at the area where I need him most.

He pulls away from the kiss as his hand covers my hip bone. "You can't go anywhere."

The teasing tone in his voice does nothing to quell the heat burning my skin.

"What is this?" I ask, trying to push my legs together. A bar is in the way and I frown.

"Spreader bar," he answers. His hand moves inward, his thumb brushing over my clit. "I told you. Tell me what I want to know, and I'll free you. Until then, I will use whatever resources at my disposal to get you to talk to me."

And what incredible resources he has, I think, as he presses his hips against me. I can feel his hard erection straining against the cotton of his tight boxer briefs.

Briefs he fills out incredibly well. He could be a model with a package like this.

His forehead drops to mine. His thumb presses against my clit, sliding through my wet folds. "God," he groans. "I love how wet you get for me. How much this turns you on."

I shake my head, unwilling to admit it. But it does. Something snaps inside me when Donovan takes control.

Perhaps because for the last several years, I've had to control so much. So many people depend on me, and now with my dad…

I blink the memory of him in his nursing bed away.

I tilt my head back, his lips falling into mine. "I don't want to talk."

He licks my lips, tracing my bottom lip with his tongue. "Tell me."

"Why is this important to you?"

He pulls back, emerald pools swirling in his eyes. "Let me in."

My heart clenches. It aches to burst free from the safe, free from the wrap, and jump into his worthy hands.

I don't know what face I make, but Donovan laughs and he slides a finger inside me, crooking it so it hits the most delicious parts of me.

"Stubborn woman," he murmurs. "I'll get you to tell me, one way or another."

"Please," I gasp, arching into him. With his weight on me, I can't plant my feet into the bed like I want. "Donovan."

He slips another finger inside, and his thumb presses my clit.

My lower stomach trembles as my orgasm climbs. His fingers continue pressing in, pulling out, his thumb doing deliciously torturous things to my clit until my mind feels like it's mush.

"What happened today?" He leans down to my ear, whispering the question. The words dance across my skin, igniting me everywhere.

My body shakes as it heats and tightens. "Please."

"Please what? Let you come? Is that what you want?"

"Yes."

His fingers thrust inside relentlessly. "I will, T. Just give me this."

Something in his tone, the desperation in it, makes me focus on him. "Why is this important to you?"

"Because I want to know you."

His sincerity makes my eyes burn. "Let my hands go."

He smirks. "Tell me first."

"I can't think with your fingers inside me." They had stilled when he made his confession, and at my reminder, he removes them.

I whine.

My pussy clamps around nothing, feeling the loss.

I throw my head back into the pillow and groan. This is horrendous. Sweat lines my skin and my pulse is pounding wildly. I've never been more aroused.

I turn my head and my eyes widen as his hands move to the waistband of his boxers. He pushes them down, pulling them over his erection, so thick and beautiful as it bounces free from its confines.

I lick my lips, unable to take my eyes off him. My chest heaves, and without his weight on me, I'm able to move my legs, plant my feet onto the bed. They're spread several feet apart and the movement is awkward.

His tantalizing smirk turns into a full grown smile. "Going somewhere?"

"Ugh. I hate you."

His playful expression disappears. "Don't say that."

I blink. This is too much. I was just on the brink of an orgasm that was going to make me scream, and now we're talking.

I want sex instead.

It's so much easier.

Donovan wraps his hand around his thick shaft, stroking himself from base to tip. I lick my lips, straining against my wrists to get to him. My eyes cloud with desire.

He arches a brow and continues stroking his erection. "You want this? Me?"

"Yes."

"Eyes on me."

I lift them at his command, obeying instantly.

"What happened?"

He takes a step toward the side of the bed, and with one hand sliding slowly up and down his shaft, leans over and unties the ribbon on the front of my lingerie with his other hand.

He grips one of my breasts, feeling its fullness before he slides his thumb over my nipple.

"My dad," I gasp, unable to hold myself back.

Every touch shoots straight to my warm and throbbing sex.

He rewards my honesty and leans down over me, sucking my nipple into his mouth. His tongue swirls around the painfully hard nub. "More."

He slides his hand down to my other breast, fully opening my black lace babydoll before his hand trails slowly down my abdomen, skimming along my sensitive and overheated flesh.

I whimper as pleasured goose bumps break out on my skin, chasing his touch.

"He had a stroke," I quietly admit, closing my eyes.

His hand stills and my eyes snap open, remembering what he

likes.

His eyebrows are knitted together in obvious concern. "Today?"

"No."

Whatever he sees in my expression, the fact that this obvious isn't sexy-time talk makes him nod.

"Thank you," he says, his eyes still weighted. But his hand begins moving again, and that concern quickly shifts to a smirk as his eyes gleam with something else—something much more enthralling.

He slides his fingers through my still wet folds and makes a hum of approval.

He's there and gone before I can fully enjoy it, moving to the end of the bed.

I lean forward as much as possible. "What are you doing?"

"As much as I love to see you spread for my pleasure, I want to feel your legs wrapped around me, squeezing me tight when you come and scream my name."

His arrogant smirk makes me want to smack him.

"So confident."

He slides up my body until his thick cock rests against my pussy. Shifting his hips back, he grips himself with one hand and pushes himself inside me. He steals my kisses like he steals my breath as he pulls out. "I've earned it."

And then he spends the next few hours showing me exactly why he has the ability to be confident.

Chapter Nine

I wrap up the last of the sandwiches and slide them into a picnic basket I picked up on my way to Donovan's house after work yesterday.

After feeling guilty for disappointing Jeremiah the other day, and after hanging out with him Friday at the center when he showed up after school, I decided we needed to do something fun.

That Jeremiah and Donovan both need to spend time together. They're both too stressed, too uptight, and too angry at things I don't fully understand. I'm hoping that today brings them closer, but also fills their chests with deep, rumbling, stress-relieving laughter.

Yesterday, Jeremiah spent some time talking about his mom and his family—how they didn't see Donovan or his grandmother that much when he was younger. It seemed to me that somehow his mom, Emily, didn't have much interest in the impressive Lore lifestyle. She married a construction engineer, made their home near Lansing, and was a stay-at-home mom to her two kids.

Jeremiah made their life seem idyllic. He began opening up about how much he missed his friends and missed playing football because his new private school only has a lacrosse team in the fall.

My heart hurts for him even more now, but as I grab a few water bottles from the freezer, using them as ice packs to keep our lunches cold, I can't contain my smile.

Today is going to be fun.

At least for me. I haven't been on a roller coaster in ages, and I can already feel the adrenaline zipping through my veins, filling me with excited anticipation for the upcoming day.

I look up when Jeremiah stomps into the kitchen, his familiar and standard scowl making him seem angry.

"What's going on?"

He points his thumb in the direction of his shoulder.

Behind him, Donovan is walking down the stairs dressed in a light blue buttoned shirt, brown dress pants, and shiny brown shoes.

He looks like he's dressed for a casual day at the office, not a day at the park.

"What's going on?" I ask, this time to Donovan, suddenly terrified that he may, in fact, be going in to work and not staying with us.

Donovan slides his hands into his pockets and frowns. "He's upset with me about…whatever." The man looks genuinely confused.

I press my lips together.

"Are we ready to go?" Donovan asks, one eyebrow raised.

But it's his tone…or something…that's off. He sounds like we're taking him to jail.

I cross my arms over my chest. "You can't wear that to the park." I scan his outfit and watch as he looks down at his feet and up at my disappointed gaze. "When did you become so uptight?" I ask, almost ashamed of myself.

I can't help it. The Donovan I dated in college played video games. He laughed often. He didn't want to take over his father's company, and he certainly never would have entertained Cassandra for more than a necessary greeting at some stupid party.

He's completely different from the man I remember—and he's not altogether better, either. Even the nights of sex and his whispered words of regret don't sway me enough. I see hints of the Donovan I remember occasionally peeking through his hard exterior.

But has he really lost so much of himself that he can't

freaking let loose for one day?

"I'm not uptight. And my clothes are perfectly acceptable."

I snort and roll my eyes. "Yeah, for lunch with your mother—but not for a day riding roller coasters. Jesus, Donovan. Go change and look like you want to be with us."

"Told you he wouldn't think this is fun," Jeremiah mutters, and my heart instantly clenches inside my chest.

His voice—or the disappointment on his face—changes something in Donovan. Maybe it's my own scolding. His shoulders relax and he takes a moment before he nods, mischief lighting his eyes.

He smirks, points a finger at Jeremiah, and then his smirk widens into a full grin. "I can be fun."

Jeremiah lifts his chin, daring him. "Prove it."

Donovan scoffs and heads up the stairs. "Be ready to eat your words, J."

As he disappears, I turn to Jeremiah and see him fighting a smile. He loses, and his lips spread wide in a grin that almost matches Donovan's.

I throw my arm around his shoulders. "See? Told you this would be fun."

He doesn't say anything, but his grin stays in place until Donovan comes back downstairs dressed in jeans and a simple gray T-shirt with the word Michigan screen-printed across the front in cream lettering.

The shirt is ancient and must be from his college days.

The idea that he threw something on, so ugly and worn, with its frayed hems around the edges of the sleeves and the collar—and if I'm not mistaken, a bleach stain down near the bottom—makes me grin.

He winks at me and grabs the basket with one hand, resting his other at the small of my back.

He leads us out of the house, and by the way my cheeks are hurting from my own smile, I am certain it rivals Jeremiah's.

But even with the thrilling victory of simply seeing Donovan relaxed and casual, something niggles at my mind during the drive to the amusement park.

We have so much to discuss. His words of regret at leaving me make me question if this thirty-day plan he had for me was just a way to manipulate me back into his life, or if he doesn't want anything more.

He might just need someone to warm his bed after leaving his wife…which he doesn't discuss. These are all things we need to talk about if there's any hope of something real happening between us.

I just don't know if I'm brave enough to broach the subject first.

* * * * *

"That was wild," I say, my hand to my chest trying to hold my rapidly beating heart inside my body. My legs are wobbly as I climb out of the roller coaster's harness when it pulls to a stop. "My feet are shaking."

Next to me, Donovan rests his hand on my back, guiding me to the exit lane.

Jeremiah laughs. "That was freaking awesome. Can I go again?"

I hold up a hand. "You're on your own this time."

He pouts and looks at Donovan. "Will you go with me?"

We get to the end of the exit and I move toward a bench. I'm all for roller coasters but the last one, a suspension ride, was almost too much for me.

Donovan looks down at me, his brow pinched together. "Are

you okay? You look a little green."

"I'm good. I just need to rest for a minute."

He looks uncertain, but I press a hand to his forearm. "Go. I'll wait right here for you." Looking at Jeremiah, I see him biting his lip and bouncing back and forth on his feet. Anxious to ride, worried no one will go with him. "Take him, Jeremiah."

He doesn't waste time in reaching for Donovan's hand. Donovan's eyes widen slightly at the contact and he turns, smiling hesitantly. "All right, man. Let's do this."

"Awesome."

I watch them walk away, a grin on my face that has rarely disappeared all day. We've been on countless rides, most of them more than once. We've stuffed our faces with corn dogs and funnel cakes and devoured the lunch and snacks I brought.

The locker we rented as soon as we walked into the park is jam-packed with jackets that we stored once the warm fall sun came out, and stuffed with animals that Jeremiah and Donovan won playing the carnival-type games.

Whatever Jeremiah wants to do, Donovan has followed. They seem to be in some unspoken masculine competition to win… something. I don't know what it is, but I have never spent a day laughing so hard at testosterone-filled antics as I have today.

It's like being in college, hanging out at the fraternity house, all over again.

It's been absolutely perfect, and with the sun warming me, tanning my skin for probably the last time of the year, I can't help but lean my head back and let the heat beat down on me.

I'm relaxed.

I might have needed this day as much as Jeremiah and Donovan.

It's the first time I've seen Donovan act like the man I remember: relaxed, easygoing, carefree. I hadn't realized truly how much he had changed until he shed his harsh exterior with his work clothes this morning and started acting like the man I once knew.

It makes it nearly impossible to not want to whisk him away to a dark corner and have my wicked way with him.

So lost I am in my dreamworld, where Donovan takes me roughly in some hidden corner, I jump when a soft touch brushes across my cheek.

"What the—" I gasp, my eyes flying open only to find Donovan and Jeremiah standing in front of me. Matching smirks twist their lips.

My hand is on my chest and I shake my head. "You scared the crud out of me."

Jeremiah grins. "Have a nice nap?"

I feign a scowl and stand up. "I wasn't napping. Where to now?"

"Maybe we should head home if you're tired," Donovan says, his green eyes bright as limes as he scans my flushed cheeks.

The heat on my skin increases from his concerned perusal. No way I can tell him what I was just thinking.

"I'm not tired."

"You sure?" One eyebrow arches.

Jeremiah gives a fist pump. "Awesome, then. Water park time."

Donovan's jaw drops. "Water what?"

"Really?" I ask, my hands going to my hips. "You haven't seen the water rides? We've been here all day."

"Perhaps I was hoping you two wouldn't see them."

"Cute." I bump my hip into Donovan's, enjoying that his arm wraps around me. His hand settles on my hip like it's the most natural thing in the world. "Let's go."

"You'll get wet," he whispers, and peers down at my shirt. It's white, and I press my lips together. He has a point. The last thing I need is a teenage boy seeing my pink bra beneath my white shirt.

The way Donovan's staring at me makes me almost feel bad for him, too.

"No worries," I say and start walking. "I'll just pick up a new shirt to throw over it."

It's a good idea, anyway. When we got ready for the park today, I figured it'd stay too cool to enjoy the water rides, but now that the sun is out, I could use some cooling off.

Or perhaps that's still from my daydreams.

Whichever.

We head to the water park, where we wait in line for thirty minutes only to dive down a waterfall in an inner tube built for six. I'm thankful for the black shirt I bought, because by the time we climb out of our ride we're all soaking wet from our toes to the top of our heads.

"This is the best day I've had in, like, forever," I say wistfully as we head out of the park.

Donovan has his arm wrapped around me, his hand on my hip on one side of me, and Jeremiah walks next to me on the other side.

I link my arm through his when he looks up at me, a large, genuine grin on his face. There's no hint of sadness or anger as he simply says, "Yeah, it was fun."

I elbow Donovan in the ribs only to watch him nod, his own lips mirroring both Jeremiah's and mine.

"Fun. Definitely."

* * * * *

I'm sitting on his deck, wrapped in a thick fleece blanket and staring out at the dark water in front of me.

The sun set and brought with it a cooling breeze that is rolling off the lake. My blond hair blows from a sudden gust and I shiver, gripping my blanket tighter with one hand, my wine glass in another.

This weekend has been incredible. Not only did we all have a blast at the amusement park, but Donovan hasn't worked once this weekend. Earlier this afternoon, when I woke up from a nap on his couch in the living room, I searched the house only to find him involved in some motorbike racing game with Jeremiah.

Their shouts of victory and disgust at losing coupled with the manly ribbing or humorous insults being slung at each other made me smile, and I disappeared from the game room before either one noticed me.

All around me, I see Donovan changing. It's beautiful and terrifying at the same time.

I squeeze my eyes closed briefly at the sound of the sliding door opening and closing behind me.

Donovan doesn't speak while he walks to me huddled in one of the lounge chairs that circles his fire pit.

"Do you want a fire?" he asks when he comes close. "You look cold."

"Sure." I turn my head, needing to tilt it back to see him. The outside lights from the house cast a shadow over his features. "That'd be nice. Thank you."

"Want company?"

I frown, momentarily thrown. He's not an ask-and-wait kind of guy. "Of course." I smile through the hesitance in my words. Right now, he's not the easygoing guy I've spent the weekend with.

He walks toward the fire pit, stacking logs and kindling with ease, his body and limbs moving with graceful, lithe movements until the fire is crackling in front of me.

The flames heat my cheeks and I relax my hold on the blanket.

I frown when Donovan leaves the deck, the sliding door opening. I thought he was staying, and disappointment begins to slide through me when I think he's gone.

But he returns quickly, refills my glass, and sets the bottle of red wine down before taking a seat in the chair next to the table. A simple, domestic beer bottle is in his hand.

"How's your dad?" he asks, breaking the thickening silence.

I take a sip of my wine and focus on the dancing, colorful flames shooting ash into the air.

We haven't spoken of my dad or his stroke since the night he snuck into my bedroom, and then when he woke me up the following morning, his fingers stroking my sex before he slid inside me, bringing me to a quiet, slow-paced, but nevertheless intense orgasm, as he kept his unwavering gaze on me.

The reminder of the quiet, peaceful moment sends tingles to my toes, and I curl them under my blanket.

"He had a stroke just over a month ago—a massive one—and he's not well."

Silence passes between us for several heartbeats. "I'm sorry."

I wave off the apology. "Not your fault." I take another sip of wine, debating how much to tell him, how much to open myself to him, before I just go for it. At some point, we need to start talking. "He can't move. He doesn't recognize me, and he seems to be barely holding on by a thread. His therapist has told me that recovery from his type of serious stroke sometimes doesn't begin for months, but…" My voice trails off. Tears burn my eyes.

"Where is he?"

"Centerville Nursing Facility."

Donovan makes a disgusted sound and I turn to face him.

"You have him there?"

My spine stiffens at his tone. "I can't exactly afford luxury. I know the place sucks, but his therapist seems to know what he's doing."

I trust Dr. Getting, even if I despise the administrator, Ms. Zelder.

"You can afford it now, though."

My lips twist and I turn back to the fire. Its heat is less intense than Donovan's gaze. "That's for the center."

I feel his tension rolling off him in palpable waves before it settles into something else. Something weightier and heavy in a different way.

He reaches over and takes my hand, gently removing my wine glass. Slowly, he entwines our fingers together and squeezes. "I'm sorry about your dad. I know how close to him you are."

I shrug, trying to stay unaffected by his touch. "He's all I have."

His hand squeezes mine again before he lets me go. I reach for my glass and take a large swallow of wine.

Donovan breaks the next silence when he says, "I think this weekend was the best one I've had since college."

I try to smile, but I falter. I'm happy for him, thrilled that I could do something small to help his relationship with Jeremiah, but his reminder brings too many questions to my mind.

Taking a fortifying breath, I stare at the fire and whisper the question I've been dying to know the answer to for eight long years. "Why did you leave?"

I want to say "Why did you leave me," but my lips refuse to form the last word.

He sighs and I look over at him, see his head dropped to the back of his chair, beer bottle at his lips.

His throat works as he swallows, and I can't help but follow the movement.

"My dad died and everything changed." Swinging his legs to either side of the lounge chair, he straddles it, planting his feet flat on the deck, his elbows go to his knees and he rolls forward, hunching his shoulders. His head falls down and he shakes it. "You have no idea how much I wanted to call you then, how much I needed you—wanted you there. But somehow I was thrown into meetings and there were wills being read, decisions being made, lawyers and my mom telling me what to do. Everything snowballed and before I could blink, I was practically running a company."

"I would have been there for you through all of that." I don't hide the pain in my voice. It sounds like he ditched me thinking I wasn't good enough for all of it, wasn't capable of handling it, when all I'd ever wanted was Donovan.

Just him.

"I think on some level I knew that," he says, turning and meeting my pained gaze with his regretful one. "But there was so much going on, and my mom kept pushing. I was just a stupid, scared, and hurting kid, and it was easier to simply do what I was told."

My nose twitches, my anger rising. "And you were told to get rid of me."

He reaches for me, but I pull back. I get it. I always suspected his mom had something to do with his silence, considering she looked at me like I wasn't worthy enough to lick the dirt off her shoe.

"She was hurting enough with my dad's death, and we were all trying to keep everything together, keep his company running… I didn't want to upset her further." He swings one leg over the chair and twists so he's facing me. Then he's up, his hands are under my legs and behind my back and I'm lifted, placed in his lap back in his chair. His legs are on the lounger, mine thrown over his and hanging to one side. "If I could go back and change anything, walking away from you without an explanation would be the thing I'd do different. I'd be stronger."

My breath stalls in my chest, and his hand slides down my hair, letting it fall through his fingertips. I've always loved having my hair played with. It's calming, and I fight the urge to relax into him.

He makes it sound so simple, but it wasn't.

"It hurt," I say, my emotions overtaking me.

My body tenses as he wraps his arms around me and pulls me against him.

Pressing his lips to my temple, he murmurs, "I know. And I knew it would. And it made me feel like the biggest asshole in the world after leaving you that night…especially it being your first time. But I was young and naïve and doing what I was told to do. It doesn't make it right at all, but I thought it'd be easier than calling you. I didn't know if I had the strength to walk away from my family."

I almost want to ask him if he does now. Because as sure as I am that the sky is blue, I'm equally positive that if his mom finds out I'm here, her reaction will be the same.

"What about Cassandra?" I ask, because I need to know.

How could he marry a woman who despised me like his mother? He was there. He saw how bitchy she was to me and he avoided her as much as he could, constantly defending me to her endless rants about how I wasn't good enough for him.

Donovan's chest heaves and dips against my side, his lips pressing into a firm line against my temple.

"Another ridiculously stupid decision when I was in the phase of doing what I was told. I didn't love her, she knew it all along. We were married because her dad is an investor in my father's company. It made us larger, more respected as a company to have the Lores and Kyles connected." He throws his head back to the chair and sighs. "God, it's so fucking stupid. And I just went along with everything until Emily's death. Losing her, getting Jeremiah, and seeing Cassandra as she truly is began changing things for me."

His eyes open and he sets them directly on mine.

I can't pull away. He's so intense, so distraught. I reach out and run my palm against his cheek. He leans into my hand, turns his head and presses his lips to my palm.

"And now?" I ask, uncertainty clogging my throat.

I don't know if I've forgiven him for hurting me, and I don't know if I understand his reasons, either. But I didn't come from a family with unrealistic expectations and the need to always be perfect. I was simply raised to follow my dreams and be happy.

Fortunately or unfortunately for me, the man holding me has always been the only thing that made sense in either of those things.

"I pissed my mom off by leaving Cassandra. She's been horrific, to be honest. I'm certain she's helping Cassandra delay the divorce somehow. I'm getting in contact with a new lawyer tomorrow, who has no connection to my family in any way whatsoever, to try to get it taken care of. But Cassandra said some horrible things to Jeremiah shortly after he moved in with us, and I can't have that—won't tolerate it—around him. Despite what you might think, I do truly love him."

"I believe you."

That, I don't question at all.

"God, Emily loved him so much." His voice clogs with emotion. And I decide we've had enough emotional upheaval—hashing out our past, my dad, his marriage, his family.

There's so much between us that doesn't make sense, that should make me stay far away—because as hard as I try, I simply can't imagine a happy ending between us, even if I want one.

His lips quirk, shaking off his thoughts of Emily, and he leans forward, tightening his hold on me.

I turn my head, lean forward, and tenderly brush my lips against his.

His hand cups my cheek, his fingertips by my ear. The slight movement of his skin against mine creates a fluttering low in my belly.

"I want nothing more than to take you to bed and make love to you until you can't walk tomorrow."

Make love. Not fuck. Not just sex.

I smile coyly and say, "Then what are you waiting for?"

Chapter Ten

"Do you need any help with this?" I ask, leaning over Jeremiah's shoulder.

He turns his head, looking up at me. "I think I got it."

His smirk tells me he wouldn't accept my help anyway.

As far as I'm concerned, math should never, under any circumstances, contain letters and numbers.

I nudge his shoulder. "Thank goodness. I'll be just outside if you need anything. Okay?"

He nods, already back to scribbling pencil on paper and frantically erasing. Poor kid. I always hated math in school, too. As much as Jeremiah loves to read and write in one of his many worn notebooks I've seen him use, algebra comes about as easy to him as it does to me.

Leaving him alone to do his work, I head out to Marisa's desk and prop my backside on the edge.

"What's going on?" I ask, watching her look over a spreadsheet. It contains columns and rectangles filled with more numbers.

I might never escape them today.

"Just looking over our projected budget now that we have the funding."

My interest piques. "And?"

The million dollars is sure to do everything we want, plus some. Even with the amount I've set aside to help my dad, there's way more money than we could ever imagine.

"You know that place on Beacon Street? The one next to the coffee shop?"

I nod. It used to be a large exercise gym, one of those twenty-four-hour places, but apparently Denton doesn't have the interest in our small population to maintain it, because it closed down six months ago. I've had my eye on it ever since as a place to expand our business.

"What about it?"

Marisa's smile is huge and excited when she looks up at me. "We can buy it straight up. Even with the renovations, we'll still have more space to add in another therapist and space for social services to have an office so they can meet with kids there."

I close my eyes, sighing gratefully. It's what I've always wanted.

I can see my dreams for the future taking shape in my mind, and it's all thanks to Donovan. Twenty-one more days and I'll have money beyond my wildest dreams, and all of it will go toward helping more teenagers.

With how close we've become since our talk last weekend, it almost feels as if everything I've ever wanted, including Donovan Lore, is within my grasp.

I don't know what sort of look is on my face, but I can feel my cheeks heating when Marisa playfully punches the side of my leg.

"What's going on with you?" she asks. "You've been walking around here on cloud nine all week."

I shrug, not willing to admit anything yet. "Nothing. It's just been a good week."

Her lips pull to the side. "All thanks to our favorite benefactor, I assume."

I scrunch my nose. "Shut up."

"It's okay to fall in love with him, you know. He seems a lot different from how he used to be, from what you've said."

I finally broke down and admitted everything to Marisa over lunch at Sal's Italian Restaurant on Monday. I couldn't contain all the emotions rushing through me after Donovan's confessions on

Sunday night. She was kind and quiet as always, with a little bit of sexy sarcasm thrown in for good measure.

She's no substitute for Mrs. Bartol, whom I miss dearly, with her wicked sexual innuendos and conversations, but Marisa has been like an aunt to me for years, and she knew I just needed to process, out loud, everything I was feeling.

It helped some. The fact that Donovan has been more relaxed at night, and more fierce in his bed at night when I join him there, has most likely helped more.

But I'm still hesitant to admit to anyone that it's not that I'm in danger of falling in love with Donovan all over again…

It's that I already have.

"I should let you get back to work," I tell her as my phone in my hand begins vibrating. I instantly recognize the number and slide my thumb across the screen to accept the call.

"Hey," I reply, blushing instantly.

"Hello, T." Donovan's voice rumbles through the line. I can practically see his slight smile as he taps his pen against his desk. A desk I would love to see. If his house is new—and from what I've learned, he bought it fully furnished—I'm dying to see what his office looks like. "I just wanted you and Jeremiah to know I'm going to be here almost all night tonight. This new contract I'm trying to win is more difficult than I thought it would be."

"Okay." I pout. I can't help it. I was planning on cooking dinner for him tonight, doing something for him instead of him constantly being the one giving.

"You're upset."

"No." I run a hand through my hair and saunter down the hall for privacy. "Just disappointed. I was looking forward to seeing you."

"Hmm. I like that. How about if I promise to make it up to you later?"

That seductive tone. The deep timbre in his voice hits my ears and shoots straight to my sex. My body instantly heats and my breath catches.

"I take it from your reaction that you like the way that sounds."

I nod, forgetting he can't see me. "I do," I finally admit. "I like that idea a lot."

"Wear something special for the occasion," he says wickedly.

The perfect outfit comes to mind. I saw it at a boutique lingerie store in town just the other day, clothing a mannequin. I had halted in my steps and peered at the scraps of white lace and satin with a matching garter belt. I had to force myself to keep walking so I didn't stop in and buy it.

"I have just the thing in mind."

He groans. "God, I'm not going to get anything done now, imagining you naked."

I lick my lips and rest my head against the wall. "I could come visit you later, show you what I have in mind."

He stumbles over his words for a moment, and I grin. It's rare that I fluster him. "I wish you could, trust me. But I'm going to be in meetings and on conference calls for most of the night."

"Okay then, I'll see you later. Can't wait."

"Me neither, Talia."

I hang up then, loving that he said my name, and the way it sounds coming from him. He's mostly stuck to calling me "T," his old, tender name for me. It's just a letter, but it's the closeness it implies that I love. But when he calls me by name, on those rare instances like he just did, my entire body warms and I feel the need to curl my toes.

I head back to my office, a plan forming in my mind, while I decide to completely ignore Donovan.

A man needs to eat.

When I reach my office, Jeremiah is standing and facing my

wall where all my wood-painted quotes hang.

I stop and watch as he gently brushes his finger, tracing the words It may be stormy now, but the rain doesn't last forever.

"That's one of my favorites," I say quietly, still standing in the entryway to my office.

He jerks his finger back and I feel bad for startling him. "Where did you buy these?" he asks, looking over his shoulder.

"I made them."

His eyes widen in shock. I love that I can surprise him. I'm learning that underneath all this anger and scowling and classic teenage angst, Jeremiah is a really sweet kid with a big heart. He feels everything. Sees even more. Just like his uncle.

"That's so cool."

I enter my office and walk until I'm standing next to him. My finger traces a similar line on the distressed wooden plank, except mine follows the natural grooves in the wood. "When I was young, after my mom died, I used to spend a lot of time at my dad's auto shop. There was this teenage kid who was working there part-time, mostly cleaning up and taking the trash out. But he loved art and when we had free time, he showed me how to do it."

We're silent for a minute before I nudge his shoulder.

"I could teach you. I have everything in my garage at my place, but maybe Bentley or Donovan could have someone bring it to his."

I expect him to jump at the opportunity, considering he's not taking his eyes off the wood in front of us. Instead, he says, "I miss them."

Tears beckon, but I fight them back and place my arm gently around his shoulder. He freezes for a moment and then relaxes, so I pull him closer to me. He's so tall that his head is above my shoulder. We're almost eye-to-eye. I'm not that tall, at only five-foot four, but I know that soon I'm going to be looking up at him, even in my three-inch heels.

"I miss my mom, too. Every day. She was amazing."

"How'd you do it?"

I know what he's asking. Only someone who has lost a parent can understand that kind of pain. "I was about your age, you know. And I was lucky because my dad was still around, loving me and helping me through it. But I know I hurt and was angry for a lot of years, especially when it came to birthdays and holidays and all the big things that a kid wants their mom for."

Tears fall from my eyes, clouding my vision. I wipe them away and my chin trembles.

"But slowly, over time, I began to see her in everything. I remembered what she wanted for me. I held onto the wisdom she gave me when I was too young to understand it. All she ever told me was to chase my dreams, be who I wanted to be, and not worry about other people. And I found that as I grew up, if I could do that, I could keep her with me all the time."

His shoulders shake a bit and I hear him sniff, knowing he's either crying or fighting back his own tears. I don't look and I don't ask, I just allow him time as the silence settles between us.

Suddenly, he twists his body and throws his arms around me. His sobs fill the room and my own tears quietly fall as I watch this boy completely fall apart.

I place my hand on the back of his head, holding him to me, and allow him to cry. I don't whisper soothing platitudes that don't really help. I simply allow him to feel whatever he's feeling and to get it all out.

Something tells me that he hasn't done that much.

"Sorry," he says when he pulls away. He looks away and sniffs, his fingers rubbing furiously beneath his eyes.

"Don't worry about it," I tell him sincerely. I'm not overly gushy, knowing how much teenage boys mostly hate it, but I let him take his time. When he's composed, I scoop up his backpack and slide his homework inside. "How about I take you out for some ice cream? We can finish your homework later."

* * * * *

The rest of my afternoon with Jeremiah went by quickly. After I plied him with a triple-scoop waffle cone that we devoured in a small ice cream parlor overlooking the pier and Lake Michigan, we slowly began sharing memories of our parents—things we remembered about them, places we went.

None of it was serious, but I hope by helping Jeremiah remember how great his parents and little brother were, that it helps him think of the good times instead of dwelling so much on his loss.

I know he'll never get over it. I only hope that as he grows, he can heal from it in a healthy manner. I was fortunate to have my dad around when I lost my mom. From running the center, I have also learned how easy it is for people to become so lost in grief and despair that they are never able to pull themselves out, and their lives are ruined before they ever fully begin.

I don't want that for Jeremiah, and I let him know that regardless of how long I stay in his house, I would always be there for him.

He nodded, seemed deep in thought at the realization that I won't always be in his house with Donovan, but he didn't say anything, so I let it go.

After he ate dinner and went to play games in the game room, I made sure it was okay with him if I left for a few hours, only slightly hating that I was telling him I was going to run some errands.

Now that I'm making my way into Donovan's building, even

though most of the employees have left for the day, my nerves are increasing.

He told me not to come.

I'm hoping that I can persuade him to take a few minutes to rest. I figure the delicious aroma of Cazador's wafting from the plastic bags in my hands will help.

I'm almost surprised to see his assistant, a man about my age with slicked-back black hair and a thick but neatly trimmed full beard, sitting behind his desk outside Donovan's office.

I know his name is Patrick because I've heard Donovan talk about him often.

"Can I help you, ma'am?" he asks when I reach the desk.

I hold up the bags of dinner, feeling bad that I didn't think to get extras for him. If he's working this late, he's probably hungry, too.

"Hi, I'm Talia. I stopped by to see Donovan for a minute and bring him some dinner."

His eyebrows pull together in confusion. "I...um...Mr. Donovan is busy right now. If you'd like to leave the food, I can ensure he gets it."

I don't know him, but I don't like the way his eyes flicker to Donovan's office before returning to mine. "Can I wait for him?" I ask, thinking of the lingerie that is beneath my skirt and blouse.

"Um. You can. But he might be awhile." He stops, presses his lips together, and then nods. "Yes, that's fine. You can wait."

Uncomfortable, I turn and slide into a seat just outside Donovan's office. His office is fully enclosed, so I can neither hear nor see what's going on. I knew he was going to be busy, but the way Patrick continues to look at me makes me feel like I shouldn't be here.

With each passing moment, unease spools in my gut, and I decide to give up. I stand up to leave the bags at the front desk, figuring I can leave my dinner for Patrick as well. I'll just go home and wait for Donovan like he suggested.

"Here," I say, sliding the bags onto Patrick's desk. "I need to get going, but perhaps you and Donovan can enjoy this when you have—"

My sentence is immediately cut off when Donovan's door opens. I shift, turning to face it, and then all the blood drains from my body when I see Cassandra walking through the doorway.

She's laughing, that grating laugh I remember so well, and smiling wide as she looks at the man who is gripping the door to his office.

His scowl doesn't match her laugh, but she doesn't seem to notice.

I can't move, and I don't have time to decide what I should do before Donovan speaks.

"I'll see you later this week, Cassandra. Don't be late."

She opens her mouth to speak when he notices me standing outside his office, gawking at him.

Cassandra turns to me to see what's taken his attention, and her brow furrows as she quickly scans my face.

"Talia," Donovan says, and recognition immediately lights in her eyes.

They flash in confusion before they turn to cold blue steel.

I can't speak, but my eyes dart to Donovan and back to her.

"Talia Merchant?" she asks, her voice practically a sneer. "What in the hell are you doing here?"

"That's enough," Donovan hisses. "Go, Cassandra. I'll see you later."

"That's right," she says, and turns to him so I can only see their profiles. Donovan's shocked green eyes stay on me, his back stiff and straight as she drags a perfectly manicured bright pink painted fingernail down his sternum. "Our appointment. How could I forget?"

She leans up and presses her lips against his cheek, and when she drops back I fight the urge to gag at seeing lipstick on his skin.

Sauntering by me, she quietly hisses, "I should have known he'd come to you."

"Go!" Donovan shouts, and Cassandra jumps slightly before glaring at me.

She doesn't say another word as she walks away.

In fact, none of us do—and poor Patrick looks like he wants to vomit.

"You told me that you shouldn't be interrupted for any reason," he begins, stuttering over his words and looking at Donovan.

The poor boy. I almost want to soothe him. This wasn't his fault.

It was mine.

For trusting Donovan.

For believing that things were over with him and Cassandra.

But if the lipstick on his cheek and at the top of his collar is any indication, I'm struck with the sudden realization that I've been the mistress all along.

The paid whore.

For one million dollars, I've warmed his bed.

I close my eyes and take a step back. "I brought you dinner," I say lamely. "I think I'll just go, though."

"No," Donovan says, and before I can open my eyes, his hand is on my wrist and he's pulling me into his office. "You're not going anywhere."

I stumble on my feet from the sudden movement, and barely catch my balance before I'm inside his office and the door slams shut behind me.

Chapter Eleven

He stalks to his desk and presses an intercom button. "Patrick, cancel the teleconference we have in fifteen minutes. Reschedule for tomorrow."

I don't hear a response before his finger releases, and he presses his hands flat against his dark wood desk. His gaze hits me with a ferociousness I've never seen, but I can feel his palpable anger as if he's shooting solar flares from his eyes.

"That is not what you're thinking it was."

My lips twitch and I swallow my heart, which feels like it's lodged in my throat. "It looks like your wife came by to see you while you're working late."

His muscles tighten and his chest heaves with barely bridled fury. "What you saw is Cassandra trying to make a play when there's none to be made."

I run my fingers across my lips. I no longer want to be here. The lingerie against my skin feels scratchy and uncomfortable.

I blink, knowing he's waiting for an answer, when he's suddenly in front of me. Damn, he's fast and quiet.

His hands wrap around my upper arms, his fingers digging into my skin. And stupid me, I feel that touch radiate warmth beneath my waist.

"Let go of me."

He shakes his head, that deep line appearing above his slightly crooked nose. "I told you I was meeting with a new lawyer today. She got word of it, came to convince me we have something left between us. That's all you saw, Talia."

I lift a finger and point to his cheek and his collar. "You're wearing her lipstick."

He scowls and runs his thumb across his cheek, rubbing it off.

I stare into his green eyes searching for lies I can't find. But it still hurts. I've just been smacked with the reminder that even if I am in his bed, I'm not truly his.

He's not mine.

"What did she want?" I ask, and I see relief flicker in his eyes.

"My former lawyer called her, which breaks about a thousand attorney client privileges and I plan on suing him for it." His hands leave my arms and he scrubs them down his face, sighing heavily. "There's shit going on that I haven't told you, mostly due to my mother and her perceived hold on me. She hates that I'm no longer her puppet and blames Jeremiah, blames Emily. She's using Cassandra to keep me under her thumb, except what she hasn't realized yet is that neither of them have any control over me anymore."

I want to ask him who does, because by the way his eyes are searching my face, looking for understanding, I think he might say me.

But I'm too raw. The last thing I expected to see here tonight was Cassandra. His wife.

Guilt churns in my stomach like curdled milk.

"I should go," I tell him, taking a step away.

"Don't. Tell me why you came."

I shake my head and wave in the direction toward his door. "I brought you dinner, thought we could eat together since you were going to be home late." And then I thought I'd screw you on your desk so you'd always remember me.

The satin shifts across my breasts, causing my nipples to harden.

Donovan grins and walks toward his desk. He presses the intercom again and I hear Patrick answer.

"What can I do for you, Mr. Lore?"

Donovan's green eyes keep me cemented in place. I should go, but I can't.

"Warm up whatever you can from the dinner Miss Merchant brought and bring it to my office. What would you like to drink?" he asks, his question clearly for me.

"Water," I croak. My throat feels parched. My tongue thick.

He nods. "And two waters."

"Certainly—"

He hangs up on Patrick and I frown. "That wasn't very polite." I nod toward the intercom.

"I pay him a lot of money to do what he's told, so I don't have to waste my time with manners."

Well, that's rude. My lips twitch with the need to scold him, but then I remember that he's not one of my kids.

"So." He rounds the corner of his desk and reaches out his hand for me to take. Even with my pain and my anger, I know I trust him. I just hate that I can't claim his as mine. "You missed me so much you had to see me?"

I think of the lace and satin beneath my clothes and my cheeks heat. "Partly."

"Really?" His voice drops to that seductive tone, sending shivers to my pelvic area. "What was your other reason?"

My eyes dart to his desk. To his chair. I look away, feeling warmth climb up the column of my throat to my cheeks. My lips burn.

"I was going to surprise you," I mutter, running my hands down my thighs. I feel the clasp of the garter belt beneath my thin skirt and my panties grow damp.

"Something tells me you mean more than dinner."

I can't think with his amused but desire-filled voice. I swallow thickly and my bottom lip finds its way between my teeth.

His thumb pulls on it and moves to my chin. I feel that one

small touch roll through my system as adrenaline and arousal build inside of me.

"What is your surprise?"

I wrinkle my nose. "I'm not sure now is the best time, anymore. I'm feeling sort of thrown by everything."

Disappointment flashes in his eyes, but not enough to quell the passion I see in them. He sighs. "Talia, you are the only woman I want. The only woman, if I'm being honest, I've ever wanted."

Replaying the few moments I saw them together suddenly makes sense. He was not happy to be around her, the way he flinched when she touched him. He didn't make a scene, but he made it obvious that she wasn't wanted. Relief spreads through my shoulders and they loosen.

Cassandra's hissed words replay in my mind. "What did she mean? When she told me she knew you'd come find me."

Donovan's lips twitch, fighting a smile. Then they spread into a chagrined grin, and if I'm not mistaken, his cheeks turn pink. His fingers run along the outer edges of his mouth. He's fidgeting and nervous. My curiosity piques.

"I may have called her your name once."

"My name?" I ask, and then my eyes widen. "You...you didn't...did you?"

He has the grace to look ashamed—whether for admitting he had sex with her or that he called my name while doing so, I don't know.

I take a step back. This information is tasteless...yet oddly, I'm turned on by the thought.

He thought of me while having sex with other women.

He nods and his hand reaches for my hip, stopping me from moving further away. "She was my wife."

I shake my head. She still is.

Slowly, a grin spreads my lips wide. "I can't believe you'd do that."

"I told you," he says, looking oddly perplexed. "You're the only woman I've ever wanted."

I'm torn with this new information.

Fortunately, our spell is broken by a knock on his office door. Donovan goes to it, unlocks the door, and opens it. "Thank you, Patrick. You may leave for the night."

I hear a muted conversation between the two, but can't hear the words Donovan returns, pushing in a wheeled tray.

I inhale the aroma of burritos, enchiladas, fried rice, and beans. The chips are in a bowl, and the salsa and guacamole are as well.

"Come join me," Donovan says, pushing the cart toward a couch.

I take a seat next to him and we settle in, eating our food.

"This is delicious," he murmurs over bites. "Thank you for doing this for me."

"My pleasure," I tell him. It's been a rocky, mind-bending night, but I can't deny the way I feel around this man.

He quirks a brow and holds a chip to his mouth. "It will be."

* * * * *

"What was your other surprise?" he asks.

Our bellies are filled with delicious, spicy food. I take a drink of my water, trying to ease both the slight burn of the question and the hot salsa in my throat.

I cross my legs, and Donovan's eyes drop with the movement. They narrow, and I watch as he notices the hint of my thigh-highs ending and the clasp of the garter. He looks at me through long, light-colored lashes.

"This?"

His hand reaches out and slowly runs along my thigh, pushing my skirt up higher. I uncross my legs to give him easier access.

His touch sends a shock to my core. Quivering sensations spread from my sex to my inner thighs.

I hesitate before nodding. "Yes."

Leaning forward, Donovan brushes his lips against mine, once, and then twice. His hand pushes my skirt up further, until his fingertips brush against the edge of my lacy panties.

Then he claims his kiss in a movement so slow, so tender, I feel like reaching into my chest and simply handing him my heart on a platter.

The warm rasp of his tongue against mine combined with his tender caresses create a silent riot inside my needy body.

I lean forward, into the kiss and into him, clasping my hands behind his neck.

He leans forward until I'm on his couch, splayed out before him. Shifting his body over me, he settles once his erection presses against me in the perfect spot. I can't contain the shivers that roll through my body in response.

"Always so ready for me," he murmurs, pulling away from me slightly.

I meet his gaze and hold it, loving the emotions I see swirling inside his green eyes.

He wants me.

A rush of confidence floods through me and I push him back until I'm sitting, legs spread wide, Donovan on his knees.

Inhaling a deep breath, I slide my hand down his chest. "I wanted you to fuck me on your desk, so you can remember me when you're working late."

He swallows slowly and his lips spread into a smirk.

With quick movements, he grabs my hips and pulls me to him. "That sounds like the best idea I've heard all week."

A laugh escapes my throat as he stands up, lifting me along

with him, and wraps my legs around his waist.

Holding my ass with one hand, he clears off files and sets me on the edge of his desk. My heels drop onto the floor. His eyes roam my body and then they narrow.

"What?"

"I can't decide where I should start first." His hand brushes across my covered breasts, and I inhale a gasp. "Here?" he asks, and trails his hand down the side of my ribcage. All the anticipation I've felt all day begins heating my blood, and I can't take my eyes off him as his hand moves to cup my already hot, wet center. "Or here?" He looks at me, his eyes bright with mischief and lust. "Any preferences?"

I shake my head and lean back until I'm propped up on my elbows. With the sexiest voice I can muster, I reply, "Wherever you want."

His lips crook to the side, and an uncommon tender look softens his features. "God, you're perfect for me."

Without wasting any more time, I watch as Donovan slides off his suit coat, unbuttons his shirt, and removes the belt on his pants. His hands stall on the button on his pants and he quirks a brow. "Are you going to undress?"

I fight back a laugh and sit up. "Romantic, aren't we?"

"Horny. Yes, I am." His forehead drops to mine and he clasps the back of my neck with his hand. "You have no idea how many times I've sat at this desk and envisioned sinking into you, tasting you until you're all over my mouth and my lips."

Shudders wrack my body and I moan. "Then you should probably get started."

Pulling back from me, he plants a quick, firm kiss on my lips. His hands begin removing my shirt from my skirt, and I shift against him until I can feel his erection press against me.

"God you're sexy," he murmurs, and removes my shirt.

I raise my arms to help him, loving the way he looks at me, and rest my hands on his hips. "You're not so bad yourself."

"And good for my ego," he mutters with a grin on his lips.

"I think your ego is probably big enough." I'm about to make another sarcastic retort when he silences me with a kiss. This one is not fast, but his tongue plunders inside my mouth, instantly claiming me, and I succumb to the taste of him, the feel of him, and the heat from his body rolling off him as he lays me down on his desk.

"Yes," I whisper.

His hands find my underwear, and he pushes it to the side before two of his fingers slide inside me.

My breath hitches. I'm overwhelmed with emotions and the need to have him inside of me, when he suddenly pulls his fingers out and presses them against my lips.

I open my mouth instantly, sucking his fingers inside. Keeping my eyes open, I hum at the taste of me mixed with his salty skin. He overwhelms me in the most delicious way possible, pulls emotions and sensations from me that I never knew existed, and all it takes is a confident touch, a commanding tone.

"Stand up," he orders. Not giving me time to comply, he pulls me off the desk. One of his hands pushes down on my shoulder. Knowing what he wants, I keep my eyes on his and sink to my knees in front of him.

My hands run down his rippled abs until they stop on his waistband.

In quick movements, I finish unbuttoning his pants and pull them down his legs, along with his boxers, until his erection springs free and is directly in front of my mouth.

I lick my lips, wetting them, and look up at Donovan.

One of his hands moves to the back of my neck and he pushes me forward. "Suck me."

I can't think of anything I want more. I wrap my hand around his cock and tug once, then twice. A groan falls from his parted lips, and his eyes close as I lean forward and lick the tip of his cock.

"Fuck, yes."

Wanton lust spreads through my veins as I watch him turned on just from me. I want to play with him, drive him absolutely crazy, but I want him too much.

When I have his attention, I open my mouth and wrap my lips around his cock. His hand continues pushing me forward until I have most of him inside me. I pause, taking a moment to loosen the muscles on my throat before he pulls me back.

With one hand still on his shaft, I begin sucking him, loving the taste of him and inhaling his scent. I rock back and forth, moving along with his firmly guiding hand at the back of my neck, yet he never takes full control.

"Jesus, Talia. You're so fucking good at this."

I hum my approval as I feel him thicken inside my mouth. I know he's close. His thighs shake slightly and his grip on my hair tightens. Another pained groan is ripped from his throat before he roughly pulls out of me.

"Enough. Stand up."

I smile wickedly. "Was that not good enough?"

His hand cups my cheek. "I don't want to come in your mouth. I want to come in your pussy. Now turn around."

I move slowly and fall forward when his hand on my back pushes me forward. "Grip the edge of the desk," he growls. And I smile for just a moment before he unclasps my garter belts and yanks down my underwear.

He doesn't see if I'm ready—he knows I am.

Instead, he lines his cock up at my pussy and plunges inside.

"Yes," I hiss, my walls clamping around him instantly.

He pushes me up onto my tiptoes before pulling out.

"So good, Donovan."

And then I'm rendered speechless as he pulls out and forcefully pushes back inside me again.

My fingers tighten their grip on the desk and my head falls forward.

"Tilt your ass, let me have all of you."

I do, and instantly moan from the change in position that makes me feel like he's splitting me in two. I don't care.

It's incredible. Earth-shaking.

My thighs begin to shake and tremble and his hands hold onto my hips, pulling me back against him, making me fuck him.

His growl fills the room, mixed with my whimpers, and I shatter. With one final push as he seats himself inside of me, I come around him, knowing that I have just become Donovan's.

Completely his.

Permanently.

Irrevocably.

"Talia," he groans, and I feel his own orgasm ripped from his body. His muscles tense. His hands tighten on my hips, and then he falls forward, pushing me until the edge of the desk digs into my hips.

"Holy fuck," he mutters. "How does it always keep getting better and better?"

He whispers it into my hair, but I'm far too lost in my own realization that he owns me— everything about me—to answer.

Instead, I murmur my acknowledgement.

When he's calmed down, he pushes off of me, and I frown as I feel him pull out of me. With a hand on my lower back, he keeps me still.

"Seeing my come fall out of you is so fucking hot, T." His quiet but reverent voice sends sparks to my sex and I feel it clench, feel more of him slide out of me. His finger swipes along my inner thigh and then it's in front of me. "Taste us."

I wrap my lips around his finger and close my eyes, relishing our mixed tastes.

"So fucking sexy," he mutters, and pulls his finger from me. I look back at him over my shoulder and my breath hitches when I meet his gaze.

Unknown emotions flash in his eyes, and I know he's feeling the exact same thing I am.

Overwhelmed.

Owned.

He doesn't know what to do about it any more than I do.

Chapter Twelve

I can barely focus on the faint blue lines marking the walls and doorways on the initial blueprints of our soon-to-be new counseling location.

It has been a week filled with the most blissful experiences I can possibly remember. Every day I see the wall that had been built between Jeremiah and Donovan crumble a little bit more.

A quiet knock on my door makes me lift my head, breaking me out of my thoughts.

"Hey," I say looking up to see Marisa smiling mischievously. I lean back in my chair. "What's up?"

"You have a visitor." She sings the words happily and winks.

I make a face. Donovan? I mentally slap myself. He's busy this week. I've barely seen him. The fact that he's the first person I think of these days is telling enough.

"Who?" I ask, uncurling my legs from under my lap and standing from the desk chair.

I walk toward her and laugh softly when Marisa wiggles her eyebrows.

"You're shameless. And too old to be this goofy."

She scowls playfully. "You're never too old to be goofy."

True. Her words make me think of Mrs. Bartol. The two of them together would be a riot, and I have to remember to stop by her house soon.

Or wait two more weeks until I'm back at home.

I frown at the thought and am distracted with the realization that my time with Donovan and Jeremiah will soon come to an end.

He's held to his end of the bargain, using my body whenever

he sees fit.

I've made good on mine, helping Jeremiah and being there to create a relationship between the two.

"What's wrong?"

The familiar masculine voice clears through my frumpy thoughts and I snap my head up.

My jaw drops and that recognizable tingle of awareness awakens when I see Donovan standing at Marisa's desk, his elbows perched on top, his head cocked to the side and his eyes narrowed.

On me.

"What are you doing here?" I ask, unable to hide my shock. It's three in the afternoon. Jeremiah should be here any moment. "Is everything okay with J?"

Donovan nods. "Everything's fine. I'm here to whisk you away."

Surprise and confusion swirl inside me, making my thoughts jumbled and unclear.

He rolls his eyes and smacks the desk once, pushing off. "Come on. I have plans for you, and they don't involve a teenage chaperone."

My interest is piqued and I look down at my simple tunic sweater, distressed jeans, and black boots. Donovan is, as always, dressed impeccably in a suit. "I should probably change."

"You look beautiful the way you are. Come run away with me." His eyes twinkle with interest, and I can't help it.

I smile. I want him.

I love him.

In order to avoid the question he's sure to ask by my expression, I point my thumb toward my door. "Just let me grab my things."

Marisa shoves them into my hands. "Here you go. Go on and

have some fun."

I twist so I'm facing her. "You have something to do with this?"

"Me?" she asks, her hand over her heart in mock outrage. "Would I do something like that?"

I scowl again and take my purse and coat from her hands. "Fine."

"Come on or we'll be late."

"Wouldn't want that, would we?" I mutter dryly. Tossing on my coat, I meet Donovan on the other side of the desk and allow him to escort me outside.

He slides his fingers behind mine, and the last thing I hear before the door closes is the overdramatic, romantic sigh from Marisa.

"She's quite fun," Donovan says, a crooked smile on his lips.

"She's a pain in my ass."

He laughs. It takes my breath away. What I wouldn't do to see him laugh so loud and free more often. My earlier thoughts that I'll be leaving him soon pop into my mind and I look away.

He ushers me into his car, and once he's seated he doesn't seem to notice my change in mood.

I should be thrilled. He's surprised me at work, and I have a feeling his real surprise is going to be much better than mine was last week.

"How'd you meet her?"

"Marisa?"

He nods and pulls the car onto the street.

I look out the window and wonder where he's whisking me off to. "I've known her for years. She was friends with my mom. When I wanted to open my own free clinic instead of going to work in someone else's office, taking cases I wasn't really interested in, Marisa helped me start this place."

The mention of my mom seems to sober Donovan, like it does so often and he reaches over, resting his hand on my leg.

We spend twenty minutes in the car, driving from one side of Grand Rapids to the other. I'm on pins and needles the entire time.

Donovan has the ability to break my heart worse than he did the first time, and I don't know if he fully realizes the impact he has on me.

And maybe that's my fault for not being honest with him, but I don't know how I can be when there's already an expiration date on our relationship.

Two more weeks and I'm outta there. He hasn't once mentioned a relationship past our thirty-day arrangement, and the idea of leaving not only him, but not seeing Jeremiah every day, makes me rub a pain that aches inside my chest.

My eyes are closed and I'm trying not to think about the future—to enjoy the present and keep my heart from becoming too involved. But who am I kidding? That ship sailed weeks ago.

"We're here," Donovan says, pulling the car to a stop.

My eyes open and almost bug out of my head.

He looks at me nervously and my hands ball into fists.

"Why are we here?" I ask, looking at the entrance to the best long-term care home in the area. I know exactly why we're here, but I'm stunned.

And pissed.

He can't even think to offer this to me. I know the expense of having a patient stay here. Even with the additional million dollars he's promised to give me, it wouldn't cover my costs if my dad stays alive and needs extensive rehab.

It's why he is where he is.

"I strongly encouraged them to make room for your dad." He opens his door and comes around to mine.

I'm frozen in his lush leather passenger seat, and don't move when he opens my door.

"Let's go take a tour."

"You already have this set up?" My voice hardens. I don't look at him.

How dare he chain me to him for longer?

"Hey," he says and crouches down. He brushes hair off my shoulder, but I flinch away from his touch. "What's going on? I wanted your dad to have the best."

"And how am I supposed to pay off this debt?" I seethe, and he flinches.

I can't help it: all my insecurities, all my fears, and all my jealousies over the fact that he's got so much freaking money that he doesn't understand the stress of not having it bubble over, and before he can answer, his mouth agape with shock, I blurt, "You're still married, and I'm only at your place for two more weeks."

I stare out the front windshield, but not quick enough to escape his reaction from the painful lashing I just gave him. It shows in his pale skin and his eyes.

"You think I'm trying to buy you?"

"Isn't that what you do?"

"Holy shit, Talia. What the hell is the matter with you today? You love your dad, and I...I wanted him to get the help he needs. That's all this is."

I notice the way he trips over his words and close my eyes. "I want to go home."

"Talk to me." He reaches out and I shake my head.

I can't have him touch me again. I'll fall apart, and I hate being emotional—especially in front of him.

Suddenly I can't see anything except his mother's disgust, Cassandra's evil smile, the money he tosses around, and the way he strong-armed me into his house in the first place. I can't become any further in his debt.

"Take me home," I tell him, already feeling tears burning my eyes.

"Fine," he clips. I'm pretty sure I hear him mutter something about irrational women right before my door slams shut, the car rocking from the impact.

The drive back to Denton is filled with tension. Several times Donovan asks me to explain, but I cut him off.

I'm being a bitch, I think. This should make me happy, right? Him taking care of my dad. Taking care of me.

But if it doesn't come with promises of a future, then it just makes me more of his mistress/whore.

I can't do this anymore.

When Donovan reaches Denton's city limits, I whisper, "My house, please."

His jaw clenches and he presses his lips together. "You agreed."

"I agreed to a million dollars. Not a long-term contract where you think you can continue to buy me to sleep with you."

His hands twist on the leather steering wheel, making an eerie squeaking sound.

"That's not what that fucking was. Jesus Christ, T, can't you just take a gift?"

Not when it comes with these kinds of strings. This is my dad, the man who has always taken care of me, and now it's my job. I might be failing, but it would crush my dad's heart to think I lived in some guy's bed to move him into the lap of luxury.

"You don't get it," I mutter. I focus on the winding street, the trees, the cars that get junkier, and the houses that get older the closer we get to my house.

"Then explain it."

I let out a sigh of relief when he pulls into my driveway. "Do you see this?" I point to the houses. "This is my world. It's not mansions and tossing money at everything that comes my way. I might have taken your first offer because I was willing to do whatever it took to save the kids I care about, but my dad would shit a brick if he found out I did something like that for him."

Hypocritical, since I already have. But most of that went to the kids. This is different.

"I told you—"

"It's a gift, I know. But your gift comes with unspoken strings that I can't accept. Jesus, Donovan. You're still married."

"For two weeks," he bites out. The veins popping out on his neck tell me how frustrated he is with me.

"Funny." I laugh sardonically. "That's how long our arrangement is for."

His eyes widen and his hand clamps down on my wrist. "That's what you think? That I'm actually thinking of a timeline with you? For fuck's sake, Talia, I just got you back." He drops my hand like I burned him. Maybe I did.

With disgust clear on his features, he turns away from me. I feel the loss of him instantly.

It hurts deep in my chest, a burning distaste I already feel in my mouth, but I can't take it back.

Not when my head is pounding and I'm so confused.

"I'll give you the weekend to realize how ridiculous you're being. If you don't know how I feel about you yet, I'm not sure there's any hope for us." He looks at me, sad eyes hiding behind thick lashes, and my heart jumps to my throat. "Take the weekend and run, Talia, but for fuck's sake, I hope it's the last time you do it."

He waits while my trembling fingers open the door and my wobbly legs carry to me to my front door before I hear his tires peel away.

Tears stream down my cheeks before I open my front door,

and once I'm finally inside, I'm hit with the emptiness of my home.

It may be filled with clutter and look cute, but compared to how I've just spent the last two weeks, it's empty of everything that really counts.

* * * * *

"Well, I'm just not sure I see the problem here." Mrs. Bartol huffs and tosses her gray hair over her shoulder, throwing herself into the couch.

I roll my eyes, but inside, my gut is churning.

It could be the excess wine.

Or I'm a liar.

"He can't just buy his way into my life." I'm repeating myself. I think something has happened to Mrs. Bartol's hearing in the last few weeks.

I turn to Laurie. She's sitting in a chair on the other side of the room, her thumb languidly running up and down the side of her wine glass.

She's staring into the dark red liquid as if it holds the answer to my problems.

I'm not sure wine is helping me at all. It sure isn't giving me answers, and it's only going to leave me with a headache in the morning.

It already hurts enough. I set my glass on the table next to me and frown.

When she showed up after Donovan dropped me off, only a few hours after I called her, I crumpled into her arms before she had walked through my front door, weekend traveling bag behind her.

This is why she rocks as a best friend.

When Mrs. Bartol showed up, seeing me at home and with company, shortly after, the drinking and confessing began.

"What?" I finally ask Laurie.

"I think you should give him a chance," she mutters quietly, as if voicing her opinion might cause me to go ballistic.

She might be right. I'm angry at Donovan. I'm more angry at myself for not thinking clearly earlier. It was just…too much.

Having dinner and drinks with two women I respect more than anyone has helped me see things more clearly.

Sort of.

Maybe he was just trying to help.

"He's married," I reply, and watch her flinch. Laurie's husband cheated on her and their marriage was put through the wringer when, in her anger and confusion, she turned to a man—her now ex-boss—for physical affection. While she and James have been trying to put it behind them and move on with their lives together—including a move back to their hometown of Ann Arbor—I know the reminder that I've been sleeping with a married man forces all of this to the forefront of her mind.

"He said two weeks. Did he tell you what that means?"

I shake my head. In my anger and confusion I'd glossed over that comment Donovan made earlier. Last I knew, Cassandra was delaying their divorce and making everything difficult for him. The fact that he has an end date in sight now makes my head spin.

Next to me, Mrs. Bartol starts laughing quietly.

She must be drunk, and perhaps becoming slightly senile in her old age.

"What?" My lips pull to one side.

"You girls today." She shakes her head in total befuddlement. "You're all so intent on wanting to be these strong women, independent, having everything you can possibly dream of. You know what's important to a woman?"

I press my lips together. Whatever she's going to say is going to make me think of two old people bumping nasties. I'm not sure there's enough wine in the world to wash away the visual images Mrs. Bartol creates with her slurred words.

"Hot sex and a man who can give it to you—a man who wants to give it to you hard and fast every day of your life."

Laurie sputters. Her wine splashes into her glass and into her lap, and I look at her to see her covering her mouth. Wine spills through her fingers as she tries to regain control.

In all the years we've been friends, her interactions with Mrs. Bartol have been minimal.

She's getting the full effect of advanced-age crazy tonight.

"That's not all we want."

Mrs. Bartol silences me with a look. "It's the only thing that's important. Trust me, Harold and I have been married fifty years this summer, and if there's one thing that always works, it's his pecker."

I snort. She continues.

"That can get us through anything—and on top of that, you have a man who wants to not only do that for you—and he sounds quite capable of providing it—he wants to take care of you and your family. He's lightening your stress, making your life easier. What in the hell is wrong with you?"

I'm taken aback by her bluntness, although I shouldn't be.

I rethink my ability to be sober with her in my house, spewing things I don't want to have in my head about Harold, and take a large swig of my wine. "He's trying to trap me."

"Girl!" Mrs. Bartol howls. She throws her head back and cackles so loud I shoot Laurie a wide-eyed look. The woman's losing it. When she recovers, she sets her glass down and stands up. "That man is trying to love you, and you're so wrapped up in the pain of your past with him you can't see that he's trying his damnedest to make you see what you mean to him. He might be going about it wrong, but that's because he's a man and they're usually pretty stupid. Doesn't mean he's not trying."

Donovan's last words filter through my ears. *If you don't know how I feel about you yet, I'm not sure there's any hope for us.*

He couldn't have meant what Mrs. Bartol is proclaiming.

Could he?

I stare into my wine glass and frown.

"I'm an idiot, aren't I?"

She pats my shoulder as she shuffles by, flashing me a wink. "I knew you'd see reason eventually. Call him. Beg for forgiveness, and his cock, and he'll make everything right."

"God, you're horrible."

She shrugs and I stand up, following her to the front door. I see Laurie doing the same thing with a grin the size of the Cheshire cat on her lips, too.

"You're young, honey. You'll see. A man who gives good sex, a pocketbook that's open for you to not have to worry about anything, ever, and a heart big enough to take in his nephew? That's too good to pass up, even if there's obstacles like bitchy soon-to-be-ex-wives in your way."

I pout. "She's still his wife." And still just as gorgeous as ever. Anger boils at the mere memory of Cassandra.

"On paper. Wait the two weeks out if you have to, if that makes you feel better, but if what you've told me is true, you're the only woman he wants."

She rolls onto her tiptoes and kisses my cheek.

"Thanks, Mrs. Bartol."

"Bye. Have a good night, and it was good to see you again," Laurie says from behind me.

I open the door and grin when Mrs. Bartol shoots me a

scathing look. "Now, all this talk of sex has my womanly parts raring to go. If you'll excuse me, I'll go pop some pills into Harold and let his energizer bunny wear me out."

I blanch at the image. Not enough brain bleach in the world will erase that.

But still, I laugh. Because she's insane.

And awesome.

"On that note," Laurie mutters.

"G'night!" Mrs. Bartol gives her final farewell, and Laurie and I stay in the doorway, watching her make it safely back across the street.

When she reaches her front door, it flings open and I catch a brief glimpse of Harold, butt naked, scooping her into his arms before he shuts the door again.

Next to me, Laurie leans on the doorframe and sighs. "You know, that woman is batshit crazy, but if what she says is true, I want to do whatever she tells me just so I have a husband who still looks at me like that and wants me like that after fifty years."

I smile. "I think you have that."

"Yeah." Her grin matches mine and she runs her hand through her dark brown hair. "I think you might too."

My smile falters and my eyes mist over.

She might be right. And I was a complete bitch to the man who wants to give it to me.

Chapter Thirteen

In my garage, with my iPod blaring Ellie Goulding in my ears, I am calmer than I have been in the last forty-eight hours.

I have my plan in place to make amends with Donovan, and I'm anxious for tomorrow afternoon when I can see him. Unfortunately, I've tried calling him a half-dozen times to speak to him and he hasn't answered, nor has he returned my calls. I'm trying not to be worried, thinking that maybe I've screwed us up before we truly began again, but it's hard. It won't stop me, though, from continuing to try to explain what happened last Friday. That I was just afraid.

Saying goodbye to Laurie earlier this afternoon made tears burn my eyes. Fortunately, I have an aching belly from the countless amount of laughs we shared over the weekend.

Spending time with my best friend, who I rarely get to see anymore, was needed more than I could imagine.

I sent her home with a hug and a kiss, and she left reminding me that sometimes it takes giving someone a second chance to truly see what they're made of. I admire her strength—her ability to forgive and admit her own mistakes.

Mrs. Bartol's morning wakeup with mimosas and cinnamon rolls left me sated and sleepy.

It's really been the perfect weekend.

If Donovan had been around to see it, to hear our laughter and Mrs. Bartol's disgusting sex comments, it would have been perfect.

I've had days to think about my overreaction to Donovan's gift on Friday.

His words and the pain in his eyes speak more clearly than my doubt and fears.

I'm lost in the feel of the wood and sandpaper beneath my fingertips and my chest heaving from exertion. It doesn't seem like it should be difficult, but it can take me hours to prepare the wood to ensure the paint and stain will hold properly.

My biceps burn and my fingers are numb from the hours I've spent sanding wooden planks.

I'm almost done, taking a moment to wipe the dust from the wood, when lights shine in my driveway, an engine purring quietly as it pulls up to my garage.

I usually work with the garage door closed, but the fall weather is beautiful—cool and calm—making it easy to work and get fresh air at the same time.

Turning around, wood plank in my hand and covered in dust up to my elbows, I feel my eyebrows jump high on my forehead as Jeremiah hops out of the back door of the black vehicle in my driveway.

"Hey," I say, surprise evident in my voice and expression. I remove the earbuds from my ears and tuck them into my shirt pocket.

"What did you do? Uncle D has been pissed all weekend and you haven't been there."

"Jeremiah." My voice is calm and soothing.

Based on his expression, it's also completely patronizing.

"I came home yesterday and you weren't there. Uncle D told me you left."

His chin trembles and anger and sadness battle inside me.

"Not you." I reach for the young adult in front of me, who looks completely shattered. "I wouldn't leave you, Jeremiah."

His hands ball into fists. "You already did."

I shake my head. "We had a fight. It's adult stuff, but I'll always be here for you. Donovan should have told you that."

He scoffs, looks past me at my workbench, and his eyes

narrow.

Wretched guilt curdles in my stomach like sour milk.

"Jeremiah," I say again, my voice still quiet. I move to him like he's an injured animal. And he is, just in kid form. "I'm so sorry if we hurt you. But our fight had nothing to do with you."

He rolls his eyes and I try again.

"It was really my fault," I admit. "Donovan did something and I took it the wrong way. I plan on apologizing."

"When?" His head snaps to mine. "Because he's being a jerk again and I don't like it."

"Soon." I watch his tight shoulders loosen a little bit.

With a slight jerk of his head, I know he's forgiven me—know he believes me.

Slowly, he walks toward the bench where I've been working. Almost reverently, his hand reaches out and slowly trails along the wood. "It's smooth."

I watch him for a moment before I join him, standing next to him as he glances at the words I have printed out on a simple scratch piece of paper.

My lips pull into a gentle smile. "It is. I need to brush it off, wipe it clean, and then I start painting." I nudge him with my shoulder, getting his attention. "Want to stay and help me?"

He glances at Bentley…in the Bentley, and looks up at me. "Can I?"

"Of course."

For the next hour, I teach Jeremiah how to use the brushes and rags to finish prepping the wood. Then after showing him how to carefully stencil the words, I stand back and watch him work.

He's precise with his movements, and intentional. It makes me smile when he sucks his bottom lip in between his teeth and his brow furrows in concentration.

He looks so much like Donovan that it makes my heart hurt.

"I think we're about done for the night," I say once he's stenciled the final word.

He sets his brush down, and both of us are silent for a moment while we read the deep navy-painted words: Smile often. Forgive easily. Love freely.

"It's kinda lame," he mutters, his lips fighting a smile.

I bump his shoulder with mine. "I know. It's a girl thing."

Handing him a rag to clean off his hands, I take one too, and nod toward the car that's been waiting for him. I thought about inviting Bentley to join us, but if he was content sitting in the car for an hour, I decided to let him so Jeremiah and I could have this time together.

"You probably have to get home and get ready for school tomorrow."

His eyes sparkle with something. "Yeah. New school tomorrow."

"What?" I ask, dropping my rag. "What do you mean?"

Jeremiah nods like it's unimportant. Then he shrugs. "Uncle D said I could go to the public school starting this week. Basketball starts soon and I want to try to make the team."

"You need some help practicing?"

He scoffs at me, but I watch as he takes note of the basketball hoop next to my driveway. I don't play often, but I used to love it, and sometimes when I'm bored or in need of some exercise, I still practice my layup drills and free point throws.

"Like a girl could beat me," he says, full of mirth and cockiness too old for a young teenager.

I laugh and toss my arm around his shoulder. "You'll eat your words someday soon."

He rolls his eyes but sobers when Bentley sees us headed toward the car. He climbs out of the driver's seat to open Jeremiah's door.

"Master J," he says, tipping his head and pressing his lips together.

I chuckle as Jeremiah scoffs.

"I'll see you soon, okay?" I tell him as he slides into the backseat. "And we'll finish the sign if you want."

"Sure. Whatever. It's not like it's that important."

But I catch his gaze on my garage as he says it and my heart aches. I've damaged a relationship we were building by taking off this weekend, and while I know it can be repaired, I hate that we've taken two steps back. I genuinely care for this young man.

Nodding goodbye, I shut his door and then look at Bentley.

He's dressed as casually as he always is, in perfectly pressed khakis and a white button shirt. "Can you help me with something while I'm at work tomorrow? I know it's not your job," I say, hoping I'm not overstepping my bounds.

"My job is to help you and Jeremiah in whatever capacity you need, Miss Merchant."

"Talia." I smile.

He nods.

Nodding toward the garage, I ask, "Can you bring my workbench and a few other things to Donovan's? I'd like to be there to help Jeremiah finish the sign."

And a part of me hopes that Donovan will accept my apology and allow me to continue staying there for a few more weeks. I'd like to be there to help Jeremiah adjust to his new school and repair the things I've broken this weekend.

"Certainly." Bentley nods and we begin walking toward the front of the car.

"Thank you. I'll have everything I need set on the workbench. It won't be much, but I appreciate it."

"It's not a problem." He gives me a kind smile, and in a way that I assume is uncharacteristic of him, he reaches out and places his hand on my forearm. I look down at his touch and then at his kind blue eyes. "And now, if I'm not overstepping my bounds, I would like you to know that Mr. Lore has been truly horrific this weekend. He misses you greatly."

My throat swells with unnamed emotion and I swallow thickly. "I hope to fix that tomorrow."

He smiles, fine lines appearing around his lips and his eyes, and I almost want to lean into him and have him wrap his arms around me. He reminds me of a kind uncle that I never had. But I love how he seems to genuinely not only love his job, but caring for Donovan and Jeremiah.

"Very well, then. Goodnight, Talia."

I smile as he uses my first name for the first time unprompted, and tip my chin goodnight. I stand in the driveway, watching the car pull away until the rear lights have faded from my view.

Back in the garage, I clean up my mess, preparing everything to be moved tomorrow.

And when I'm done, showered and dressed for bed, I close my eyes and dream of Donovan.

Sweet dreams where he forgives me. Where our past is inconsequential.

Where he pleads for my love and my trust and desperately wants me to be with him.

And then I dream of love that feels more important, more necessary, than the daytime sun.

How it warms me from the inside out as he slides inside of me, his fingers and tongue and cock bringing me to overwhelmingly emotional and physical orgasms…over and over again.

* * * * *

"What are you doing here?" Donovan's voice is hesitant, but

his lips quirk into a slight smirk that says he's not altogether unhappy to see me.

My lips roll together and I take a fortifying breath. I thrust a plastic-covered pie container toward him, and he reaches out, grabbing it before it hits his chest.

"What's this?" He looks down and then up at me, our eyes meeting—his a warm green filled with amusement, mine tremulous.

"Um." I lick my dry lips and suck my bottom one in between my teeth when Donovan's eyes drop and watch the movement.

His chest expands and those warm eyes change. Darken.

When his eyes meet mine again, something flips and warms deep in my belly in the best way possible.

"Humble pie."

His lips twist, lines crinkling at the edges of his eyes. "And what does that taste like?"

His rich, deep voice sends a pleasured sensation down my spine, straight to the area between my thighs.

Humble pie is well…humiliating. I hate admitting when I've been wrong.

I shrug, lips pulling to the side. "Cherries?" It's more of a question than an answer.

Donovan's grin spreads wide and easy. He takes a step back, opening the door further. "Get inside, you pain in my ass."

I take the final step, shaking in my gray stiletto ankle boots, and smooth invisible wrinkles out of my tunic top at my waist.

"Thank you," I say when I think I can speak without a trembling voice. It works—barely.

Donovan simply nods once, questions in his eyes, and leads me toward the kitchen.

"Did you make this?" he asks. He slides the container onto the counter and takes off the top, inhaling the rich aroma of freshly baked pie.

"I did."

"It smells delicious. Join me for some?"

My eyebrows knit together as I watch him move about his kitchen as if we hadn't argued the last time we saw each other. That I hadn't essentially called him a pimp and thrown a gift back in his face.

"Donovan," I whisper, walking toward the counter. "Don't you think we should talk?"

His hand stills for a brief moment before he scoops two pieces of pie onto two bright blue plates. "I think we should have dessert first."

He turns to me, looking at me over his shoulder, and his gaze slowly slides down my body and back up again. Nodding once, as if by simply scanning my body he's come to a conclusion of an unspoken manner—a scan I still feel even when he's done looking—one side of his lips rises. "Yes. Dessert first."

He slides a plate across from him on the counter and I take the silent cue to take a seat on a bar stool and join him.

"Mmm," he murmurs over a mouthful of freshly baked pie, his eyes locked on mine.

My spoon freezes as it reaches my lips. That sound.

It steals my breath, and I feel my panties grow damp.

Feeling a heat creeping up my neck, I force my attention back to my cherry pie. It's delicious—and a recipe from Mrs. Bartol, who has declared that it will not only melt in your mouth, but make any man melt at your feet.

Based on Donovan's lust-filled eyes as he continues eating, I suspect she's not wrong.

When he's finished eating, wiping away a morsel of cherry sauce from one edge of his lips, he slides his plate to the side, leans forward, and braces his forearms on the counter. "You ran."

I focus on my pie like it's a lifeline. I can't think straight when Donovan sets those eyes…that voice…on me in this way. Everything inside me feels warm and tingly, which is not entirely unwelcome.

"I'm sorry," I whisper, my voice hoarse.

"Forgiven."

My head snaps up and I meet his gaze, his lips pulled into a wide smile. He looks so relaxed, so thrilled. There is no hint of the anger or horrific personality I have heard he was displaying over the weekend.

Is it possible that my presence calms him this much? Makes him this happy?

I shake off the thought.

"That easily?" I arch a brow and slide the last bite of cherries into my mouth.

Donovan's eyes dip, an intense expression in them as he follows my movement. "No," he finally says, shaking his head. "Not that easily."

"Oh."

"Come with me." He extends his hand as he walks around the corner of his kitchen bar and waits until I slide off my stool to meet him. My hand slides into his as if it belongs there, and electricity slides smoothly up my arms when his fingers wrap around my palm.

"Where's Jeremiah?" I ask as he leads me into his living room. "He told me he was starting a new school today."

Donovan's lip twitch into a grin. "Yes, the sneaky little guy told me he saw you last night."

"He was really angry with me."

I don't know what my voice betrays, but in a second Donovan has spun around and wrapped our entwined hands around me so they're resting at the small of my back, and his other hand cups my cheek. "Hey," he says soothingly. His thumb caresses my cheek tenderly and I lean in. I can't help it. I love this man, even if loving him terrifies me. "He'll get over this. He was already in a much better mood when he returned last night."

"You knew where he went?"

He rolls his eyes in an arrogant I-know-everything gesture. "Bentley called me while you were working in the garage. Until then, no, I didn't know, but I knew he was with Bentley so I also wasn't worried. Usually he just takes off on foot."

He walks me forward, keeping his hands on me until we're in front of his couch. His hands release me only to slide to my hips, and then he pulls me down so I'm sitting on his lap, my legs draped over his thighs, my back against the armrest.

His arms wrap around me and he smirks. "Now you can't get away."

When I'm in his arms like this, my shoulder against his and feeling his breath against my neck, I don't want to be anywhere else in the world.

"So where is he now?"

"Bentley took him shopping. Apparently all of his clothes weren't cool enough for public school."

He rolls his eyes like he's put out by this, but I hear the affection in his tone.

"That was really nice of you, letting him change schools."

"Yes, well, it's occurred to me in the last several weeks that a lot of things around here need to change. Apparently," he says, arching one brow teasingly, "I'm quite the control freak, and it's been brought to my attention that not everyone appreciates the gesture."

I flush crimson and look down at my hands in my lap.

His thumb grazes my chin and he tilts my head back so I'm forced to look him in the eye.

"I want to take care of you, Talia. I want to make up for when I hurt you years ago. That's all that gift was. By making your father's life better, giving him the best therapy I possibly can, I make your life easier."

Tears burn in my nose and I can't stop them before they fill my eyes and spill over.

"Don't cry," he murmurs, brushing them away with his thumb.

"It just..." I sniff and disgustingly wipe my nose. "It scared me. I don't know what this is between us, and I'm not used to people helping me."

He cups my cheeks and brushes his lips against my forehead. "This is our second chance, Talia. I want it. I want you. I want you in my house, in my life, in Jeremiah's, and I want us to make up for all the time we've missed. I know I messed that up, but helping your dad wasn't about making you indebted to me." He pauses and I feel the swell of his chest against me as he inhales a breath. "It was about me showing you how much I love you. How much I always have."

My heart thumps painfully inside my chest. Love me?

My eyes must widen at the admission, but my breathing has faltered and I'm frozen in his arms.

He licks his lips and brushes them against mine. Magically, his slight touch restarts my heart. I lean forward, needing more.

"Tell me you feel the same."

With his hands pulling me toward him, I can feel his arousal growing beneath him, pressing into the area between my thighs.

I can't think, much less speak.

"Talia," he whispers, "tell me."

"I do. I love you. I always have, but it's scary this time." I pull away, collecting my thoughts and my breath at the same time. "You still have Cassandra."

He scowls, as if the reminder of his wife disgusts him.

It does the same for me, throwing an icy chill over a heated, romantic moment. But it can't be helped.

He opens his mouth to speak, but I quiet him by pressing my finger over his lips.

"I can't be that other woman. Even if it's a technicality, even if it's a matter of weeks. I can't do that...be that person anymore."

His lips part, and I move my finger when his hand reaches up and clasps around my wrist. His tongue darts out and swirls around my finger before he sucks it into his mouth.

My fingertip is apparently connected to my clit, because everything begins heating and pulsing as my shocked eyes stay fixed on his lips. His tongue. His warm grip on my skin.

He pulls my finger from his mouth with a pop.

I chuckle, trying to fight the insane attraction between us.

"What would you say if I told you that Cassandra is no longer an issue and that papers are signed, sealed, and we are officially divorced?"

I shoot him an incredulous look. I'd say I want to jump him, have my wicked way with him right here on his couch—but I don't believe him.

Three days ago he said two weeks.

Finding humor in my silence, he presses a kiss against my forehead, his hands move to my hips, and then I'm being lifted, twisted, and set down on the couch next to him.

"I'll be right back."

He pushes off the couch and disappears down the hall.

He quickly returns, leaving me barely any time to consider what he said about Cassandra.

A manila envelope is in one hand and he smacks it playfully against the palm of the other.

I stand up. "What is that?"

"The reason I wasn't able to answer your calls this weekend."

He flicks his wrist, and I can see the stamp of a law firm on the upper left corner.

My brow furrows. "Jensen Rhodes is your new lawyer?"

"You know him?"

"Not really," I mutter quietly, my thumb sliding over the envelope and its brass clasp on the back when I turn it over. "He used to be James's boss."

"James worked for Rhodes?"

I nod, somehow feeling that if I open it, I'll be intruding on a relationship that's none of my business.

"Yeah, before he and Laurie moved back to Ann Arbor. From what I know, Jensen is a master. He's wicked and evil and does anything he needs to do—some things not always aboveboard—to make his clients happy."

"Well, he made this client thrilled when he discovered in the course of a matter of days that Cassandra has been unfaithful for the last two years with the CFO of her father's company."

I pull a face—disgust mixed with shock.

Donovan doesn't look like he cares.

"I'm sorry," I tell him, and he throws his head back and laughs.

"I couldn't care less about Cassandra and what she does. But… her actions violate the prenup she signed, and technically she should be walking away from this marriage with nothing. In order to get her to sign the papers over the weekend, I promised not to go public with her indiscretions, and I'm giving her five million dollars to leave me alone."

I look at him, see that he's looking at me, and then he glances down at my hands on the envelope. "Aren't you going to open it?"

It's tempting. Five million dollars is a shock, and a part of me wants proof.

I thumb the clasp, feeling the rigid metal dig into the pads of my fingers before I toss it to the coffee table next to me.

"No." If I want to move on with Donovan, I need the past to not matter. I need to trust him.

His eyes gleam with wicked intent, and like a slick, smooth panther, he is in front of me before I can blink.

His arms wrap around my waist and he pulls me to him, sliding one hand up until he's clasping the back of my neck and searing his lips to mine in a scorching kiss.

I relax into him immediately. His touch and his taste enflames every nerve in my body until I feel completely consumed…

Completely taken by this man in front of me.

This man who has broken my heart, and who has the ability to heal it as well.

Pleasured moans rip from deep in his throat as he deepens the kiss, and I'm totally done for. My hands grip his shoulders and then claw at the fabric of his dress shirt, needing to feel him, needing more of him.

And then he suddenly rips his mouth off mine, both of us gasping for breath.

Behind us, I hear the front door slam closed and I look at Donovan.

"Later, we'll finish this," he growls with his lips against mine.

If I don't spontaneously combust first.

I lick my lips, tasting him on my tongue, before Jeremiah is in the room.

"Oh God. You guys were making out, weren't you?"

I whip my head over my shoulder, only to see him grinning. Biting my lip, I look down to see his hands carrying a massive amount of plastic and paper bags.

"Hey," I say, smiling nervously.

"You're here." His voice sounds hopeful. Perhaps because he's absolutely right and Donovan and I were just making out.

And it was delicious.

"I am." I nod and see his smile widen, a little bit freer than it just was.

"She always will be." Donovan's voice rumbles down my spine, his intention clear as his hand snakes around my waist. It settles on my hip and he pulls me to him, my back to his chest. His erection is evident against my backside.

I bite my lip to prevent a needy whimper from escaping my lips.

"How was school?" I ask, trying to erase the feel and taste of Donovan from my mind. Now that Jeremiah is home, it will be hours before we can continue anything.

A part of me is thankful for the interruption: I didn't come here tonight to fall immediately into bed with him.

The rest of me feels more alive than I have in possibly ever.

He wants me.

He loves me.

I feel like running around the house and tossing handfuls of glitter dust into the air.

He clearly makes me insane.

"It was…good," Jeremiah says. But his voice is lighter and happier than it was last night.

"Homework?" Donovan asks.

Jeremiah shakes his head. "No, I'm a bit ahead in most things."

An awkward silence fills the room before Jeremiah finally lifts his bags into the air. "I'm just going to go put these away."

He scuttles off before either of us can stop him, or offer him dessert…or anything.

But when he's gone, that awkward silence thickens into something much more pleasurable.

"You're in my bed tonight," Donovan whispers into my ear.

I can only stand frozen in my spot, nodding in agreement.

Chapter Fourteen

He thrusts inside of me and my head pushes back into the pillow.

"Yes." My fingers cling to his shoulders as he moves.

His weight is supported by his elbows as he pulls his hips back slowly and then pushes inside me even slower.

"Stop teasing me," I say with panted breath.

His lips quirk and brush against mine. His hands frame my face tenderly.

His sharp green eyes are intense.

I'm in heaven.

Waking up in Donovan's arms only to have him roll over, his fingers working their magic before he rolled on top of me…

"Donovan!" I cry out, my body on fire. Completely enflamed for him.

"Give it to me, T." His voice is a growl. Needy. Husky and filled with his own lust and desire.

My body convulses. My thighs spread wide and my orgasm spasms through me until my entire body falls apart beneath him.

"So beautiful," he murmurs before his brow pinches together, his face twisted into concentration.

His thrusts become wild.

Fast.

Powerful.

I gasp and whimper as one climax quickly warms into another.

Or one long one.

I have no idea.

The only thing I do know is that being with Donovan is the most erotic experience of my life.

"Talia," he groans, and slams his hips against mine.

Another climax reaches its peak and his mouth seals over mine, claiming my mouth, my body, and my heart at the same time as his own orgasm takes him.

I feel his erection, the thickness of him inside me as I clamp around him and we finish together.

His thumbs brush my cheeks and he leans in, brushing his lips against mine one more time.

Our hearts beat together.

My hands roam his shoulders and his back as I catch my breath.

I can't pull my eyes off him.

"You're amazing," I whisper, my lips against his. Our breath mingles together along with our bodies, which are wrapped in sheets.

"I'm in love with you."

He says this as if it's the reason.

It's not. But I take the compliment with a shy smile, my cheeks flushed from amazing sex and compliments.

"I love you, too." It says everything and not enough. What word is there to describe what I feel for him?

"I want to hear those words every morning." His breath and voice brush along my ear, his scruff tickles my overly sensitive skin.

My eyes flash surprise. He can't mean what I think he's saying.

"Donovan," I say, warning him. Sated from sex, it lacks effectiveness.

He silences me with a kiss, stealing my breath in the best of ways. My body shivers beneath him and when he pulls back, his grin wide and free, he states, "It'll happen. Soon."

I lose the ability to argue when he rolls his hips, languidly shifting inside of me.

"Again?" I tease, quirking a brow.

"I wish. I have to get to work."

I pout. So do I. I just don't want to leave this bed, or this moment. From the moment I climbed into his bed last night, our solitude and our lovemaking have felt like a safe haven.

It's given me hope that we can do this. We can be together.

Maybe we can withstand anything.

He taps my nose with his fingertip. I pretend to bite it, mewling as he slides out of me, feeling the loss more than just physically.

He leans back to his knees and looks down at me, still spread wide open for him.

"You are the most beautiful woman I've ever met."

I flush under his praise, my skin prickling as his hands slide up my legs, around to the back of my thighs.

With one graceful movement he leans down, slides an arm around my back, and pulls me up and to him.

I shriek from the suddenness of it but wrap my arms around his neck, my thighs draped over his.

"I forgot something," he murmurs, his cheek sliding against mine.

"What's that?"

His green orbs meet my blue ones—his bright and light, as if he's been set free from something. There's been a playfulness with him I haven't yet seen except for the day at the amusement park.

Donovan stiff and serious is sexy.

Donovan playful and free…it's unnameable.

"I forgot to tell you good morning," he whispers against my lips, sliding his over mine before seductively licking them.

I huff. He feels so good. "I think you showed me."

"Still." He pulls back and frowns. "There will never come a

day when I don't want to wake up wrapped around you, seeing you happy and unburdened, where I want to forget the simple things."

My heart leaps to my throat.

I'm speechless.

"Good morning, Talia."

I return his carefree smile. "Good morning, Donovan."

He spins, taking me with him, and carries me into the bathroom before he sets me on my feet.

"Shower?" he asks, his eyes glimmering with arousal.

How can I say no?

* * * * *

Dressed in my typical jeans, sweater, and boots combination, I drape a silk infinity scarf around my neck, grab my purse, and head downstairs. I can hear Donovan moving around the kitchen, pots and pans banging together and the muffled voices of him and Jeremiah enjoying breakfast together as I make my way through the living room.

I stop for a moment in the doorway of the kitchen, my presence already known by the loud clacking of my chunky-heeled boots on marble.

Two sets of male eyes, mirror images of each other, are immediately set on me where I stand, my shoulder resting on the wall.

"Good morning." I smile.

Jeremiah nods before scooping a large bite of granola into his mouth. "Muh moning," he mumbles.

I shake my head, winking in his direction. "Boys."

"Men," Donovan states, wrapping an arm around my waist and pulling me to him. "Not boys: men."

"Don't be so offended." I lean in and whisper in his ear so

Jeremiah can't hear. "You've proven your manhood."

"Seeing you dressed in those boots and those tight jeans, I have the sudden urge to do it again."

Heat creeps up my neck and I press my cheek to his shoulder. "Stop it."

He chuckles and rubs my back with his hand before dropping it. Grabbing my hand, he pulls me further into the kitchen. "Come eat with us."

"I'll just have a yogurt." I pull my hand from his and make my way to the fridge, pilfering through a sea of leftovers until I find what I'm looking for.

Sliding onto the stool next to Jeremiah, I have a hard time taking my eyes off of Donovan as he moves around his kitchen. His body is muscled, but trim, too. I can glimpse just a hint of his navy tie under the folded area of the collar.

My fingers itch seeing just that glimpse with his back to me. What would it be like to undress him at the end of the day? Remove his suit, his shirt, his tie…all of it, piece by piece, until he's exposed only for me.

I blink the thoughts and the vision out of my head.

Now is not the time, and I really am running a bit late for work.

"When do you leave for school?" I ask, turning to Jeremiah. He's slurping his milk from the bowl.

He sets it down and wipes his mouth with the back of his hand. I fight the urge to remind him of his manners.

Boys are odd creatures—animals, really.

"Five minutes ago," Donovan mutters from the stove. He glances at me over his shoulder and then flashes a warning to Jeremiah.

"I won't be late. Bentley speeds," he says, taking his bowl to the sink and tossing it in.

"Dishwasher," Donovan growls.

Jeremiah rolls his eyes but does what he's told. Based on his slight grin he's hiding from Donovan, I almost get the sense that he simply likes to push his uncle's buttons.

He raises a hand over his shoulder as he leaves the room. "See ya later!"

With a slap on the side of the doorframe, he disappears, and then seconds later I hear the front door slam closed behind him.

Now that we're alone, I focus all my attention back on Donovan.

He's giving me a strange look as he brings a plate of eggs and toast to the kitchen counter.

"What?" I ask. Food on my chin? I wipe to see but my fingers are clean.

"You like him."

"Jeremiah? Of course I do. He's a great kid."

His eyes soften. "He is. He just…hasn't had that many people be good to him lately."

I sit back in my chair. "Are you worried I won't?"

"No," Donovan snaps, setting his fork down and staring at me intently. "That's not it. I just feel like I've failed him these last few years, and now I'm working to make it up to him."

I sense that he's not saying something and I frown, trying to figure out the piece I'm not understanding, when the front door opens and closes in the distance.

The telltale click of shoes on marble echoes in the house and Donovan's eyes flash to me.

The air between us freezes to arctic temperatures and he jabs his index finger in my direction.

"Stay here."

He pushes off the counter and disappears.

I close my eyes, sighing.

So much for our good morning.

I have about five seconds to figure out what I'm going to do—sit and stay, or stand next to Donovan—before I hear her voice.

"Well, isn't this just despicable."

Instantly, I'm on my feet. As I move, I brace myself for the fallout that might come from this decision.

Eight years ago, Donovan cowed to his mother, her desires for him, and one of those was to clearly scrape me loose. I can't sit in a kitchen, alone, twiddling my thumbs and waiting to see if he's going to make the same decision again.

"That's enough," Donovan says as I walk through the kitchen. His back is to me, but by the way his shoulders stiffen I know he knows I'm here.

He doesn't move and my blood chills a bit at the thought.

His mother—Claire—does, though. Her eyes flash from annoyed to vehemently disgusted when she sees me.

I keep walking until I'm standing next to Donovan.

Her perfectly groomed eyebrows arch into two sharp points in the middle of her forehead, and she scans me from top to toe.

It's obvious that she finds me wanting…or inconsequential… neither of which I care to think about, when her gaze flicks to Donovan.

He reaches out and wraps his hand around mine, squeezing my fingers. The minute gesture instantly warms my chilling skin and I relax into him, exhaling quietly.

We're in this together.

"Cassandra told me you had a plaything, but I didn't realize just how low your tastes have dropped."

"I'm going to give you three seconds to apologize before I ask you to leave."

Her lips press together into a fine line, not a wrinkle on her face. "You need to get serious, Donovan. You are too important, too visible, to be carrying on with someone of her caliber." Her hand waves in my direction but her eyes stay fixed on his.

His hand tightens around my fingers and he takes a step forward, as if to block me from her venom.

"Decisions have already been made, Mother. My divorce is final, Jeremiah has left a school he hates, and you no longer have any say in my life or who I choose to have in it. Accept it or get out—I don't really care anymore."

She huffs as if this is all a mere annoyance, and it's in this moment that I realize, to her, it probably is. I'm a simple stumbling block to what she wants for her family, her son.

My heart swells when I realize that this time, Donovan isn't backing down.

He also doesn't seem to care that her three seconds are up, because he has more to say to her, and he quietly states, "Emily would hate you for what you've done to that boy."

She dismisses him with a gesture like she dismissed me. "Emily was never strong enough."

"Emily was in love and wanted her son to be happy because you never gave a shit if your own kids were."

"There is more to life than happiness! There are responsibilities and honor and traditions."

Next to me, Donovan scoffs. His grip tightens on my hand until I'm certain that he's cutting off the circulation. Still, I stay silent, giving him whatever strength and support I can while staying by his side. "Get out, Mother. And don't speak to me again until you can apologize for the way you've treated every single person I love."

Her eyes widen and her jaw goes slack. "You can't be serious."

"As a heart attack."

Holy shit. That's how his dad died, and I watch his mother's face pale at his horrific word choice. My eyes snap to Donovan's and I see his tighten as if he's just realized what he's said.

She recovers more quickly than I do. "I still own controlling interest."

"Then fire me if you want, but that also means you lose any relationship you and I have. You have already lost your husband, your daughter, and your grandson. It's your choice if you want to lose me too."

"This is ridiculous." With a hitch of her handbag, fixing it in place on her shoulder, she fluffs her shoulder-length brown hair. "Have your fun if you must. But when you're ready to be serious about your future and the future of our family again, don't expect me to say anything other than 'I told you so'."

Donovan takes a step forward, jerking me with him.

I recover, barely, and brace myself with my free hand on his bicep, turning toward his side.

"For almost a decade I have allowed your decisions to rule every single one of mine, and they have been, other than in the business, some of the worst choices I have ever made. You are not welcome in this family, or in this house, until you are able to understand that the decisions I make from this day forward have nothing to do with you."

Her skin pales with the intensity in his voice, but she doesn't speak.

She simply spins on her heels, and both of us are frozen solid until the door clicks shut behind her.

Several thundering heartbeats pound against my ribcage while I wait for Donovan to speak.

He runs his hand through his hair and down his face, huffing while he does.

Then he turns and his chin dips to me. Even in heels, I tilt my head back to meet his gaze.

He searches me for a moment before he asks, "Are you okay?"

I flex my fingers, still in his grip, and grin. "Besides the fact that I think you might have just broken my fingers? I'm good."

"Shit." He relaxes his grip and begins to rub circulation back into my hand. "I'm so sorry."

I'm not sure what he's apologizing for…for his mother or my fingers…or for the last eight years and everything that just happened. While quick, it was painful to watch.

I'm silent while he runs his fingers along mine, soothing them. I let him, mostly because even this simple gesture has me thinking of other things I'd like him to do with his fingers.

"I have never spoken to my mother like that before."

He murmurs this and brings my fingers to his lips, kissing my fingertips and then my knuckles.

"I'm sorry you had to do it on my account."

He lifts one of his hands, tangles it in the hair at the back of my neck, and then he pulls me to him until our foreheads are pressed together. "I'm not. Should have stood up to her eight years ago. Or five. Or three. Today was long overdue."

I allow his warm words to wash over me.

With his skin against mine and his hands on me, I inhale a deep breath and just revel in the fact that I'm with him.

Finally.

After all this time, I have the man I've always loved right in front of me, loving me back.

I pull back just enough to rise to my toes, press my lips to his, and whisper everything I'm feeling in three little words.

"I love you."

"Hell, that's good to hear."

Our lips press against each other's, our smiles mirror images. His hands drop to my waist and then I'm being picked up, my legs wrapping around him instinctively and my hands going to his shoulders.

I laugh, surprised. "What are you doing? We have to go to work."

"It's a good thing we own our own businesses, because we're going to be late."

Chapter Fifteen

Dr. Kasey McGarry is younger than I expected, but she's been incredibly kind as we get my father settled into his new room at the Rolling Oaks Rehab Facility that Donovan brought me to last week.

Once I decided that I was all-in with our relationship, it took very little convincing on Donavan's part to allow him to do this for me.

It came with multiple orgasms, and a discussion when I was too satisfied from sex—after he'd made me come with his tongue—twice—then his fingers, and finally him.

I could barely think straight, much less argue about the fact that I didn't want anyone to think I was with him for his money or his connections.

When he set his softened green eyes on me early in the morning, with the sun peeking through the curtains in his bedroom, and simply stated that he did this because he wanted to take care of me…I decided to let him.

Now that we're here, after getting my father moved and filling out massive amounts of paperwork due to his transfer and updating medical records, my hand is cramped from signing my name so many times.

But there's a peacefulness in this brightly lit place. His room looks as if it was decorated by the best interior designers in the country. Gone are the stark hall lighting and linoleum floors and water-stained ceiling tiles of his old center.

Instead, I'm standing in a room where my father seems to be lounging peacefully in a queen-size bed with plush bedding, staring out a window with a view that lives up to the center's name. Next to me is a lush microfiber sofa, and in the corner is a small but elegant writing desk for visitors to use.

I'm welcome here anytime, for as long as I'd like to be.

This place is so cozy and warm, it feels as if I'm in his bedroom at home.

"Thank you, again, for making room for him."

Dr. McGarry flashes me her elegant smile and nods. "It's our pleasure. We will do everything we can for your father during his stay here."

Her gentle words and kind tone spark tears in my eyes. I fight them back, though. She's seen enough of my emotions today already.

"What's the plan moving forward?"

She gestures me to join her on the couch, where she slides a small stack of papers out of her binder. For the next thirty minutes we review his physical therapy plan, as well as new cutting-edge treatments they have found to be successful in victims of massive strokes.

By the time we're done, her hand resting gently over mine, she has reassured me of their abilities to bring my father back to me.

"Thank you." I laugh softly. It seems to be all I can say.

"It's our job, Miss Merchant. One we take pride in. The success of our patients is what drives us. Trust me, there is nothing to thank me for."

But there is, because for the first time since my father's stroke almost two months ago, I finally have hope.

She leaves the room, the mahogany door closing quietly behind her, and I pull up a chair next to my father's side of the bed. He looks gaunt and small in the large bed, and a part of me wishes I could climb in next to him and wrap his arms around me, just to feel him again.

But I don't. Tucking my feet under my behind, I sit on my

knees, hold his hand, and squeeze.

"You're going to get better here, I just know it."

My words are whispered into the air in hopes they reach someone who has the power to make them true. I don't say anything else for the next few hours while I simply hold his hand, praying for a miracle.

* * * * *

"How is your father today?" Marisa asks as soon as I walk through the door.

I shrug off my jacket, gently folding it over my arm. "The same. But I like his new place."

"I can tell."

I smile hesitantly. It's small but it's there—and it's usually not after a visit with my dad. Marisa has to notice, because she gently squeezes my forearm when I reach her.

In the living area just off the entryway, the television is muted and three young boys and one girl are zoning out to what looks like a ghost hunter show.

"What's new here today?"

She leans in and points to one boy who I'm thankful to see. Ben.

This is the second time in just a few weeks he's been here. At sixteen, he's certainly no stranger to us. We see him around town and sometimes have to convince him to come with us for a night of hot food and a shower along with a warm, safe bed. He doesn't open up to us at all about why he's on the streets, but the first time I saw him, early in the spring, the telltale bruises all over his body and the way he flinched from contact told me everything I needed to know.

He's on the streets because it's safer than being at home.

He's currently sitting in a chair in the living room, separate from the other four kids, who are watching the television. His chair is by the window, and while there is nothing there to see other than a quiet street lined with cars and small, boutique-style tourist shops, his gaze is fixed on the outside.

I pat Marisa's arm and sigh. "Some days, I hate this."

"Someday you'll have room to house them all."

I have an appointment with the architect tomorrow to look over the building one more time and finalize the blueprints before our reconstruction process begins, and I can't wait.

Her reminder of our new building, where the second story will house twenty-four beds in four rooms—two male and two female—makes me smile as I head toward Ben.

He has two years left, could easily go into the system, but even I know that with as many wonderful parents that are out there, there are some that aren't so great. Getting Ben to trust anyone—even fantastic, loving parents—would be difficult.

And because he's so old and has never filed a complaint or pressed charges against whoever has beaten him in the past, he's more likely to be sent home or into a juvenile center.

It's my job to report abuse, and while I've tried to convince Ben I'm here to help him and not hurt him further, every time he shows up and it's mentioned, he takes off. But since I don't know his last name, or that Ben is even his real first name, I've done little to push the issue.

It's breaking the rules and possibly risking my license to allow him to stay here without contacting the authorities, but sometimes rules are made to be bent a little bit.

"I've missed you," I say quietly, and slide into a chair across from him.

His eyes stay on the window for a moment, his curly, dark brown hair almost flopping into his eyes. His posture is defeated but hardened. His clothes are dirty and the cuffs of his long-sleeved flannel are ripped. His cheekbones protrude more than they should for a boy his age.

I want to hug him, but know that I can't.

Slowly, he blinks and turns to face me. When he does, I gasp and instantly touch his chin.

He flinches from my fingertips on his skin and my sudden movement. I immediately drop my hands into my lap.

"Who did this to you?"

One of his fingers reaches up and runs along the black-and-purple bruise that surrounds his left eye. It was hidden from my original view of him, but now I have to force myself not to cringe as I see it.

He shakes his head and shrugs.

"Ben, you have to give me something here."

His hands ball into fists in his lap and his nose scrunches. I watch him flinch in pain from the movement before his dark brown eyes go ice cold.

"I tried to go home and get some warmer clothes." He sniffs and stares out the window.

I can feel the tension radiating off him, permeating the space between us. I fight the urge to hold him in my arms, let him cry on my shoulder, and promise him everything will be okay.

Instead, I stay silent while he works his battle silently.

"Thought he wouldn't be there," he mutters and blinks slowly.

God. These kids. They make every single problem I've ever had in my life seem completely inconsequential.

"Your father?" I whisper it, leaning close to him without touching, but ensuring no one else in the room can hear us. The kids who come are pretty good about minding their own business, though. They've had lots of practice.

He swallows heavily. "You can't call the cops."

"It's my job."

"I'll leave." His lips twist into a menacing sneer. He won't hurt me, I know this. He's just scared. "I'll leave and never come back."

"Please," I say, pleading. "I just want to help you."

He snorts. "Calling the cops won't help me."

His eyes seem to tell me what his words don't, and I close my eyes, leaning back into my chair.

"Fuck," I mutter under my breath. "Your dad's a cop."

His lips twitch minutely and he mouths one word: manners.

I grin and hold up my hands. "Busted. Sometimes it's necessary." My mind begins spinning, trying to figure out how to help this young boy in front of me. But there are some things that can't be fixed in the span of moments. For now, he's safe. And that's what is important.

"Will he come looking for you?" I ask, and before he can answer, I continue: "Is there anyone else at home?"

His lips pinch together. "Just my mom. But she doesn't do shit." He doesn't answer the other question, and I let it slide.

It's not like it's any big secret that I take in runaways. If Ben's dad wants to find him, my place is the first one he'd probably look.

"Stay here as long as you need," I tell him, standing up. I need to talk to Marisa about this. Hiding him can risk my license as well as any state funding we receive, which dwindles by the year. "There are beds upstairs, closets full of warm clothes, and dinner at six. You know the drill…be honest and respectful, but give me time to figure this out."

He stares at me, his one eye swollen and almost completely shut, and I see the wariness in his good eye—the fact that I'd help him, knowing what I now know. He must understand the significance because he mumbles a quiet, "Thanks, Miss M.," before he turns back to the window, staring as if he's watching…

waiting.

And he very well might be, but he won't be found by his father. Not if I can help it.

* * * * *

Donovan's house is quiet when I enter, my shoulders slumped after a long day.

I have no idea what to do about Ben, but after speaking with Marisa, she agreed that he should stay at the center for as long as he needs. She's prepared to deny that she's seen him if someone does come looking for him.

It's putting us both at incredible risk, but one of the things I love about Marisa is that she's willing to make those decisions when it comes to the good of the kids.

I drop my purse on the console table just inside the front door and slide off my shoes before I begin wandering through the vast space, looking for Jeremiah.

I was told he'd be home. Due to his new schedule, he won't be coming to my office anymore. It's simply easier for him to just come home after school.

But I missed him today, and I'm still concerned that I have a relationship to heal from my sudden departure last weekend.

It's been a few days since I've been back in Donovan's house, and already I'm making myself more comfortable, treating it like it's my own home instead of one I'm simply obligated to stay in for another week or two. I've refused to consider what will happen when my thirty days are done, and I'm choosing even more stubbornly to ignore the comments Donovan has made this week about wanting to see me every morning.

It's implied, but until he comes out and specifically asks me to move in, I have one foot in his house and one foot still in mine.

I hear the zombie moans before I reach the playroom, and a smile tilts my lip.

Jeremiah is exactly how I pictured him in my mind when I walk through the doorway, my footsteps muted by the plush carpeting.

With one leg thrown over the armrest of the chair, his posture is relaxed but he's intent on fighting the dead walkers on the enormous projection screen in front of him.

I don't say anything when I take a chair next to him. I just reach for my controller and wait until he pauses the game so I can enter.

"How was school?" I ask when he waits for me.

"Good. I like it. It's better."

I glance at him, notice the slight blush on his cheeks, and press my lips together.

Only one thing can make a thirteen-year-old blush like that. Or one person.

"What's her name?"

He slides me a look. "Don't know what you're talking about."

"Sure you don't."

He's only been at his new school for a few days, but with his size and looks, I'm not surprised he's already caught the attention of girls. They're just at that age when the girls begin to get giggly and boys begin to notice developing bodies.

I shake off the thought of what comes after.

"When are basketball tryouts?"

He shrugs like he doesn't care, but I know he does. The lack of sports at his private school was one of the reasons he hated it so much.

"Couple weeks."

"Wanna practice after dinner?"

I had noticed that with my reappearance on Monday, also came the addition of a basketball hoop in the driveway.

Jeremiah huffs. "Like you'd be much competition."

I grin, facing the screen, and proceed to chop his head off with a machete.

"Hey! You're supposed to kill the zombies, not your partner."

"That's for thinking girls can't be competition."

* * * * *

nner with Donovan, and it's after spending an hour all three of us outside on the driveway, shooting baskets and playing HORSE (in which I was the winner of all five games), and it's after Jeremiah is in bed for the night when I finally sit down on the deck, mug of hot cocoa in hand, blanket wrapped around my lap, and Donovan next to me.

The fire in his fire pit provides the only light.

I've been quiet, although the night was an absolute blast. Kicking Jeremiah's and Donovan's butts at basketball was the icing on the cake.

As if reading my thoughts, my reasons for my distance even through my earlier laughter, Donovan reaches over and presses his hand against mine.

"You're quiet tonight. Something happen?"

Ben happened. I can't keep my mind off him—his bruises or his fear.

"Just a kid at the clinic today." I shake my head, trying to erase the memory of his swollen eye, but I can't. I press the mug of hot cocoa to my lips and blow gently, cooling it. "Some days aren't that easy."

"I can imagine."

"Sometimes I wish I could save them all."

His hand squeezes mine. It warms me from the tips of my toes to the tingles on my scalp. The gesture is so comforting, I turn my head so I'm looking directly at him.

"How was your day?"

He arches a brow, and one side of his lips turns up. "Changing the subject?"

"Trying to avoid thinking about it, to be honest."

He nods slowly, his eyes roaming my face as if he's assessing my sincerity over the reason for my avoidance.

"The same as always: bought some companies, sold some others."

"Ah...sounds thrilling." I smirk.

"Tell me about your day."

He sounds so sincere, his eyes pleading me with me to open up to him. I can't help not to.

"There's this boy. Shows up sometimes, sleeps on the streets others. Today he showed up with a black eye, bruised and swollen."

I watch Donovan's face harden, his eyes narrow and his jaw tightens.

"Pretty much admitted his dad's a cop, so calling them to file a report could hurt him more than help him."

I sigh heavily and close my eyes. I hate this. When it seems like there's no easy answer.

"I don't know how to help him. Legally, I have to report it. Morally, I can't...not if what he says is true."

"Do you doubt him?"

I shake my head. "No."

My eyes still closed, I listen as Donovan stands from his chair, the scraping of metal against the cement. Opening my eyes, I smile when Donovan reaches down and lifts me up. Then he shifts until his back is in my chair, his legs spread wide, feet on the ground, and he settles my back against his chest.

I relax into him when his hands immediately move to my shoulders and he begins massaging them.

My head falls forward. "That feels so good."

Pleasured tingles slide down my arms and back, up my neck. Little hairs stand on end and I close my eyes, groaning my approval.

"You're tense."

"Long week."

I feel his lips brush against the back of my neck and I shiver.

"I want to make it better. What can I do?"

I sigh as his thumbs find a knotted muscle just inside my shoulder blade. "This. Just this."

"I can do that."

And he does. He does it so well my eyelids grow heavy and my head flops forward. My breathing calms, and the only thing I'm concentrating on is the feel of Donovan's fingers and his breath brushing against the exposed skin at my neck.

I'm turned on. My thighs press together. I can't help it. My reaction to him is visceral, and based on the hardness I can feel pressing against my backside, he's not immune either.

"Stop it," he growls huskily into my ear when I shift against him.

"Please."

"Tonight is about you. I want you relaxed, de-stressed."

My lips twitch. "That's what you do to me."

He nips my ear playfully, his hands holding me still. I squeal from the sudden sting of pain that is quickly soothed by his mouth and tongue on my earlobe. "I'm glad you think so."

Slowly but firmly, his hands slide down my shoulders to my hips and he pushes me forward.

"Come on." He climbs out from behind me and holds out his hand. "Let's get you upstairs."

I grin. "That's what I'm talking about."

He rolls his eyes, his smile wide and carefree. I love it. Love him. "Not that," he scolds. "I want to run you a bath."

My voice is wistful. "I don't think anyone's done that for me before."

"Good." He takes my hand and pulls me to him—chest to chest, body to body. His arms wrap around my lower back and he lowers his head, brushing a kiss across my lips that's gone before I can feel it. "I've never run anyone a bath."

Chapter Sixteen

"So, what do you think?"

I smile at Jeremiah's controlled excitement. His nervous fidgeting belies the uninterested look in his eyes.

"I think you did a wonderful job."

"Yeah?" He looks down at the finished wooden board. We've just finished the piece he originally started helping me with last Sunday.

I meant to get to it with him earlier in the week, but with him adjusting to a new school, moving my father, and the new developments of Ben—who was still at the center this morning when I arrived—the week has been hectic.

"I think it's perfect."

"It will look great on your office wall."

I rest my hip on the workbench that Bentley brought over just like I asked. "Actually, I'm thinking of talking to Donovan. See if maybe we can hang this one here."

His hand gently brushes over the still-drying polyurethane coat. It's sticky and won't be fully dry until tomorrow, but he doesn't smudge it.

He shrugs, and I see him fighting a smile. "Yeah. Whatever. That'd be cool, I guess."

But I see the hope and excitement in his eyes—as if he wants to be excited but is too afraid he'll be disappointed.

I long to reach out and hold him, assure him everything will be fine. The relationship between him and Donovan has already changed so much in the few weeks I've been around. I'm not taking credit for it, Donovan's done all the work, but my heart swells thinking that maybe he needed me in his life to see the importance of the decisions he's now making.

Giving Jeremiah a good life.

A life Emily wanted for him.

We're momentarily blinded by bright lights pulling up to the open garage door, and both of our heads turn to see Bentley pulling up.

My pulse picks up before Donovan is even out of the car. As the car lights dim and both men exit the vehicle, my eyes are immediately on Donovan. He steps gently out of the car, buttoning his suit coat as he stands up. I watch every movement.

His fingers on the buttons.

His long, slow strides toward me.

The slow quirk of his lips as he catches me checking him out.

His eyes and how they slowly roam down the length of my body, taking in every inch of my covered skin. I may be wearing an oversized sweatshirt and yoga pants, but I've never felt so naked in my life. My hair is in a sloppy ponytail, my makeup washed off. I should feel like a slob, but as Donovan continues closing the space between us, I know he doesn't care about any of that.

He simply cares about me.

"Hi," I say, my voice a little breathless from the realization.

"What are you two doing out here?"

I step away from my workbench and wave my hand in its direction.

"We were finishing this."

His brows pull together and Jeremiah steps back hesitantly. I watch as he takes in every move Donovan makes, every glance of his eyes, with trepidation.

"You made this?" Donovan asks, turning toward me with awe in his eyes.

"Jeremiah did most of it."

His head snaps back in surprise before he looks at his nephew. "She did most of it, I just helped."

Donovan reaches out and clasps a firm hand around Jeremiah's shoulder. "It's fantastic. You did a great job."

I watch as Jeremiah rises to his full height, his confidence growing under Donovan's praise.

I know what it's like to have those satisfied and thrilled eyes on you.

I smile for both of them. There's ease in how they can talk now and show affection.

The moment is gone when Donovan asks, "You have homework to do?"

"Maybe a little."

"Get to it, then. I need to speak with Talia."

Jeremiah mutters something indecipherable, frowns at me, and then slowly walks toward the house through the garage.

"He was really excited to show this to you," I tell Donovan once we're alone.

He looks down at the board, runs his hands tenderly over the words like Jeremiah did only minutes before, and looks at me.

I'm stunned by the heat and desire in his darkened eyes. "You do this?"

"It's just a hobby."

"It's incredible. Truly. I had no idea."

My cheeks flush from the compliment and I lean forward, wanting to touch him, to show him my thanks. I'm not given time when he picks up the completed piece and moves it to a shelf along the back wall of his garage.

When he walks back, his fingers move to his suit coat and he begins unbuttoning it, sliding it off his shoulders as he walks toward me.

My nipples harden, my entire body comes alive watching his

slow, slick movement toward me.

"What'd you need to tell me?" I ask, my voice husky. Needy.

"Nothing." His hand comes out and cups my cheek. "But your ass in those pants, your hair all messy, your face so beautiful…I just needed you and didn't want Jeremiah to see my erection."

I gulp and lean into his hand gently caressing my heated flesh.

I look behind me to see that Bentley has disappeared. We're alone, but in the open—not far from his nephew or his driver.

The thought terrifies me and turns me on.

"What did you have in mind, then?"

He leans forward and pulls me against him. The soft fabric of my sweatshirt brushes against my nipples, and they harden further when I collapse against his chest.

My hands reach for his waist.

His lips brush against my ear. "I'm going to fuck you out here. Over the workbench. Hard."

Oh my.

"And fast."

Yes, please. I rock my hips into him, whimpering when I feel his thickness beneath his trousers.

"Talia?"

"Mmhmm?"

Words have disappeared—vanished into the dark night and chilly air.

He laughs, low and deep. It rumbles over me and through me.

"Talia?"

I drag my eyes to his, forcing myself to move. My jaw is slack, and I lick my dry lips. "Yes?"

"Turn around and grab the edge of the workbench."

My eyes widen in shock and I find my voice. "You can't be serious."

He grins, a slow-spreading smile that turns predatory, showing his teeth. "Turn around and let me give this to you."

I've suddenly never wanted anything more.

I listen, letting his hand on my waist guide me until I'm in front of my workbench. He pushes me forward, stretches my arms in front of me until my fingers curl around the far edge.

His hands move to my hips and he tugs, pulling me until my behind is lined up perfectly with his erection. He rocks against me and I drop my head.

God. So hot.

"Are you wet for me?"

Drenched. I can feel myself grow wetter with every word he speaks, every slow second that ticks by as his hands run down my sweatshirt until they reach the waistband of my yoga pants.

I nod my answer, my words caught in my throat.

A slow, delicious shiver rolls down my spine as I hear the clink of his belt buckle, the pop of a button, the tinny metal sound of his zipper.

Then his hands are back on my hips, my pants and underwear pulled down to my knees.

"Spread those legs for me as wide as you can, baby."

I almost orgasm on the spot, but do what he says, shuffling my feet wider, my movements constricted by the fabric that somehow tickles my skin at the back of my knees.

"Donovan," I breathe out his name. It's a request. A need. A plea for mercy.

"Yes?" he asks, and his hands are on my rear end, massaging it, before he slides one hand around to my front. "Holy shit, T."

Our groans are the same as he finds my slick, swollen flesh. My thighs shake from the pleasure when he brushes his fingers through me, around my clit, down my slit and then inside of me.

"Yes," I beg. A whispered plea ripped from my throat.

"You're incredible," he murmurs. "Hold on, honey."

My fingers tighten around the wood and I mewl when his fingers leave my sex, but then he's there, the tip of him sliding through my wetness.

Everything inside me clenches as I feel him at my entrance.

And then he slides in. His hips thrust against my backside, his hand on my hip preventing me from moving forward.

I throw my head back and moan.

"God, you're so tight like this."

I know. I can feel him everywhere inside of me. Stretching me and hitting the end of me.

So amazing.

He doesn't wait to move. Just slides out, my body clamping around his cock to hold him inside. And then he pushes back. His hips, his cock, his hands on me...everything tightens and pushes. Pulls and thrusts.

The movement shakes my unhindered breasts inside my sweatshirt. The fabric scrapes my already sensitive nipples. It's deliciously torturous.

Everything inside me coils as he continues his thrusting, plunging in and out of me with abandon.

His aroused groans filling the garage, escaping into the air.

It's too much, and it takes minutes before my climax comes powerfully and quickly.

The wood scrapes the flesh of my fingers and my palms and I arch my back, loudly groaning Donovan's name.

"Yes!" he hisses. His hips slap against my flesh, his balls hit my clit, and then he pushes himself fully inside me. "Talia."

I feel him orgasm, the pulsing of his cock against my inside walls.

Everything explodes as we orgasm together. Stars burst behind my closed lids and I let my head fall forward until it rests against the harsh wood.

His hands slide under my sweatshirt, soothing me. He rolls his hips, that delicious tingle as he prolongs my orgasm, pulling out every little wave until it's too much.

Way too much.

"That was amazing," I say when I can find my voice.

He leans forward, brushes his lips against the back of my neck. "You're amazing. I don't want to separate from you."

I don't either. Ever. I want him in me, and next to me, and simply near me for the rest of my life.

"We should probably get cleaned up," I tell him.

He slides out, turns me around, and bends down, starting to pull up my pants and underwear as he does it. He leans forward, gently pressing a kiss with a quick flick of his tongue at the apex of my thighs as he stands.

Reaching into the back pocket of his trousers, he pulls out a handkerchief and wipes me clean before he stands up.

My knees shake...from the orgasm and his tender touch.

He fixes himself up. My eyes stay fixed while he re-zips and buttons his pants and closes his belt.

And then he leans forward, brushes his lips against mine. "How was your day?"

He pulls back and smiles—that boyish one that makes me throw my head back and laugh.

"I've had better," I tease him through my laugh, and watch him pout.

He reaches out, and one of his fingers taps me on the nose. "I'll do better later."

It's a threat and a promise. One that—as he takes my hand and pulls me inside, and then sits me on a stool in the kitchen, declaring I stay with him while he cooks dinner—I can't wait to see fulfilled.

ENFLAME

* * * * *

It's Monday, and I've spent the entire weekend with Donovan and Jeremiah. We went and saw an Iron Man movie at the theater —one that I hated, but that the guys loved, so it wasn't a completely horrible experience for me.

Then we went to dinner at my favorite Mexican restaurant, where we gorged ourselves on chips and salsa and enchiladas.

I'm entering my last week where I'm supposed to stay at Donovan's, and as the week begins, my stomach is filled with a heavy, unnamed weight. He hasn't mentioned anything about me staying, like he did last week the morning his mother showed up.

I don't know if he still wants me here after this coming weekend.

I don't know if I'm ready to have him ask me again.

Everything has moved so quickly, yet we are far from strangers.

He's my one and only.

I woke up to an empty bed this morning, Donovan's space next to me cold, telling me he he'd been awake for a while. I found him in the kitchen, heading out the door to work as I made my way downstairs. He simply brushed his lips over mine, telling me he had an early morning but he wanted to take me out to dinner when he gets home tonight, hopefully to celebrate the close of a new deal he's been working on.

But he was distracted and distant, and it left me unsettled as I made my way to Rolling Oaks to see my father.

Here in my father's room, with the bright sun filtering through the windows, making everything seem bright and cheerful, I have been able to sit for the last hour, holding his hand and dispelling every insecurity and fear I have.

I don't know if he can hear me, but just being with him helps.

In the last three weeks, I have fallen madly in love with Donovan all over again.

I want to be in Jeremiah's life.

I want all of us to be together…forever. A family.

And it terrifies me that as my original thirty-day agreement comes to a close, I have no idea what Donovan is thinking other than that he loves me.

I just don't know if I'm enough.

Wiping away a tear from my cheek, unaware that I had started crying, I am shocked when my father's cool hand tightens around my grip.

I blink and lean forward. His hand tightens further.

Excitement and fear tumble inside me and my pulse immediately begins to thrum.

"Dad?" I brush his cheek with my fingertips of my free hand. "Daddy?"

Shaking my head, more tears forming in my eyes. I haven't called him Daddy since I was just a young child and could crawl into his lap.

His hand tightens again and I gasp.

This is not an accident.

Not like the other times.

Slowly, I watch as his eyes open to narrow slits and close. I wait with bated breath for more movement, silent encouragement bursting forth from my heart. His eyes open again, lids fluttering with strained weight.

His gaze is unfocused as his lips part.

"Bae…"

My shoulders shake, and tears of relief and surprise run down my cheeks.

"Dad." I lean forward, turning his face so he's looking directly at me.

He blinks again and a sob escapes my throat.

"Hey, Daddy."

His lips twist and push, as if he's fighting words. I have to fight the urge to run into the hallway declaring that he can talk.

He can see me.

I stay still, my breath in my throat, watching him struggle.

"Baby girl."

My head collapses onto the bed. My shoulders shake violently.

His voice is muffled. The words slurred. The left side of his lips droops more than the right.

It's the most beautiful sound I've ever heard in my entire life.

His eyes close and he moves his head. On his own.

I have never been so excited in my life, and just as I'm about to jump up and shout for joy, his unfocused gaze is back as his eyes open.

But his hand squeezes mine one more time.

And I don't care that he can't talk.

He's coming back to me.

Finally.

When he looks as if he's falling asleep, I finally remember that the nurses or doctors will want to know what just happened. Reaching over his bed, I begin slapping with ferociousness the emergency red call button that is mounted on the side of one of his bed panels.

I don't stop until his nurse hurries through the door, her eyes wide with concern.

"Is everything okay?" Amanda asks. She's young and cheerful. I liked her immediately, the first day I met her.

"He talked to me," I sob again, my shoulders still shaking as I say the words out loud. "And he squeezed my hand. Tightly. Several times."

Her lips stretch into a gentle smile. "That's excellent news."

I spend the next forty minutes watching and waiting while nurses and Dr. McCarry examine him. He seems to have slipped back into his dark world, and even though by the time I leave, I long for him to wake up, take my hand, and call me his baby girl all over again, I finally leave Rolling Oaks feeling full of joy.

All my insecurities from earlier forgotten.

My dad is coming back. He's improving.

There is absolutely nothing that could ruin the excitement of this day for me.

Chapter Seventeen

My hands are still shaking as I pull into my parking spot at the center. Before exiting the car, I try one more time to call Donovan.

I've been attempting to reach him for the last thirty minutes, but every phone call has gone directly to voicemail.

It's strange. He always answers when I call, even having Patrick transfer me immediately.

But today, he's simply unavailable. And not returning my call.

There is no other person in the world I want to tell about my dad's progress besides Donovan, and I can't reach him.

I'm still overwhelmingly thankful to Donovan for moving my father, for throwing his weight and getting him a room at Rolling Oaks. My heart believes it's made all the difference.

"…Donovan Lore, CEO of Lore Enterprises. I'm unavailable at the moment. Leave a message—"

I hang up before the recording finishes.

If his phone is on, he'll see that I've been calling. And I know I shouldn't be worried. He's probably in a meeting, closing deals and making money. But with his unavailability and distance this morning, I can't stop the small flutter of nerves in my stomach from taking flight.

Sliding my phone into my purse, I do my best to shake off the feeling.

Today is a great day. My dad saw me.

I blink away the tears that want to fall, exhale a calming breath, and step out of my car.

The cool wind instantly whips my hair into my eyes and I brush it back, pushing a chunk behind my ears as I quickly make my way inside.

"It's freezing out there today," I say as soon as I enter, shaking the cold off me.

Marisa looks up and shakes her head. "It's October."

"I heard we might get snow in a few weeks."

Marisa simply laughs. "I don't know how you can be so shocked by this. It's Michigan, for Pete's sake."

I scrunch my nose. "I hate the cold."

After removing my coat, I run my hands up and down my arms, trying to erase the chill. It's true: I hate cold. Some days, I dream of moving south. Marisa caught me searching for homes in Texas in the middle of last year's brutal winter, dreaming of places where snow never falls.

I hate it. And it doesn't matter that I grew up in the land of ski slopes and snowmobiles; my blood has never gotten used to bitter cold temps. Today's cold front only reminds me that it's coming. And it's coming sooner than I'd like.

"How's Ben?" I ask, not seeing him in the living room.

"He's been in his room all day. Hasn't come down except to eat breakfast."

I frown. He's been here for five days, which isn't uncommon for kids awaiting foster care placement, but this is the longest he's ever stayed. I'm just thankful that he hasn't left for the streets yet. I hate the idea of him outside in the cold.

"I should go talk to him, but I don't know what to say."

If he won't press charges, and if I refuse to call the cops, we're at a standstill.

Marisa must see my distress, because she lays a gentle hand over mine. "But there's good news today."

"Yes. There is." I smile just thinking about my dad. When I couldn't get a hold of Donovan, I immediately phoned Marisa, telling her I'd be late getting back to the center. She cried happy tears with me and declared we celebrate with champagne.

I had to turn her down since I promised Donovan dinner.

I tap my hand on the desk once and move toward the stairs. "I'll go talk to Ben. See if I can coax him downstairs for a late lunch."

As I do, the phone rings and Marisa reaches to answer it.

It's well past lunchtime, and it makes me sad that Ben hasn't come down to eat. He's thin from spending so much time on the streets. He's sixteen and should be cleaning out our pantry. The fact that he hasn't seemed to be able to make himself comfortable here worries me. It's as if he's just waiting for the right time to leave.

"Ben?" I ask, knocking on the door to the boy's room.

The door opens almost immediately, and I frown when it's not Ben who answers.

"Hey, Spencer," I say, drawling the words slowly. "How are you?"

Spencer, a boy the same age as Jeremiah, has been staying with us for the last two weeks in between foster homes. He's angry, like so many of the other kids who come through here, and likes to show that anger by punching walls and the face of anyone who gets in his way. He's not entirely strong enough to do physical damage, but his temper makes it difficult for foster parents. We haven't yet found the right home for him.

I reach out and ruffle his wild, copper hair. I'm one of the few people whose touch he doesn't shy away from him.

"He's not here."

"What do you mean?" I ask, my blood instantly heating with concern.

"Dunno." He shrugs. "Said he was going downstairs a couple hours ago and didn't come back. I figured he was watching TV."

A heavy weight sinks in my gut and I swallow, too afraid to let my emotions get the best of me.

"I see." I take a step back. "Thanks. You doing okay?" I ask, because I can't let him think I came just for Ben.

"Same shit, different day." His eyes widen when my mouth opens. "Sorry. Same stuff, different day."

"I know." I smile sadly. God. Some of these kids are so awesome. I hate their struggles. Unfortunately, I'm unable to focus on Spencer when my mind is swirling with a sudden, unnamed fear for Ben. "We'll find you a good place, though. Okay?"

He shrugs, that same feigned nonchalance I see in so many of these boys. "Whatever."

Before I can reassure him, he closes the door, and I know our conversation is done.

Most days it would upset me, but I'm turning around, Spencer not forgotten but pushed to the back burner while I go figure out what in the hell happened to Ben.

"He's not here," I tell Marisa as soon as I see her. She's on the phone but her mouth drops in shock.

"I'll have to call you back, Mrs. Jones. Yes, I know. I'll see what we can do for you."

"Mrs. Jones?" Damn. This day is getting out of control, quickly.

"Yes, she has a girl, an eleven-year-old in an emergency foster care placing, but they haven't been able to find a long-term care for her yet."

That's younger than we usually take, but damn it...I hate turning away kids. "That's young," I say, hesitating.

Marisa reads my thoughts. "I know. But we don't have a lot of girls right now."

She's right—we only have two staying with us right now. Usually the younger ones are at risk of being bullied and bossed around, but the other two are younger teenagers anyway.

"Have Mrs. Jones bring her by. We'll figure it out."

Marisa nods, scratches a note, and then remembers why I'm here in the first place. "How do you know he's gone?"

"Spencer said he came down here hours ago."

Marisa frowns. "I never saw him."

Her desk is at the bottom of the stairs, and she knows everything, sees everything. Between her and our two weekend guards, we know where every child is at all times.

"He must have slipped out while I used the restroom or something."

Damn it.

I can't help the tears. So much crying today, I'm almost tired of it. These tears are for a different reason, though. I hate this.

"He's gone."

"We'll find him," Marisa assures me.

She's right.

The problem is that I have no idea what type of condition he'll be in when we do.

* * * * *

"You're distracted."

So are you, I think.

As far as dates go, tonight is a bust. Donovan came home from work promptly at six o'clock, sending me a text when he was on his way for me to be ready.

I received it just as I walked in the door to his house, frowning at the lack of even a basic friendliness in his words: Home at six. Be ready.

As if I'm someone for him to order around.

My hackles instantly spiked, and even though I did change into an appropriate dress, tights, and my favorite brown heeled riding boots, I did it under duress.

I want nothing more than to curl up in my sweatshirt, stare at a fire, drink wine, and wallow.

Celebrate my dad and mourn Ben. I hate that I can't shake this kid off. He's so much more than just a regular boy who comes to our center.

Looking out the window of Donovan's Mercedes, I watch the streets, the shops, the restaurants go by without truly seeing any of them.

I also ignore his question, my sassy response still on the tip of my tongue.

We're on our way to dinner, to a destination he won't mention, and we've barely spoken except for this.

"Thinking about your dad?"

I wish. Ben, Spencer…sometimes it's difficult for me to shake a crappy day of work.

"No."

His sigh is heavy and fills the space in his luxurious vehicle, the leather smooth like butter, more expensive than anything I could ever own…would ever want to buy.

"Help me out here, Talia."

His hand drops to my thigh and he squeezes to get my attention.

I turn to him, notice the concern in his eyes. Questions immediately surface.

"Did you finish the deal?"

A line appears in between his brows and he glances at me before focusing on the road. "Still working on it."

"I thought that's what we were celebrating tonight."

"I had hoped so. Maybe we can celebrate the news about your dad, instead."

He flashes me a quick grin but it's different. That same coldness…that same wall of control that he had slowly begun shedding is back in place.

I scowl at him, turning to look back out the window. "If you're not going to talk to me, I don't know why we're doing this."

By "this," I mean dinner.

But the air chills instantly. "I could say the same."

"Jesus, Donovan. I've just had a bad day. There's too many kids, there's too few of us trying to help them. Too many are slipping through the cracks, and with winter coming it always stresses me out. Ben's gone…somewhere…more kids need places to stay…"

And you're keeping something from me, and I only have one week left in your house, and I have no idea what's going to happen come Sunday.

Who is this needy, uncertain, and scared girl? My reflection in the window looks to be me, but I'm feeling things I've never felt before, and I hate it.

I drop my head to the headrest and close my eyes before tears form.

"I'm not used to being in this position." At my sideways glance he arches a brow and then fixes his eyes back on the road. "Wanting to help someone, and not knowing how."

"You've helped enough." I admit, my voice softer. "Your funding for the center will help with a lot of the stress I'm under right now. It's just never enough. There's always more kids in bad places who need help."

"Have you ever thought about doing more? Taking kids into your own home?"

Yes. All the freaking time. Unfortunately it's a huge step over appropriate boundaries, and while I'm running the center, I have to make do with what I can. Besides, even for me—at my age and as a single woman—it's not easy to become a foster or adoptive parent.

I explain all this to Donovan, watching as he bristles with the mention of me being single. He's quiet while he finally pulls into a restaurant in Corallville, the town just north of Denton where I live. Lived.

I don't even know where my home is anymore.

"What if you could?" he asks after he parks the car. One of his hands drops from the steering wheel to my thigh and he squeezes. He turns to me and watches my expression morph into something that's probably close to peace.

Contentment.

I smile. "I'd take them all."

"Maybe with the funding you could start working in that direction, then."

"I can't stop my work."

"I'm not talking about stopping your work. I'm talking about hiring the people you need in place to keep the center going, maybe taking a hands-off approach and being behind the scenes so you're not conflicted professionally. That way you can take the steps to do what you really want."

My heart flutters with his praise. His confident look tells me that he does remember the dreams I used to whisper to him, telling him what I wanted to do when I grew up. Not only that, but he believes I can do anything I put my mind to.

"Donovan…" My voice trails. I don't know what to say to him, what that means to me.

"What if you weren't single?" he asks, and I jolt slightly. As if he knows what I'm thinking, his hand on my thigh tightens, and he shifts in his seat until he's facing me. "What if you had a home that could hold as many kids as you want? A husband who cares?"

Tears burn my eyes.

"You already know I want you in my home, Talia." His hand reaches out, brushes hair off my cheek, and pushes it behind my ear.

Everything in me awakens from that simple touch.

"It's too soon."

"For what?" He frowns. "Moving in with me? I love you, T. I want you with me all the time. I've already told you this and you didn't answer."

The insecurities I've been feeling all day bubble to the surface, somehow becoming smoother...less scary.

"I didn't think you still meant it. You hadn't brought it up."

"I was giving you time to think. To accept what's happening here."

I lean into his hand, his warmth heating my cheeks and spreading it down my neck to the tips of my toes in a pleasurable sensation.

"I thought you'd changed your mind."

His hand slides to my neck and he tugs me forward. Our foreheads press together before he runs his cheek along mine. "Never. I knew what I wanted the moment I saw you, when I came to get Jeremiah. I've just been waiting for you to figure it out, too."

"What's that?"

"Forever."

His lips press against mine, his tongue sliding into my mouth, rolling with mine before I'm able to fully consider the impact of that one word. But as I lean into him, I revel in the taste of him—the feel of him and his scent.

He tastes like my home.

Wherever it is.

"How about we go eat now?" he asks when he pulls back.

I lift my thumb, rub smeared lipstick off his bottom lip.

"Forget about the hard stuff for a while."

Chapter Eighteen

Dinner ends up delightful, as we talk about nothing and everything. I tell Donovan stories of my dad, we talk about his sister and Jeremiah.

It's lighthearted and fun. The warmth of a couple glasses of Pinot Grigio and a belly full of delicious lobster and scallops help me to laugh easily and often.

I do my best to set aside the revelation Donovan provided in the car.

The fact that he wants me with him. That he was giving me space. He's essentially said if I want to bring children into our home, he's with me.

It's heady and serious and it feels completely right. We aren't complete strangers who have only known each other for weeks. We are adults, reconnecting after years of separation. And while we still have much to learn about one another, I have learned enough in the last few weeks to know one thing for certain.

He is my future.

I tip my wine glass to my lips, swallowing the last small sip. Donovan's wiping his mouth with his gray cloth napkin and his eyes dip, watching me swallow.

"Yes," I whisper, and set my glass on the table.

One eyebrow jumps. "Yes, what?"

"I'll move in with you."

A visible amount of tension—one I wasn't aware he was carrying in his shoulders until I watch them deflate in front of me—evaporates.

His eyes shine and his lips tip up. "Champagne to celebrate?"

I shake my head slowly. I want something different.

Him.

"I'd prefer to go home."

"Home." He breathes the word out on an exhale. His nostrils flare, eyes dilate.

He looks hungrier than I am, and he quickly garners our server's attention, handing him a credit card without seeing a bill.

I watch in fascination as the young man scurries off, as if he senses the need for expediency.

I grin. The thought of that word…the realization of what I've just agreed to, blossoms inside me. It's not terrifying at all. "Our home."

"And Jeremiah?" he asks, his fingers tapping on the table.

I reach over and cover his hand with mine.

"If I didn't love Jeremiah and want to be in your family, I wouldn't have said yes."

He nods. "I know." He flips his hand, our palms touching. Our fingers lace together, entwining with the other person's hand as if it's what they were meant to do. Tingles burst on my arm, traveling to my heart.

"I love him, too," I assure Donovan.

He blinks harshly, swallows more forcefully, and nods as the server returns with our bill for him to sign. I watch as he does it, one-handed, not removing his hand from mine. Then he tugs me to my feet, draping my jacket over my shoulders and pulling me outside.

The brisk fall air causes me to catch my breath as we step through the door and Donovan pulls me to his side, unlacing our fingers only to settle his hand on my hip.

"I want to do irreverent things to your body tonight."

The apex of my thighs instantly heats and spasms.

"Good." I tilt my head, look up at him, and smile. "I want you to be wicked."

"Utterly perfect," he murmurs before pressing his lips to my forehead.

I'm ushered into the car, the door closing behind me quickly, and Donovan takes his seat. He barely pauses to look for traffic before pulling out on the road in front of us.

I laugh, startling him.

"What?"

"You," I say through my laughter. "You're in such a hurry."

"Because I've been thinking you'd say no. That you'd leave."

He scowls, a line of frustration etched in his features that I didn't understand this morning but understand completely now.

I rest my hand on his leg and squeeze. "I'm sorry I made you worry."

"Yes, well, you can make it up to me tonight."

"With pleasure."

He shoots me a look that almost makes me orgasm on the spot. "Oh. It will be."

I don't know what entirely comes over me—perhaps knowing I truly am his—but as Donovan shifts the car, his strong hands on the gearshift, my eyes trail his body, up his arms to his jaw, his slightly crooked nose, and to his eyes.

He's looking straight out the window, intent and focused on driving.

And I come undone for him.

Slowly, I slide my hand along his thigh. It tenses under my touch and his eyes slide in my direction.

My hand moves further up and I bite my lip when he widens his legs slightly.

"What are you doing?"

I cup his balls through his trousers and squeeze firmly. "Playing."

I keep my eyes on him as my fingers go to his belt.

Donovan shakes his head. "You're trouble."

Yet he doesn't move to halt my inefficient progress.

"I'm getting turned on," I tell him, my voice a hoarse whisper. The heat coming through the air vents is no match for what's coursing through my blood. I run my hand along his erection that's quickly growing hard beneath me. "I want you."

He drops a hand from the steering wheel to cover mine and stills me. With a deep groan, he squeezes my hand. "Wait until we get home."

I press against his erection, my fingernails scraping his thick cock through his clothes. "I can't."

He blinks, looks at me and out the window. I see him debating my insanity before he mutters, "Fuck it."

His fingers help mine and we quickly undo his belt buckle. With that out of my way, I lean over and undo his button and then his zipper. He shifts his hips, making it easier, the entire time a grin on his lips.

I love that grin.

"I want this," I say and slide my hand into his pants. Cupping him, I tremble at the feel of his hot erection. It pulses in my hand and I pull it out, slowly sliding my hand from base to tip. "I want you."

He groans. It's low and soft but fills his car and sends shocks to my sex. My panties are wet, and I shift in my own seat as I continue slowly sliding along his sensitive flesh.

"This is so hot." I yearn to lean down and run my tongue down his length, something I've rarely done to him. But with him in my hand, completely at my mercy, the power I have right now is heady.

"Suck me," he commands, his voice more hoarse than mine.

I lick my lips and smile. "It's like you read my mind."

I lean forward, squeeze his cock, and love the tortured groan that escapes his lips. We're just leaving town, no traffic on the roads. I feel so wanton.

In the most exciting way possible.

He turns a corner and I brace myself against the armrest only to have my hands still on his erection when I see a squad car up ahead, flashing lights.

Donovan slows, checking for traffic before he moves around the cop car, but my eyes move quickly to the sidewalk.

I know that flannel shirt.

"Stop the car!"

"What?" His dick twitches in my hand and he looks at me, but my gaze is focused on the windshield.

"Stop it. Pull over!" I yank my hand from his erection.

"What's going on?"

"It's Ben."

Donovan slows immediately. We're in front of the cop car, its lights flashing in our rearview window, and I twist in my seat to see a man in full dress uniform suddenly reach out and wrap his fingers around Ben's throat.

I fling my door open, not stopping when I hear Donovan shout my name, quickly followed by a curse behind me.

"Hey!" I yell, running toward the two men. "Get your hand off him."

The cop turns to me at the same time Ben's eyes flash in my direction.

It's night, but not dark enough where I can't see the pure evil shoot daggers in my direction from the man's eyes. "This is none of your business, ma'am. I suggest you move along."

"No way." I shake my head. "Not until you get your hands off this boy."

The cop sneers but slowly I see his fingers loosen on Ben's throat before he drops his hand completely. "This boy is under arrest."

I walk closer to Ben, my eyes staying on the cop. His dad. It has to be.

"For what?" I ask, cocking my head.

"I don't have to tell you."

I hear Donovan walking up behind us, but I don't look at him.

With his silent strength behind me, knowing he won't let anything happen, I take my eyes off the cop and turn to Ben.

His hands are balled into fists, his chest is heaving, and his eyes are brimming with tears. I take another step forward. "Are you okay?"

His lips twitch, but he stays silent.

"I'm going to ask you to step back, ma'am, and let me do my job."

I slide an angry glance in his direction. In his hands, he's holding a pair of handcuffs.

Ben's breath hitches when his dad raises them.

"No way in hell."

"Talia," Donovan whispers behind me. He reaches forward and wraps his hand around my wrist.

I grow strong from his touch but ignore the warning in his voice and square off toward the cop, putting Ben behind me. "Since when does a cop do an arrest by choking a teenager?"

He sneers and looks like he wants to hit me. I'm not surprised. "He was resisting arrest. Now, if you don't mind, I'm only going to ask you once more to step back and let me do my job."

The red and blue lights flash behind him, making it difficult to see his face or his expression.

I shake my head, but Donovan steps in.

"Very well."

"What?" I snap my head toward his. "You can't be serious."

He has a cell phone in hand and his eyes on the cop.

"Thank you," the cop says. It sounds like it's taking every evil restraint in him to be polite. I would bet money he doesn't say it often.

Donovan just shrugs. "It's no problem. I'll call my lawyer and we'll follow them to the precinct until this mess is straightened out."

Behind me, I hear Ben sigh. With relief? Or more fear?

Donovan smiles toward the cop. "And then we can file a report for the way you mishandled your authority and the way we witnessed you abusing this boy."

Victory slices through the air. The handcuffs jingle in his tightened grip. The muscles in the man's neck grow visible. He looks like a panting bull. Pissed beyond belief.

His eyes slide down Donovan's body, and if he doesn't recognize the face, I see him clearly recognize that Donovan comes from money. A lot of it. And he's not fucking around.

His lips curl in and he takes a step back, raising a finger to point at Ben. "I'll give you a warning tonight, boy. You hear me?"

His voice cracks as he replies, "Understood…sir."

His dad steps back and whips the cuffs around his hand before pocketing them at his waist. Without another word, he climbs into his cruiser and peels out into the street, tires squealing, lights still flashing.

As soon as he's gone I turn to Ben and pull him into my arms. "I was so worried about you. Are you okay?"

His hands grip my biceps and he pushes me away.

He doesn't look at me when he says, "You just made everything worse."

"Ben…"

He shakes his head and steps back, putting his back to a brick wall. "I need to go."

"Let me take you to the center," I say at the same time

Donovan says, "Come home with us."

My eyes widen and I look at him over my shoulder. He just shrugs.

"I'm Donovan," he says holding out his hand in Ben's direction. "Talia's boyfriend."

The word rolls off his lips so easily. It sounds perfect. And silly.

He's way too masculine to be simply a boyfriend. I bite my lip, fighting a grin, when I see Ben's hand reach out tentatively and shake Donovan's hand.

"Come home with us for the night. We'll feed you, give you a warm, safe bed, and you can play video games with my nephew."

"Jeremiah," I tell Ben. They've been at the center together before, and while they're practically strangers, I know he'll be familiar.

Indecision wars in his eyes, and I wait with bated breath while he evaluates his options.

"Please, Ben. It's either our place or the center, but I'm not leaving you on the streets tonight."

He nods briskly once, still not looking me in the eyes. "Fine. Your place."

He starts walking toward Donovan's car and Donovan reaches for his phone. "Bentley? Yes…I need some help. Take Jeremiah to the store and go pick up some clothes. Two weeks' worth, everything…boy, sixteen years old—" He looks at me for confirmation and I nod. My head is spinning. "About five-ten, one-seventy…yup. Thanks."

He hangs up and opens the back door to the car.

No one says anything when Ben slides in and I slip in next to him. But I catch the smile on Donovan's lips as he nods in understanding and closes the door behind me.

I quickly take Ben's hand in mine and squeeze it tight. I can see red marks on his throat, and the taste of bile rises in my throat.

"Are you okay?" I ask and he shakes his head. "Can you tell me what happened?"

As Donovan pulls onto the street, Ben is silent, staring out the window, but slowly he squeezes my hand back and says, "Same shit. Different day."

And I don't know what comes over me in that moment, but I make my decision.

There is no way in hell he's ever going to have to be around his dad again.

* * * * *

Low, quiet laughter filters into the hallway from the game room and I stand there, my back against the wall in the hallway, just listening.

The last two hours have been insane, to say the least. As soon as we got home, Donovan gave me a kiss on the cheek and then picked up his phone and excused himself to his office. While I was left alone with Ben, I gave him a tour of the house and showed him one of the guestrooms next to Jeremiah where I figure he can sleep.

I have no idea what Donovan's been doing and haven't had much time to think about it.

Jeremiah and Bentley showed up just as I was finishing the house tour, where Ben had been silent for most of the time until I showed him the game room. Then his eyes lit up like the Fourth of July.

I had smiled and rolled my eyes. Boys.

After I settle the boys in the room, explain that Ben is staying the night, and tell Jeremiah to show him how to work the gaming system, I leave them alone to search out Donovan.

He's in his office with the door shut, and while I hear his voice murmuring but can't make out what he's saying, I don't know if he'd want me to interrupt.

Walking away from his office, I decide to head back into the game room but pause again outside when I hear Ben ask, "You like your uncle?"

Several quiet moments pass until Jeremiah, almost so reluctantly it makes me smile, says, "Yeah. He's pretty cool."

I rest my head against the wall, turning it to the side, when I hear quiet footsteps headed my way.

"You're eavesdropping," Donovan whispers, his lips stretched into a smile.

I press my finger to my lips and head his way, pushing off from the wall. "Jeremiah thinks you're pretty cool."

He scoffs quietly. I don't think either of us want to be caught spying. "That's because I am."

"Thank you." I slide my hand to the back of his neck and roll to my toes, pressing my lips to his. "For everything tonight."

"We should talk about this."

I drop to my heels and frown. "Everything okay?"

"Come with me." He takes my hand and pulls me down the hall to the living room.

Technically, I'm breaking about a thousand ethical codes having Ben in my house.

I also don't care. All night long, I've been replaying my earlier conversation with Donovan in my mind. It's as if running into Ben tonight has opened the door for what Donovan suggested, and I can't stop thinking about what-ifs and why-nots. What if I hadn't seen Ben? What would his dad have done? What would Ben have done? What if I—we—could take in more kids? What if I stepped back from the center a little bit?

They're looping through my brain and making it hurt, but

filling me with unknown excitement at the same time.

I take a place next to Donovan on the couch and lean back as he drops an arm around my shoulders. He's turned slightly so he's facing me, leaning in, and all I want to do is close the space and show him exactly how thankful I am that he stepped in tonight.

"I talked to Jensen," he states with no preamble.

"And?"

He runs a hand through his sandy-brown hair. I can see the tension lining his eyes, and when he sighs, I feel the weight of it. "Technically, I'm breaking laws by bringing him here. Sort of. I think it's complicated, but since he's sixteen it might not be so bad. But his dad could easily file kidnapping charges if he wanted to, if he finds out who I am."

He pauses, runs his hand over his mouth. "We need more information, but Jensen's already looking into doing whatever he can to help make sure Ben doesn't have to go back to that home again."

"That's good, though." I lean in and rest my hand on his thigh.

One of his hands covers mine and he squeezes.

"Isn't it?"

"It is, but there's a lot to figure out. I know you already have a foster care license, but I talked to Jensen about getting me certified as well." My eyebrows shoot up my forehead and Donovan reaches out, smoothing my surprise from my face with a firm brush of his fingertips against my skin. He laughs softly. "What did you think I was willing to do when I brought it up earlier?"

"I don't know." I shake my head. "This is all happening so fast."

He simply shrugs and brushes his lips across my forehead. I sigh at the gentle, calming contact and lean in.

"Perhaps it's happening the way it was meant to be."

Perhaps. Emotions clog in my throat. "This is fast, though."

He laughs softly. "You already said that, and I know it is. Before we can do anything at all, we need more information from Ben. I need to get you officially moved in, and I need to talk to Jeremiah about all of it, too."

I squeeze his leg and close my eyes. Everything's changing in the blink of an eye, and while it's overwhelming, so much of it feels right. Perfect.

"Can I be there when you talk to Jeremiah?"

He looks at me hesitantly, and I suck my lip in between my teeth. Then he nods. "Of course. I was going to, but yes…of course I want you there."

I smile and his lips drop to mine.

He kisses me briefly but passionately before he pulls me to my feet. "It's late. Let's get these boys to bed."

I wrap my arm around his waist and let him walk me to the game room. When we get there, a football game is on the big screen and I look over to see Jeremiah shout, "Game on, man! I totally kicked your ass."

Ben is quieter, but he still raises his hand into a fist-bump. "Good job, kid."

"I'm not a kid."

"Younger than me." Ben shrugs.

Jeremiah slinks into his chair, affronted at the nickname.

"Time to turn in," Donovan says, standing behind me in the doorway. Immediately, the screen goes blank.

Apparently, threatening the loss of video games for six months if Jeremiah didn't turn them off as soon as Donovan requested, game saved or not, was enough of a worry for Jeremiah that he always listens.

Both boys clamber to their feet, Jeremiah relaxed and smiling, and Ben…hesitant and sad and bruised and so freaking broken I want to pull him into my arms.

"You still want to stay?" I ask Ben as Jeremiah heads out of the doorway. Donovan gives us a few minutes alone, which I appreciate. "I can take you anywhere."

Ben looks around the room, the leather furniture, and I know he's probably as overwhelmed as I was when I first showed up here. "It'll do for the night, I guess."

I smirk. Yup. My exact reaction.

"Come on." I nod toward the door. "Let's turn in. You've had a hard night, and I have a feeling tomorrow will be just as difficult." He doesn't say anything until we get upstairs and I rest my hand on his shoulder. There are so many things I want to say… promises I want to make…but I can't lead him on and I don't want to hurt him by not following through. "We'll do whatever we can to help you, you know. But at some point you're going to have to let me know how I can do that."

Ben licks his lips, staring at his feet. With a simple nod, he turns and opens the door to his room. It closes behind him, almost in my face, and I stand there for several moments, until I hear the lock click and I know I've lost him.

At least for the night.

Chapter Nineteen

When I woke up this morning, I knew today was going to be difficult. I just didn't know how hard it was going to be to listen to Ben tell us, after much gentle prodding, that his mother lets his stepdad do whatever he wants because "he's better than his first dad."

I don't know if my heart has ever hurt so much. There's a pain in my chest as I slowly glance at Donovan, watching his hands ball into tight fists at his sides and a muscle tic in his jaw.

He might be more upset than me.

Ben scoops a spoonful of oatmeal into his mouth and chews slowly, acting like this is no big deal.

"I'd like for you to talk to my lawyer about this today, Ben."

"No." He takes another bite and Donovan blows out a slow, calming breath through slightly parted lips.

"Your stepfather won't know about it," I say, and move close to him.

He stiffens his shoulders when I sit on the stool next to him, but I don't touch him.

"But if we talk to Jensen, he might be able to help us figure out what to do now. You can't go back there."

He relaxes slightly and shovels another mouthful in, scraping the sides of the bowl with his spoon.

"I can get you more food."

He pushes the bowl away. "I'm done. What do I do now?"

It's the first time he's asked. The first time I've seen helplessness flash in his eyes instead of arrogance.

"Have you been going to school?"

He rolls his eyes but shrugs. "Most of the time. Not doing

good, though."

I suspect he goes to school to avoid his home, but at least he's going.

"I can call your school and get your absence today excused. We'll meet with Jensen, and once he knows your story we can figure out how to proceed."

"What are my options?"

I look at Donovan and he nods his head, seeming to understand that even with as little as this kid trusts anyone, he has some level of respect for me. I'm not a stranger like he is.

"You're sixteen, so you have a few. The first is we can try to see if you qualify for emancipation, which means the state determines if you're able to live on your own, or at a home of your choosing, and your mom will relinquish all rights to you."

He flinches but says nothing.

"The second is foster care."

"Hell no." He jumps off his stool and scowls, crossing his arms. "Fuck if I'm taking my chances on a new dad to kick my ass. I'll do the first one and be on my own."

I stand slowly from the stool to not scare him or push him away. He reminds me of a cornered animal, and I don't want him to dart. "We have time to decide all of this, but I'd like for you, in the long-term—even if your emancipation goes through—to consider staying here. With us."

His eyes dart from mine to Donovan's. Then his eyes take in Donovan's scowl, his hardened jaw, and his muscled body. I don't have to look at Donovan to know that Ben sees what I did this morning when I hit the kitchen: designer, well-fitted jeans, a dress shirt untucked, and hardened eyes that are still caring and compassionate despite his anger with what he saw last night and what he's heard this morning.

I give Ben time as he continues looking everywhere, taking in every part of the house that he can see.

Minutes seem to pass before he shrugs. "We'll see."

"Of course. Take your time."

Without another word, his shoulders slump, and he walks out of the kitchen toward the living room. When I hear his footsteps on the stairs, I exhale a breath.

Warm hands wrap around my shoulders from behind and I feel Donovan's breath at my neck. "You did good."

I raise my hand to my shoulder and cover one of his hands. "So did you."

"He's terrified."

I nod. "And angry. Hurt. Confused." My chin trembles and I bite my lip so I don't cry.

He twists me, spinning me slowly until I'm facing him, and his hands slide up the sides of my neck until they're under my jaw, tilting my head back. "I love you."

"I love you." Leaning forward, our lips brush against each other.

The kiss is soft and slow but full of passion. A promise. I lean in and rest my hands on his hips, pulling him to me. Even with the stress and the exhaustion from last night, and—at least for me—not being able to sleep for fear that Ben would sneak out in the middle of the night, my body still responds to Donovan's lips and his tongue as it tangles with mine.

I love it. I want more of it. A whimper escapes my throat, showing my need, when Donovan's phone begins buzzing on the counter.

He pulls back instantly. "It's probably Jensen."

I nod, and watch as he answers the phone without looking at the screen. "Hello?" And then he scowls, and everything in his shoulders tightens. "Good morning, Mother."

Ugh. A very unfeminine snort escapes my mouth and Donovan

shoots me a look, shushing me with his finger over his lips.

"This isn't a good time…yes…no…Talia and I will be there. Jeremiah will not."

I frown, showing my displeasure as his stance hardens and he runs his hand down his face. I can't hear what his mother is saying, but if his expression speaks for his response, then she's not being any nicer than she was just a few days ago.

"Fine," he clips harshly. "Saturday brunch. But I warn you now," he says, his eyes piercing mine with sincerity, "you say one incorrect word to Talia and we're gone, and you'll never see me again."

He hangs up almost immediately after and heaves a frustrated sigh.

"She's a piece of work."

He rolls his eyes. "She's conniving and I don't trust her, but she wants to get together. Claims she's considered what I had to say and wants to get to know you."

"I don't trust her."

"Good." He grins and wraps an arm around my back, pulling me to him. "You shouldn't—and I don't, either. But I'm curious to see what she's planning."

I'm picturing a brunch with a dozen women who are more wealthy, more fancy, and more schooled and refined than me, being paraded in front of him like a cattle ranch. Ripe for his pickings.

"Hey." He tilts my chin up with his thumb and brushes his lips against mine. "Don't worry about it. I can handle her."

I'm not so certain.

But when his cell rings again, and this time it is Jensen, I excuse myself to go get ready for a meeting with an attorney.

I have no idea if we can even do anything to help Ben, and my nerves are already shot. The thought of spending an afternoon with

Claire Lore in just a few days is not what I need in the back of my mind.

*****

I have met Jensen Rhodes only a handful of times, when I'd joined James and Laurie at events through James's old law firm. To me, Jensen is hard and unyielding. His deep brown, almost-black eyes match his hair almost exactly. His suit screams power. And while he's always been polite to me, showing a professional indifference, I have never seen him interrogate a client.

And that's exactly what he's done today.

I have no idea how Ben has answered all of his questions, but the four of us, Donovan included, have sat in a small conference room for the last two hours and I've listened, biting my tongue to keep from lashing out at some points and crying at others, while Ben has described the horror of what he's lived with.

Physical abuse. Emotional Abuse. Parental neglect from his mother, who simply turns a blind eye.

I have crescent-shaped grooves in my palms from my hands being curled into fists with rage.

Never have I been so angry with another human being in my life.

At the same time, never have I been so proud of a teenager for being so honest and forthcoming. I expected Ben to whither under Jensen's demeanor. Instead, he seems to have flourished, as if he somehow trusts this man to get him out of hell.

I would throw my arms around Jensen and cry into his shoulder if I wasn't so afraid of his reaction.

Emancipation. That's the route Ben agreed to, and when I spoke up and questioned Jensen if it was really possible for him to do that, he slid his narrowed, dark chocolate eyes in my direction and stated, "Let me handle it."

I stiffened my shoulders and rolled my lips together to keep quiet, nodding once. James always described his former partner as ruthless and cunning.

I see a man who wins. And if I were ever opposite him in the courtroom, based on his behavior today, I'd probably pee my pants a little bit with fear.

Having him on my side, however, makes me feel formidable. Undefeatable.

Sliding paperwork into his folder, Jensen closes it and rests his hand on top. "You will not have to speak to them if you don't choose. Everything will go through a judge, and I can guarantee that with the amount of judges I know personally, we will get you the earliest court date possible."

Ben says nothing, but his shoulders seem lighter, less burdened than they did three hours ago when we were getting ready to head to the office.

We have Jensen to thank for it—although I'm sure he couldn't care less about a simple "thank you."

"When will we know?" Donovan asks, his hand still on my thigh in comfort.

"End of the week. I'll get working on this right away."

"I appreciate it." Donovan nods once and stands.

Sensing the meeting is now officially done, I do the same.

"Thank you, Jensen," I say, shaking his hand across the table. "I really appreciate this."

In addition to helping Ben, he also spent time discussing the legalities of a minor staying with us, or with me, and the risk to my licensure. Until Ben is emancipated, him staying with us is still inappropriate, but Jensen assured me with utmost confidence that he'll handle any problems that may arise. His tone leaves no room for arguing. He's also assured me he'll have someone in his office handle everything I'll need to take a more backseat, office role with my center.

It makes me sad, in some ways, to be stepping away from some of the kids, and I know I'll have a busy fall with hiring new counselors as well as getting construction started on the new place. But I have Donovan to thank for all of it. And now, Jensen.

"It's my job," he simply states, releasing my hand from his firm grip. "How are James and Laurie?"

I smile lightly. "Good. James likes his new job, and Laurie says they're happy."

He nods once. A slight glimmer in his eyes appears before it vanishes, so quick I almost missed it. "Good."

Then he turns to Donovan. "I'll keep you posted as soon as I hear."

"Appreciate it." The men shake hands while I usher Ben out of the office.

"You did really good today," I tell Ben, walking quietly next to him.

He's showed no emotion, and I wonder if he's in shock, scared, or just relieved that someone is stepping in to help him. It can't be easy for him to trust me. Sometimes this seems too easy. But until he shows signs of trouble, I decide to roll with it and take things as they come. There's always the possibility that he'll be emancipated and on his own and want nothing to do with us.

A simple shrug of his shoulders is his acknowledgement to my words.

"Do I have to stay with you until the court stuff?"

I press the button on the elevator, watching as the numbers climb to our tenth floor. "You don't have to—" I start to say, but Donovan interrupts, coming up behind us.

"But we'd like you to."

Ben whips his head around, looks uncertainly at Donovan.

"Why?"

"Because Talia likes you and I want to help." He shrugs, sliding his hands into his pockets. "It's as simple as that."

For all the honesty he's given us, I know Ben is having a harder time trusting Donovan with anything. Not that I blame him. But even now, he takes a small step next to me, away from Donovan.

Donovan notices like I do. I can see it in the quick flick of his eyes to Ben and then to me.

The elevator dings, doors open, and Ben turns to step in. We follow him, giving him space on his own side of the elevator while he stares up at the number pad.

"I guess it couldn't hurt anything."

The doors close with a ding that seems to echo. At his acquiescence, I release a breath I didn't know I was holding. "You're safe with us, Ben. I swear it."

Donovan slides his hand out of his pocket, a key ring between his thumb and finger. "This is for you," he says, handing the keys to Ben. There are only two keys on the ring, and I watch, brow furrowed, as Ben sticks out his hand.

His lips are twisted. "What is it?"

Donovan shrugs, easily sliding his hand back into his pocket after he drops the keys into Ben's palm. "A key to the house. And your car."

"What?" The kid's eyes practically bug out of his head.

Mine do the same and my jaw drops. "Donovan."

His eyes slide to me and he smiles. "This is your freedom. You can go anywhere you'd like. Do anything you want."

Ben stares at the keys as if they could bite him, and my blood begins to boil in my veins.

"But I'm hoping you don't," Donovan says sincerely. "You're sixteen, so you should have a car. You'll need it to get to school.

ENFLAME

But I expect you back at the house by ten on school nights, midnight on weekends. We're not trying to control your life, just make it easier for you. And only you can decide if you want the help."

A pure, heated love for this man next to me slides through me. He's giving Ben the decision, and even though I'm terrified he could just take off, I sincerely hope he doesn't.

"You have your freedom to go anywhere you want. I'm just hoping you choose to stay—even past your court date, whenever that might be."

Ben's fist tightens around the keys in his hand and his head drops. I have no idea what he's thinking, but I see his chin tremble slightly.

When the doors ding and open on the main lobby floor, he slowly lifts his head and looks Donovan directly in the eye. His jaw is hardened, his eyes tight, and his entire expression is firm. "Thank you."

Then his eyes slide to mine, which are quickly filling with tears. My fingers tangle together, my heart filled with uncertainty. I want to pull him into my arms, but don't want to push him away by doing so. "I'll stay. This is too much."

"It's not enough." I shake my head. "Not nearly enough."

Emotion clogs my throat as Donovan leads us out of the elevator to the lobby. He has to go into work now, and now I know why he was so secretive earlier today with Bentley.

Because at the curb outside is Bentley, standing by the car that will take Donovan to work. And in front of it is a brand new black Chevy pickup. My eyes almost bug out of my head, and both Ben and I turn to Donovan, who grins.

"Thought you'd like a truck. Didn't think you'd like some luxury stuck-up car like Bentley drives."

Ben smiles, the first full grin I've ever seen on his face, and his eyes widen with glee. "This is the shit."

I nudge his side with my elbow but don't correct him. He's sixteen. And really…this is the shit.

"It's yours." Donovan nods in my direction. "Get Talia home safe, would you?"

"Yeah." His voice trails off and he turns back to the truck. It gives Donovan and me just a moment where I throw my arms around his neck, pulling him down for a kiss.

"You're incredible. Thank you."

He pulls me to him, brushes his lips across my cheek, back to my ear. "You can show your gratitude later."

I laugh, throwing my head back. "Deal."

When he lets me go, he walks to Ben, who's still admiring his truck in awe. I have to hand it to Donovan: the truck is awesome—simple but big. And he's right: Ben wouldn't be comfortable in some sports car. He'd be too far out of his comfort zone in something flashy. But this truck is perfect. Screams Midwestern, a bit of money, cool. Perfect for Ben.

"Drive safe," Donovan says, and reaches out to shake Ben's hand.

"I will." Ben returns the handshake without hesitating.

And I stand back, tears in my eyes, and wonder how in the hell my life has changed so quickly…so easily…and hope like hell the other shoe doesn't drop anytime soon.

Chapter Twenty

"Yes," Donovan groans, and his hands grip my hips tighter. "Fuck, Talia. Ride me."

I'm breathless above him, straddling his waist, his cock deep inside of me.

One of my hands is on his chest, and I rock against him, up... down...rolling my hips.

"You feel so good." I'm trying to stay quiet. It's virtually impossible as my body heats.

When I woke up this morning, Donovan sleeping peacefully behind me, his erection against my backside, I couldn't help but roll him over and taste him.

His hand had fallen to my hair, holding me, and I looked up to see his sleepy eyes barely open but his jaw was clenched tight as if he were restraining himself.

I wasted no time pulling him into my mouth, sliding my tongue along his shaft. When I sucked one of his balls into my mouth, his hands reached to underneath my arms and he pulled me up until I straddled him, squealing in surprise.

Then he slid his cock inside of me and told me to take my pleasure.

I love having this control.

My blond hair falls like a curtain to my sides and I can only see his chest and his eyes.

They're intensely focused, his teeth gritted together.

I lift off his shaft, my eyes teasing him as I move slowly.

"Fuck me," he growls, and slams me back down on him. "Do it, Talia, or I'm taking over."

The thought of giving him control sends a spasm to my sex

and I groan. "Donovan."

The thought of sending him over the edge is more enticing.

"Yes," I whisper, rocking against him. I speed up, until my thighs are shaking and my arm is trembling. Donovan meets me thrust for thrust, rocking into me and pulling me against him.

"Get there, Talia. I'm coming."

"Ahh," I cry, his admission sending me over the edge. With a final thrust he rocks into me, pulls me down against his chest, and everything inside me tightens and convulses around his cock as he spends himself inside of me.

"Holy shit," I gasp, my breath wild, our skin hot and sweaty. "You're amazing."

His hand slides up and down my back and I feel his heartbeat racing against my chest. "I think that honor goes to you this morning."

I chuckle softly, turn my head into the crook of his shoulder, and bathe him with gentle kisses.

"Need a shower," Donovan says, his hand in my hair now, running through it. "And we've got a busy day."

I sigh, relaxing into him. We do. I have appointments with a contractor, I need to see my dad, and mostly I need to fill Marisa in on everything so she can get the ball rolling on hiring new therapists.

Everything's changing so quickly.

"I don't wanna move," I whisper against his skin. "Can we stay like this all day?"

We can't. But I love seeing Donovan's pulse speed a bit at the idea. His cock pulses inside me and I know he's getting hard again.

I smile and press my lips to his pulse.

"I wish." Then he jackknifes up, sliding out of me, but he doesn't let me go. He wraps my legs around his back, and then swings his legs over the edge of the bed, standing up. "Let's think about that idea in the shower."

I tighten my hold around his neck. "I don't really like to think in the shower."

"I do…I'm already thinking about sliding my fingers into your pussy. Fucking you from behind, your skin wet from the water, and how good you'll feel when you're milking my cock."

"Oh." I smile again, press my lips to his cheek. "If that's what we're talking about..show me what you have in mind."

"That sounds like a challenge." We reach the bathroom and he doesn't set me down as he slides open the door to his shower and turns the water on.

Then he sets me on my feet, giving me space to brush my teeth and get ready for the shower.

When the room is beginning to steam from the hot water, he takes my hand and pulls me inside the stall.

Shivers slide down my skin, from the warm water and from his hands that slide slowly down my arms. Grabbing a loofah, he fills it with soap and begins washing my body. "You're beautiful. Every single inch of you."

My knees tremble slightly and I slide my fingers through his hair. "I think you're pretty perfect too."

He slides the loofah against my stomach, looking at my skin as goose bumps trail in his wake, and then he drops the soapy sponge and falls to his knees. His fingers go to my slit, and already I feel primed, ready for him.

My head falls back out of the water. The combination of the spray hitting my breasts, his fingers sliding through my sex, and the sight of Donovan on his knees in front of me is overwhelming.

"I love your pussy," he says, and leans forward to lick my clit. "Back up against the wall."

I move carefully so I don't fall. Donovan follows, his hands on my backside until I'm against the cool, wet tiles. His hand slides down my thigh and his lips move, bathing my skin with his kisses as he lifts one leg over his shoulder. I grip onto him to keep my balance. He looks up at me and smiles a smile that would make me want to drop my panties if I wasn't already naked.

God, he's beautiful. And all mine.

"I want to see you come, feel you pulse all over my tongue."

Yes.

He leans forward, licking my slit from back to front before his tongue drives me crazy, making slow circles around my clit.

"Donovan." My head falls back against the shower wall and I'm already shaking. He turns me on in seconds, and when he slides his fingers inside of me, hooking them to rub against that sweet spot inside, I come around him, just like he wanted.

He laps me up like I'm his favorite dessert as my hips rock against him, and I take every ounce of the pleasure he gives me when he stands up, turns me around, and slides his shaft inside of me with one thrust.

"Yes," he hisses. "Damn it. You always feel so fucking good. So tight around me."

I arch back, making it easier for him to move, and as he begins rocking into me, quickly, hard and fast, my entire body quakes with pleasure.

Our moans mix together as he thrusts, filling me completely, and it's only minutes before one of his hands grips my shoulder, his other on my hip, and he's pushing inside of me…powerfully… perfectly…

"Talia," he groans as I begin to clamp around him. "Hurry."

"I'm there," I whimper. I am. He can wring an orgasm out of me in minutes, and I already feel my peak climbing as he slides his fingers to my front, pinches my clit, and then I shatter.

My screams are muffled by the shower and I press my forehead against the wall as he thrusts into me one final time, shouting my name against my shoulder and chasing his own climax.

* * * * *

"How is he today?" I ask Dr. McGarry when I enter my father's room.

His eyes are open but hazy, yet as soon as I speak, his head turns in my direction.

One side of his lips lifts slightly while the other side droops low. But it's progress, because at least he recognizes my voice.

"He's doing great." She smiles kindly and slides a clipboard to the end of his bed. "His therapy is going really well—although he's probably tired because we just got done with the physical therapist."

"Wonderful."

She leaves the room and I walk to the side of my father's bed, taking his hand in mine.

He squeezes it. "Baby girl."

My chin trembles and I fight back tears. "You're getting better."

His head nods and I can't believe how much he really is improving in just a week. I have so much to be thankful for, even with all the unknowns.

"Tired," he says, and I see him fight to keep his eyes open.

I lean over and brush my lips against his cheek. They're pinker than they were just weeks ago. More alive.

Tears burn my eyes as he turns his head so my lips brush against his. "Love you."

"I love you too, Dad."

He nods once before his eyes close, and it's only minutes before he's asleep, but I stay next to him for another hour, waiting for him to wake up.

It's quiet and peaceful in his room, and feels warm and cozy. Outside, the leaves have changed colors—a sure sign they'll be falling soon and winter is coming.

And while it's generally my least favorite time of year, this winter will bring a lot of excitement.

Earlier today, after a quick stop at the office—where Marisa and I had spent an hour going over requirements for new therapists and created an employment ad—I had then met with the contractor in our new space. He'd assured me that he could remodel the old fitness gym into what we need and have everything open by the end of the year.

Eight weeks.

My dream is occurring before my very eyes, and most importantly…my dad is healing. I had almost given up hope.

When it's clear he's going to be sleeping awhile, I brush my lips over his again and tell him I'll see him soon. Now that he's awake more often, I want to figure out a way to coordinate my schedule so I can be around during this therapy, learning how to help him get better even quicker.

I'm just reaching my car in the parking lot when my phone rings. I answer it quickly when I see Marisa's name on the screen.

"What's up?" I ask. "Need me to bring you back lunch?"

"No. But you need to get here."

My pulse thumps in my ears and I quickly unlock my door and slide into my seat. "What's going on?"

"Cops are here. Looking for Ben."

"Shit." I shift the car into drive. "What do they want?"

"He wants to search the place. Says they're looking for him."

My mind spins. I wish I had the time to call Donovan or even Jensen to see what I should do, but if Ben's stepdad is there, I don't have time, and I'm fifteen minutes away.

"Where's the cop from?" I ask, already knowing the answer but hoping I'm wrong.

"Centerville."

"Dammit. That's his stepdad."

"Sort of what I figured. I excused myself to your office to call you, but he's steaming mad out front. What should I do?"

"Kids around?"

"Just a few. Spencer and a couple others."

"Let him search," I tell her. "I'll call Jensen, but I know he's going to say without a warrant we don't have to let him in. But if you can get him in and out before I get there, that'd probably be best. He knows me from the other night, so I don't want him to see me. If you cooperate they shouldn't be there too long."

"Are you sure?"

No. My hands are shaking and I could be totally messing up. "Just do it. Call me when he leaves."

I hang up with Marisa and instantly call Donovan. While I'm driving, he assures me he'll call Jensen. After scolding me that I shouldn't have let the man inside my business without a warrant, something I already know, he apologizes and says we'll get it figured out.

I knew it was only a matter of time before a cop came to the center looking for a missing child. When I get to the office and there's no police cruiser in sight, my nerves begin to settle.

Without knowing who I am, or who Donovan is, there's no way for Ben's stepfather to figure out where he is.

I rush inside, finding Marisa at her desk like it's a normal day. "Is everything okay?"

She nods and smiles easily. "Yeah. I had all the kids come downstairs while he searched, and he was only here for a few minutes. Spencer even spoke up and said that Ben hasn't been here since last weekend."

I heave a sigh of relief. "That's wonderful. Remind me to give the kid some extra ice cream later or something."

She laughs but sobers quickly. "Are you sure you know what you're doing?"

"Haven't the faintest idea," I tell her honestly. "This could all blow up in our faces any day and I could be in hot shit, but if we can get Dick off our backs that will help."

Marisa snickers at Ben's stepdad's name. It's fitting, completely, because the guy is a total dickhead.

"Okay," I say on an exhale. Tension releases from my shoulders. "What else is going on today?"

With one altercation done, we push it from our minds, slide back into work mode, and it's hours before I think about Dick again. And even then, it's in passing while I'm sitting at the dinner table with Donovan, Jeremiah, and Ben.

The boys give each other crap about Ben beating Jeremiah at basketball.

Donovan challenges them both to a game after dinner.

And for one of the first times in the last month since Donovan and I reconnected, their dinner table is filled with laughter and easy conversation, despite the heaviness and uncertainty surrounding us.

* * * * *

"So you did have a guest house at some point," I murmur to Donovan as we walk across the driveway to his mother's house. His childhood home is definitely more like a castle. Above a four-car detached garage there is clearly another floor that looks like an apartment. I can't help but think of the first time I saw him and compared my house to his guesthouse.

By my quick calculations, the guesthouse is larger than my home.

Donovan squeezes my hand in comfort. "Did. Not anymore, never again. You doing okay?"

It's the tenth time he's asked me. I smile tightly. "Just great."

"Hey." He tugs on my hand, pulling me to him until I have to brace myself with my hand against his chest. He leans down and presses his lips to mine. "Don't let her get to you today, okay?"

"You don't sound like this will go well."

"I no longer have any blinders on when it comes to my mother. I'm trusting she has something up her sleeve, but I guarantee I won't let her hurt you."

"I know you won't." In fact, knowing that is the only thing keeping me calm.

"I love you."

I grin and step away. "I know you do. I remember you screaming that very thing this morning in the shower."

Since Ben has been staying with us, the shower has become my new favorite place to have sex. Even though his house is big and the boys' rooms are separated from ours by a large distance, I can let myself go more easily if our lovemaking is muffled by running water and an extra locked door.

"I didn't hear you complain," he reminds me with a wink. He reaches for me and takes my hand in his.

"I never will." Changing the subject, I ask, "Did you talk to the boys about what we're doing afterward?"

We reach the door and he knocks, using an elegant, lion-shaped knocker. I frown, thinking we could have just headed in, but I don't say anything. I'm still stuck on my question about later today. Bentley has rented a moving truck and after brunch, Donovan and I are meeting him at my house to move out everything I want to keep. After talking to him more this week, and with everything going on, we've decided to simply sell my house; and while Donovan's house is fully decorated, I miss my stuff and want to make his house ours by combining our things. There won't be much, but when I called Mrs. Bartol yesterday, she said she'd spend some time there last night and this morning packing up my clothes and some of my favorite things.

I'm going to miss her tremendously, but thankfully she's only twenty minutes away. She's made me promise to continue our Saturday mimosa mornings, which there was no way I could decline.

I will miss the crazy woman.

I've had Donovan and the boys in stitches all week telling them stories about her—some of the more teenage-appropriate stories that don't involve talk of Viagra and penile implants.

"They grumbled but agreed," Donovan finally admits right before the door swings open.

Claire stands in the entryway, a plastic smile plastered on her face and her eyes glimmering until she sees me standing next to Donovan, his hand firmly holding onto mine.

"Mother." Donovan nods.

"So good to see you, thank you for coming." She brushes an air kiss across his cheek and turns to me, her smile faltering. "Tanya."

Donovan growls. "Talia. Do we need to leave before we even get inside?"

She steps back, opening the door while looking completely unapologetic. "Of course not. I just forgot. Good to see you, Talia."

"You too." I smile, even though she greets me like I would greet a rattlesnake in my living room.

I see Donovan scan his mother's face before he hesitantly steps inside, his hand around mine tightening as he leads me into the kitchen.

"Fucking Christ," he mutters when we reach the doorway and

spy two young women at the dining table, their backs to us.

My heart stutters in my chest as Claire walks around us. "Well, I just thought it would be lovely to have more company today to enjoy this beautiful morning. You know how much I love having family around."

And suddenly, as the two women turn their heads in our direction, I finally have to bite back a laugh.

This is just too funny.

Cassandra, I instantly recognize. I'm not actually surprised to see her sitting in his childhood home, looking as if she's still family. I figured Claire had some reason for wanting Donovan and I to meet her for brunch.

But I am shocked that next to her, is the woman who slept with Laurie's husband, James. Becky, also known as Laurie's best friend since high school—well, ex-best friends now.

It's too hilarious, and I quickly cover my mouth as a giggle escapes.

Donovan tugs me backward. "We're leaving. Now." His anger is palpable.

My laughter turns audible and I look at Donovan to see him giving me a staggering look. "Let's stay," I whisper, my mouth hurting from the grin. "This should be fun."

Becky's eyes are wide with surprise at seeing me standing in Donovan's house, and if I'm not mistaken, her cheeks turn a pale color as I lift my hand and wave. "Hello, ladies. Becky."

"You'll explain this, right?" Donovan whispers in my ear as I begin walking toward the table.

I nod without saying anything but wait for Donovan to pull out my chair. He seats me across from Becky, who's losing more color in her cheeks by the moment, while he moves to his chair across from Cassandra. Her lips are twisted into a very unladylike scowl.

"Should I do the introductions?" I ask happily, once Donovan is seated and drapes his arm over my shoulders in a possessive gesture.

"Becky, this is Donovan." I turn to him and grin. Wide. My cheeks ache and twitch from the strain, but I don't care. "Donovan, this is Becky. She's the woman who ruined her lifelong friendship with Laurie by fucking her husband."

Becky gasps.

Donovan's jaw drops and he shoots me a shocked look. I nod once. "Yup."

And Claire says, "Young lady. I don't know what type of family you grew up with, but we do not use that language in this home."

I take my scolding with a grain of salt, because that's funny, too. I grew up in a home where parents would never pull some asinine stunt like this and find it acceptable.

Clearly, by the look on Becky's face, she's regretting her appearance.

"Nice to meet you," Donovan says casually, as if he means it. His thumb begins rubbing the top of my shoulder and Cassandra notices.

"Aren't you going to say hello to me?" she asks Donovan, purring like a kitten, her eyes like lasers where his thumb is brushing my skin.

He shrugs and drops a kiss to my bare shoulder before turning to look at her. "Not sure why I'd bother. You're not my wife, no longer part of this family, and I'm not sure why you're here."

Claire gasps again and opens her mouth.

Donovan silences her. "And you should be ashamed of yourself. I don't know what game you're playing today, but if Talia and I weren't finding this so fucking hysterical we'd already be out of here. So why don't you cut the crap and tell me what this is about, or serve your food so we can get the hell out of here. We have family shit to do today."

I fight back a laugh.

Claire's expression morphs further into disgust with every curse word spoken, until I think she might blow her top.

Across from me, Becky fiddles with her napkin.

"Cassandra is family," Claire says slowly. She reaches out and holds Cassandra's hand on top of the table. "Some bonds are thicker than blood, and she will always be my daughter. Just because you so carelessly tossed her aside doesn't mean I have to."

Donovan chuckles. He squeezes my shoulder and pulls me closer to him. I wish I had a camera for this moment. It's deteriorating quickly, and if it wasn't so ironically funny, I'd be fuming mad. As it is, I have a feeling Claire is slamming the final nail into the coffin of her relationship with Donovan.

"That's funny," Donovan says, reaching for his water glass. "I suppose you know all about her fucking the CFO of her father's company then?"

Claire's expression falters a bit when Cassandra says, "You aren't supposed to disclose that information."

"I'm not supposed to disclose that information publicly, but I also believe you were handsomely rewarded with a few million dollars to stay the hell out of my life."

"Your mother invited me."

"My mother has an agenda that far surpasses anything you can understand." As if Donovan just realized there were more people in the room than he and his ex-wife, his gaze slides toward Becky and narrows. She looks about ready to vomit. "And why are you here? Moral support for Cassandra? It sounds as if you two have a lot in common."

Becky opens her mouth but nothing comes out.

"Becky's father is running for senator soon. I think her closeness with our family will secure connections," Claire quietly supplies.

I bite back a snort and reach for my water, taking a sip when Donovan says, "If you thought I'd fuck her to get in her family's good graces, you're sorely mistaken."

Becky turns green.

I choke on my water.

Cassandra's eyes water as if she might actually cry, and she looks at Claire.

And before anyone can say anything else about the colossal fuck-up that is brunch, two servers appear and quietly set dishes down in front of us, oblivious to the tension that is bouncing around the room.

Chapter Twenty-One

"Well that was the most fun I've had on a Saturday morning since I can remember."

Donovan slides me a glance. His thumb taps a rhythm on the steering wheel to the beat from the music playing on the radio. "I'm concerned about your mental well-being."

I snort. I've long since given up ladylike appearances—not that I had many to begin with. "Oh come on, that was funny. Did she really think she'd try to whore you out to Becky and Cassandra?"

"I don't know if I should be amused that you find this funny, or worried."

I place my hand on his thigh and squeeze, laughing. "Your mom brought in two women who have both slept with married men and thought you'd find them so beautiful you'd turn away from me. Wasn't that her goal?"

"I assume so." His lips purse and a tendon pops by his temple. He's more upset about this than me. I decided during the quiet, stifled meal—that was absolutely delicious and foodgasm-worthy—to stop caring about what anyone thinks of me, especially in that trio of horrible women.

I have enough things on my mind, and worrying about Donovan going back to any of them is at the bottom of my list. Becky, maybe, if he didn't know who she was.

I'm just thankful I finally got a chance to tell her what I think of her. After she slept with James and Laurie found out, I quickly took sides, severing my friendship with Becky. Today is the first time I've seen her since, and the whole reason she was there is simply laughable.

"But I hope she's happy knowing that she's lost me for good after this stunt. If she ever wants a relationship with me, she has a ton of groveling to do."

The thought of Claire Lore on her knees begging anyone for anything makes me giggle. Which means it's never gonna happen, and I don't have to worry about her tricks in the future because Donovan truly wants nothing to do with her. I almost feel bad, but thankful he sees how truly wretched she is.

"Can we talk about more fun things now?" I ask, leaning my head on his shoulder. The move softens him and I feel his breath leave his chest in a long, calming exhale.

"Like what?" He drops his hand, threading his fingers through mine.

"Like the fact that by the end of the night, I'll be living with you."

"You've been mine for a month."

"Yeah, but it's official now."

He turns his head and presses a quick kiss to the top of my head before turning to focus on the road. "You've been mine since I slid my cock into you eight years ago and took your virginity."

It's true. No man has ever compared.

I can't even argue, but in order to not become turned on by the thought of his cock sliding into me when we're minutes from my house, I change the subject.

"Have you spoken with Jensen?"

"After yesterday's debacle with Dick, which I'm still mad at you for, by the way…"

I roll my eyes. He's pissed I let the man search the center, but I didn't have anything to hide and I didn't want him returning while I was there. No sense fanning the flames of his anger.

"Jensen said he's going to fast-track the meeting with the judge. He thinks he can find someone to look over everything in the next couple of weeks, instead of thirty days."

"That means everything could be done before Thanksgiving."

I smile, thinking of the four of us together as a family for Thanksgiving. It's a long shot, considering Ben could take off any day, but something tells me he won't.

"You like him," I tell Donovan, meaning Ben. "I'm surprised you've jumped into all of this, to be honest."

"I see something in him that I used to feel in me."

I frown, slide my fingers against his, and watch as his muscles tighten. "What?"

I pull back from his shoulder so I can see his eyes. They're lined with small wrinkles as he squints into the sun. "Fear of never being good enough. Failure. Terrified he's going to fuck up somehow." He pauses, shakes his head. "My parents never beat me, but their expectations were certainly unreachable and there was always the fear of what I would lose behind their threats."

"It seems too easy, having him stay with us—like he fits right in, but I'm worried he's faking it."

"Me too, Talia," he says and pulls into my driveway. I can't help but smile when I see Mrs. Bartol flirting with Bentley. He looks uncomfortable looking at the woman twenty years older than him donned in only a silk robe that stops at her knees. He flinches when she reaches out to touch his shoulder, and I see her laugh.

We step out of the car at the same time that Jeremiah and Ben walk out of my front door, carrying a teal buffet table I want to bring to Donovan's house.

Donovan's hand finds mine and he slides our hands together, interlocking our fingers as we watch the boys smile and laugh while they carry the table to the truck parked at the curb.

"On the other hand," Donovan says, leaning down to whisper in my ear, "maybe it's easy because we're giving him what he wanted, because he can relate to Jeremiah in some way, and because he trusts you."

I sigh, shivers dancing along my neck from his breath and then his teasing touch as his finger draws slow, lazy circles at the small of my back. "Maybe you're right."

"We'll watch him, but I trust the kid, too. Otherwise I wouldn't have handed him a truck and just assumed he would stay. Now c'mon," he says, and swats me on the behind, making me jump. "Introduce me to Mrs. Bartol and let's get you moved in with me. I want to fuck you on our bed tonight, knowing you'll never leave it."

Hmmm…how can I argue with that?

* * * * *

The sun wakes me up, and I stretch my well-used muscles slowly. It's been a week that I've woken up in Donovan's bed every day, living with him. The sex alone would have quite possibly been enough to sway my decision to get me to move in with him. He's insatiable—even more so now that he knows for certain I'm not going anywhere.

I never want to go anywhere where he isn't with me. A month ago, I never thought my life would change so drastically—and while it's been filled with more drama than I can imagine, there's also a peace deep inside me, knowing I'm exactly where I'm supposed to be.

A smile tugs at the edges of my lips as I turn my head to see Donovan sleeping next to me, one arm behind his head, the other resting on his naked abdomen. The sheets are tangled around his waist, and I know he's not wearing anything under them.

My lips twitch with mischief and a sudden need to wake him up in the same way he enjoys waking me up most mornings, with his tongue and his fingers. I don't often have the opportunity to see

ENFLAME

him sleeping, since he's usually up before me—but today, with the sun barely rising, I seem to have beat him.

And I plan to take advantage of it.

Sliding onto my side slowly so as not to wake him, I rise to my knees and shift to the end of the bed.

Pulling back the sheets, I move quietly until I've exposed his beautiful cock.

Even at half-mast, he's still long and thick and beautiful.

I lick my lips, and look up to see that he hasn't moved. His lips are slightly parted and his chest rises to a slow, deep rhythm.

He's so handsome, with his square jaw slightly covered in stubble, that crooked nose, his chest and abs that are perfectly carved with just the right amount of hair smattering his pecs.

Just looking at him causes moisture to begin sliding down my inner thighs, and I push them together, reveling in the way that I can be turned on just by looking at him.

Sliding my palms to the outside edges of his hips, I lean down, deciding if I want to use my hand or my tongue on him first.

He seems to grow and harden just by my lustful stare, and my mouth waters.

I do this to him. Even in his sleep.

"Are you going to just stare at it, or put your sexy mouth to use?"

My head snaps up and I look to see Donovan smiling, his sleepy eyes barely open.

"You scared me."

He arches a brow, pulls his lips into a smirk. "Well?"

His hips lift, and his now thick and hard erection bobs, standing straight up. I can't resist it.

Wrapping my fingers around his base, I sigh at the feel of him beneath me.

Donovan closes his eyes and arches into my light grasp.

"I think I'll put my mouth to use."

Lowering my head, I tug on his shaft once and then twice, smiling at the way a groan falls from my man's lips.

He's so damn sexy.

I swirl the tip of his head with my tongue, teasing him. Pulling on his hard, thick shaft, I tighten my grip when my hand brushes my lips, and then lighten my hold as I move back down.

I'm torturing him, and I love the sounds he makes when I do. I wrap my mouth fully around him, sliding down his shaft and tasting every inch of him, and he lets out a shaky breath that makes me even wetter.

"Damn it, Talia. So fucking good."

His hand rests on the back of my head, not controlling my movements but encouraging me to continue.

I love the feel of him in my mouth. The dichotomy, silky but hard as steel, turns me on as I continue sliding my mouth up and down his thick cock, taking him all the way to the back of my throat, opening myself so I don't gag.

"Hell…"

I pull off, my hand dropping to his balls, and I cup them in my hands, teasing him and pulling on them.

"Hurry up," he grits, his thighs tensing.

I raise my gaze to meet his and the sight of him coming undone spurs me on.

My mouth moves faster as I suck him in, my hand gripping his balls more firmly before I pull off his erection and suck his balls into my mouth. His hips arch and jump and his hand tightens on the back of my head.

"Yes…so good…damn it…"

"I love the way you taste," I whisper before putting my mouth back on him.

"I love the way your mouth feels on my dick. Now stop teasing me and take it."

I squirm, leaning back on my knees so I can take him further while my other hand slides to my own sex.

And then I quit playing. My own need is too great.

With two fingers on my clit, I rub myself, sliding around my juices while I continue bobbing on his erection. My breath is panted, my chest heaving, but I don't take my eyes off Donovan as I suck him. He groans and his muscles flex and tighten in ecstasy.

"Get there," he groans out, his head pushed back into the pillow. "I'm gonna come, T."

Me too. My fingers rub against my clit more furiously as I chase my orgasm, and just as I fall over the edge, my own pleasured moans muffled by his cock, I feel him stretch and grow.

He arches into me, hitting me at the back of my throat, and then I feel his hot, salty flavor sliding down my throat.

"Holy fuck," he gasps. His hands press against my cheeks, holding me still while he takes over, fucking my mouth with quick, sudden movements. I take every last drop, letting him use me until his climax is complete and my own has subsided.

I open my mouth, letting him slide out, and give him one last long, teasing lick with my tongue.

"Good morning," I whisper, pressing kisses against his stomach, up to his chest. I straddle his hips and rest my head against his shoulder.

His arms wrap around me, holding me close to him.

"Hell of a way to wake up," he murmurs, pressing kisses against the top of my head. "I liked it."

I chuckle softly.

"Any plans for today?" he asks, his hand sliding through my long blond hair. I love the way he plays with it. It's erotic and soothing at the same time, and my body begins to warm all over again.

I can never get enough of him.

"Not except for seeing my dad."

"How is he?"

Donovan met him earlier in the week when we both stopped by after work. I was shocked to happy tears to see him sitting up in a wheelchair, staring out the window. It was the first time I had seen him out of his bed.

"Dr. McGarry said he's improving much quicker than they expected now." I smile against him, pressing my lips to his hot skin. "I can't thank you enough for moving him."

His hand on my waist tightens and he squeezes me. "Just glad I could help."

"I know." I raise my head and push my fingers through his sandy hair. "I love you for it."

"Just that?"

"No." My lips twitch. "I love you for your dick, too."

He laughs, and I'm smiling when his arm tightens at my back and then I'm flipped to my back, Donovan hovering over me.

His hand wrapped around his dick, I look down to see him stroking it quickly and watch it harden in his hand. "You just love me for my dick?"

I nod, feeling heat spread to my cheeks. "Yup."

"Perhaps I should show you how good it is, then."

He already has, dozens of times, but I love this playful side of him.

He slides his cock through my slit, still wet from earlier but growing even wetter as he teases me.

"Uncle Donovan!"

We both jump at Jeremiah's shout and snap our heads toward the door right as a loud pounding comes from the other side. "Wake up!"

"What the hell?" he groans and jumps out of bed, quickly

moving to his dresser. I slide out of the bed too and am getting dressed in a shirt that Donovan tosses me as he shouts, "What is it, J?"

"It's Ben. He's not home and his bed isn't slept in."

My eyes widen with fear and Donovan's eyes pierce mine as he tugs up a pair of pajama pants. When he sees that I'm covered, he quickly unlocks the door and throws it open.

"What do you mean?"

Jeremiah's eyes roam the room, and for a brief moment I'm completely embarrassed to be only half-dressed in front of him. If my heart wasn't pounding with fear, I'd probably be more so.

Jeremiah snaps his head to Donovan, runs a hand through his hair that is so similar to his uncle's, and shakes it quickly—maybe brushing off his own embarrassment.

"I...uh...I just woke up and Ben's door was open, so I looked in it and his bed is still made. I went downstairs and his truck isn't here."

"Shit." Donovan scrubs a hand through his hair. "We'll figure it out. Why don't you get dressed and we'll meet you in the kitchen."

Jeremiah nods, turns to leave when Donovan stops him.

"Jeremiah?"

"Yeah?" he asks, looking back over his shoulder.

"Thanks for letting us know."

Jeremiah shrugs as if it's nothing, but I can see the worry in his own eyes. It's not like it's any secret to him what Ben's gone through, although he hasn't been around for most of the conversations. "I like him. And his life is shittier than mine was."

With that, he turns and walks away. Donovan closes the door behind him and then rests his body against the closed door.

His head falls forward and he scrubs his hand over his face. "Did you hear what he just said?"

"That his life isn't so shitty anymore?" I smile lightly. "Yeah, I heard it."

"I have you to thank for that. For helping us…reminding me who I was, what I'd lost. Being there for Jeremiah."

I shake my head and rest my palm against his scruffy cheek. "I can't take the credit for all of that."

He nods disbelieving but doesn't say anything. He pushes off the door, presses his lips to mine, and heads to the bathroom. I follow him, and we quickly get dressed and ready for the day before heading downstairs.

My mind is spinning with a thousand possibilities of what could have happened to Ben and where he could be.

Unfortunately, none of them are good.

And since we don't know anything about his friends or his life, outside the abuse suffered at his stepdad's hands, I have no idea how to begin trying to find him.

Chapter Twenty-Two

My fingers strum the countertop. Next to me there's a plate of forgotten eggs and bacon. My coffee is cold and there's a heavy silence in the room as the three of us are lost in our own thoughts and worries about Ben.

It's been two hours since Jeremiah alerted us about Ben's absence..

Donovan quickly called Jensen, who immediately said he'd sic his own team of private investigators to the task of finding him.

Two hours since we've called our lawyer, who is somehow becoming a friend, or a guardian, or…I don't know what he is, but he's helping us so that's all that matters.

If Ben wants to be found. A shudder rolls through me at the thought.

"We'll find him," Donovan whispers to me from the other side of the counter.

I chew the inside of my cheek. "I know."

His serious gaze stares straight into mine. It's as if he can see my every fear, my every thought, my every concern. He can read my mind, and as I stare back at him, I silently wish for his confident statement to be truth.

I don't want Ben to have run away—not when he's so close to being free.

As far as we know, the last time anyone saw Ben was when he left school.

"He probably just went partying with some friends."

I shrug at Donovan's idea. It would be a typical teenager thing to do, especially for someone who's used to staying away from home. I can't imagine Ben's ever had someone worrying about where he is before. Or someone who cares about him enough to want to know where he is.

The thought is even more depressing.

"You're probably right," I mutter, and push off the kitchen stool, snagging my cold coffee mug on my way.

I walk around the counter and am immediately pulled into Donovan's arms, his hand at the back of my head, his other arm wraps around my waist. My forehead falls to his chest and a shaky exhale falls from my lips.

"You guys like him," Jeremiah says when he sees tears fall down my cheeks. "I thought you just felt bad."

"I like both of you," I reply, stressing that to him. There's no way in the world I want Jeremiah to think I care about him less, or that I only put up with him because of Donovan.

He seems to get my unvoiced thoughts, because he nods once and his lips show the slightest hint of a smile.

"Why don't you go shower and get ready for the day, J?" Donovan says.

I slide out of his arms toward the coffee pot, suddenly needing the caffeine.

Once Jeremiah is gone, I turn to Donovan, holding my coffee mug in both hands. "Why'd you kick him out?"

"Maybe because even with all this shit going on, I'm still a bit annoyed that he interrupted us."

He flashes me an arrogant grin and walks toward me.

I step back, shaking my head. "Now is not the time."

"Now is always the right time," he murmurs, nuzzling his face into the crook of my neck. His hands wrap around the edges of the counter, caging me in his arms, my coffee mug the only thing keeping distance between us. "Mostly I just wanted to see how you're really doing."

"Scared. Worried. And I'll be really freaking pissed if he just decided to stay out all night with buddies or some stupid shit."

Donovan laughs quietly, and I feel his lips spread into a smile against my skin. "You sound like some protective mama bear. I like it."

I feel like one. And a part of me worries that I'm beginning to care too much about Ben. He's not my child. He might never become my responsibility, and a small part of me wonders if I'm getting too close to him. But the other part—the bigger and louder part—doesn't care.

He might not be mine, but as long as he's around, I swear to take care of him, do anything he needs, be there for him in any way I can.

I swallow down the emotion in my throat that's also burning my nose. "I just want to know where he is, even if he's not coming back."

"Hey." He pulls back, cups the back of my neck with his hand, and tilts my head to his. Two soft green pools stare down at me. "He'll come back, I know it—or we'll find him and bring him back."

I sniff, blinking rapidly. "Okay."

He takes a step back and I bring my coffee mug to my lips. I'm just taking the first sip when the front door opens and slams shut. Loud footsteps echo on the marble floor and I jump, choking on my coffee.

My eyes flash to Donovan's, but he's already moving.

I take off after him, quickly setting down my mug. Coffee splashes over the rim onto the counter and floor, but I don't stop to clean it up.

"What the hell happened to you?" I hear Donovan shout as I hit the entryway just steps behind him.

I gasp, my fingers flying to cover the sound leaving my mouth, and my eyes jump out of my head. "Are you okay?" I ask, and quickly rush to Ben.

His clothes are torn, his cheek is covered with dried blood, and one of his eyes is almost swollen shut. He stumbles into me as I pull him into my arms and I have to choke down a gag.

He reeks of alcohol.

"Have you been out drinking? Got in a fight?" I squeeze him tighter, but he puts his hands to my arms.

"I'm fine," he says and pushes away from me. "Mind your own business."

"Ben—" I take a step toward him.

"Do you have any idea how worried we've been?" Donovan asks, stepping in front of me. "You scared us."

His eyes are on the stairs, not looking at us, and I take the brief moment to look him over. He looks like he was run over by a truck. Or slammed into some heavy fists. Fury boils inside of me like I've never felt before.

"Yeah, well…" He stops to scrub his hand down his face, flinching when he hits his eye. "It was a tough fucking day. Can I go to bed?"

Relief floods me even with my worry. Because he's here. And he came on his own.

"Let me clean you up first. Please?" I ask when he shakes his head.

He shrugs lamely. "Fine. Whatever."

I reach out and brush my hand over his shoulder, not caring at all that he moves out of my way. Letting my hand fall to my side, I fight the tears that want to fall. "Go upstairs and I'll be up in a minute."

I watch his back as he walks away, feel Donovan move closer to me, and when Ben has disappeared at the top of the stairway, I allow just a few tears to fall, biting my lip to stop them. "He's here."

Donovan presses his lips to the top of my head and squeezes my shoulders. "I told you he'd come back. Go see to him, see if he'll tell you what happened. I'll call Jensen."

* * * * *

Ben hisses as the hydrogen peroxide I place on his knuckles stings his skin.

He's quiet and in pain. I can see it in his eyes and I know it's not just physical.

I've been quietly taking care of him, only speaking when needed, while a thousand questions burn the tip of my tongue.

Setting down the cotton ball tinged with his blood...or someone else's...I unwrap a bandage for his cheek.

"Do you want to talk about it?"

He shakes his head once and swallows.

"We were really scared this morning," I whisper. I don't want him to feel bad. I just want him to know we genuinely care.

"Sorry," he mutters, and looks down at his bloody knuckles while I put another bandage over his eyebrow.

The edge of his bed, which we're sitting on, bounces as his foot begins tapping.

I close up the medical kit and push it to the side. There's nothing else I can do for his physical wounds, and nothing appears to be broken, although he does have a nasty bruise on his ribs. It looks like tread-marks from a boot, but I'm trusting him that he says it doesn't hurt much. I've given him some pain meds with the promise that he'll tell me if it gets worse.

"Can we talk about it anyway?" I ask hesitantly.

For a moment I don't think he's going to speak, but then he sniffs, balls his hand into a fist, and says, "Dick found me."

I grind my teeth together to keep from lashing out a string of curse words. Not that this isn't an appropriate time to use them. "Where?"

He shrugs. "Leaving school, I guess. I don't know, but he stopped me at the gas station. I was on my way here, I swear." He looks at me suddenly, eyes wide as if he's begging me to believe him.

I nod, letting him know I do.

"He's pissed it took him so long to find me. Punched me right in the fucking face and no one said a word."

"What gas station?" I ask, immediately wondering if they have surveillance tapes. If we can get him charged with irrefutable evidence, it makes Ben's case better.

He exhales harshly, and I can tell he doesn't want to tell me when his shoulders finally collapse. "Holiday by Sixth in Centerville."

I place my hand on his thigh. "Thank you for telling me that. Care to explain the rest? Like the beer and the rest of your cuts?"

"Stupid shit," he mutters, and then laughs once. It's cold and empty and I hate that this kid, who genuinely seems to want more than what he's been given, feels so alone. "Showed up at a party, got in a fight."

He shrugs as if it's no big deal—nothing new in his world. I suppose it's not, and my guess is he took out his anger on some unsuspecting teenage prick because he couldn't do it to his stepdad.

"It's okay," I say, and rub his leg before standing up. "I don't really care about the fight. I'm just glad you're okay."

He looks away, another sniff as he focuses out the window. "You're the only one who would."

If hearts could physically break in two, the pain in my chest tells me mine just did. "Not true." I smile sadly and nod toward the door to his room. "There's two other guys downstairs who care, too."

"Yeah...maybe."

I let myself out, heart breaking in my chest and rage boiling in my veins.

I hate adults like this. Men who think they can use their power of authority to abuse it, or who take out their own insecurities on people younger and weaker than they are. It doesn't make them men.

It makes them assholes.

Once I'm downstairs, I find Donovan in the living room, sitting on the couch and talking quietly to Jeremiah, who's now showered and cleaned up. Both of their eyes snap to me as soon as they see me.

"He'll be okay, I think. Just needs some time."

"Did he tell you what happened?" Donovan asks, rising to his feet. Jeremiah does the same, and if I weren't so upset, so relieved, or so overwhelmed, I might smile at their similar stances and appearances.

"Dick found him. Didn't do all the damage, but enough that he went and got drunk and picked a fight somewhere else."

"Damn," Jeremiah mutters. "What a prick."

I shrug in agreement. "He said Dick found him at a gas station in Centerville, where he hit him. I think he might have kicked him, too."

Donovan grabs his phone and presses a button. "He say which one?" His eyes spark, and I know he's thinking the same thought I had upstairs.

"Holiday on Sixth in Centerville," I tell him.

He nods, presses his lips to my cheek as he leaves the room, and as he's walking away I hear him say, "Jensen? Yeah...we got something...get in front of a fucking judge as soon as you can..."

Then his voice trails off and I look at Jeremiah, shuffling on his feet, uncertainty filling his features.

"He really okay?"

I walk to him and wrap my arms around him. "I think he will be. Someday."

* * * * *

"Do we have to do this?" Jeremiah moans pitifully, shuffling his feet behind me down the hallway.

I ignore him. He's been like this all afternoon—ever since Ben came back. I thought maybe the best thing for him to do after his nap would be to pretend the night before never happened. Plus, I don't want him replaying the night in his mind.

He'll have to relive it once Jensen gets ahold of the security tape at the gas station, if there is one.

And since there's no way I'm letting either of them out of my sight, I've made them come with me to see my dad.

"Shut up, squirt," Ben mutters. He hasn't smiled all day and has talked very little. The familiar ribbing makes me smile.

"I can't help it. Old people make me feel weird."

I shoot him a look. "My dad isn't old. He's just sick."

"Same difference," he mutters, and shoves his hands deep into his pockets.

I shake my head and when we reach the door to my dad's room, I turn to face both boys.

I almost have to look up to meet both of their eyes. If I were wearing flats instead of heeled boots, I probably would. The boys' looks are completely opposite one another, and I can't help but take in their differences: Where Jeremiah is built, Ben is taller but lean. Jeremiah's sandy brown hair to Ben's dark hair and tanned complexion. Yet it's their sullen faces, which look like I'm taking them straight to a firing squad, that make me grin.

"Chill," I remind them. "We'll only stay a few minutes. I just want to say hi to him today."

Both boys shrug, almost synchronized.

"Maybe I just want him to meet you two, okay? I've told him all about both of you."

How much he hears and comprehends is a whole other story, but I don't let that sadness or doubt creep into my mind.

Slowly opening the door, I smile when I see my dad in what is his new favorite spot. His nurse, Amanda, is standing off to the side of him, checking his vitals, and her grin matches mine when she sees me.

"He's having a good day today," she says, and pats him on the shoulder.

His lips twist into a semblance of a smile…bigger than it used to be.

"Baby girl," he says. His voice is still hoarse, but I love that he can speak at all, even if it's gravelly and slow.

"Hey, Dad." I move quickly to the side of the chair once Amanda walks away, and place a kiss on his lips. "I brought some friends with me today that I want you to meet."

Looking over my shoulder, I see Jeremiah and Ben hovering in the doorway, hands shoved into their pockets, uncomfortable looks on their faces.

"Dad…meet Jeremiah, Donovan's nephew, and our friend, Ben."

With hesitant steps both boys nod and slowly enter the room when their name is called. Amanda shuffles out behind them, closing the door, and Jeremiah's head whips over his shoulder as it shuts.

I fight back a snicker.

"They're happy to see you," I tell my dad, running my hand over his.

He turns his hand so our palms are together and squeezes. It's faint but it's stronger than before.

"Good…to…m…m…meet…you," he stutters. I can see the strain it takes him to form the words.

"Hey." Jeremiah nods and lifts his hand in greeting.

"You, too," Ben says, his shoulders relaxing a bit as he takes in the room.

"Fight?" my dad asks and nods toward Ben.

He brushes his cheek, cringing a bit. "Yeah."

"You…win?"

Ben laughs softly, but it's sad, and I instantly see that my dad notices. His eyes flicker to mine but back to Ben when he replies, "One of them."

"Can't…win…them all."

He squeezes my hand again, and I watch as Ben further relaxes. It seems to mean something to Jeremiah, too, because he walks further into the room and takes a place on the couch.

"No, sir, you can't," Ben finally says, and then follows Jeremiah's cue. I smile at his manners and give him a thankful smile.

"How are you? Doing good?" I ask my dad, turning my focus to him.

"Better."

I smile, my lips stretching into a grin so wide my cheeks ache. "I'm glad."

We spend the next few minutes talking, and he slowly tells me about his therapy. They have him trying to hold his own silverware and lift his arms, but I know from the progress reports I get when I visit that it's difficult for him. He's doing better with major muscle movement, though—things like stretching his legs and standing with support.

I can almost imagine the day where he'll be able to walk out of here on his own. As we talk and I see him begin to yawn through his words, I know I've exhausted him. Jeremiah and Ben don't say much, but I can tell they're listening to every word. And when I finally kiss my dad on the cheek and tell him I'll see him soon, I can't stop more tears from forming in my eyes when I see Ben and Jeremiah both walk over and shake his hand.

"Be good to her," he says, through slow words and stretched-out pauses. "She's the best."

"She's all right," Jeremiah says, clearly teasing.

My dad simply smiles and pats his hand.

As we walk out of the nursing home and toward my car, I'm surprised when Ben says, "Your dad seems cool. Well, like he would have been, before…"

His face twists like he said something wrong. But he didn't.

I put my arm over his shoulders, even though I have to slightly rise on my toes to do so. "He was the best," I tell him and pull him to me.

We head home in silence, just the radio filtering through the speakers, but slowly, the further away we get from the nursing home and the closer we get to Donovan's house—my house—I feel a tension lift in the car.

When we pull into the driveway, Ben slides into the middle of the seat before getting out, and he props his elbows on the backs of the front seats. "Thanks, Miss M. You're pretty cool."

He exits the car before I can say anything in return—like tell him how awesome I think he is, too. I can't help but grin as I watch Ben run into the house, throwing a playful punch against Jeremiah's shoulder when he slides past him.

Because there's a lot of difficult things going on in our lives right now—Ben's, mostly.

But there's also a lot of good, and just like when I prayed for a miracle for my dad, I bow my head and take a few minutes to pray for a miracle for Ben, too.

Chapter Twenty-Three

I sit with my back straight in a simple black leather chair, and watch as the judge in front of us peruses Ben's file from Jensen.

He's standing behind us, due to a lack of chairs. On my side, Donovan is holding one of my hands, and I'm squeezing onto Ben's hand on the other side of me so hard I can only hope I don't break it.

We've discussed his options, discussed the proof of abuse that Jensen's investigator was able to lift from a security camera last Friday. After we sent Jeremiah to school this morning, we got a call saying Jensen had a judge willing to fast-track everything.

It includes temporary foster parent status for Donovan, with the promise he begins his twelve-hour foster parenting course immediately.

Freedom for Ben.

I can't believe it's only been forty-eight hours since Ben walked into the house bloody and in pain. It feels like forever.

Thank God for Jensen and his most likely slightly illegal views on the legal system. He's getting us what we want, and that's all I care about.

"So," Judge Cochran says. He closes the file and clasps his age-spotted and pudgy hands together on top of the manila folder. "I've reviewed everything, and while I haven't had the time to go over it as intently as I usually review a case, I think I have a good grasp of the situation." He slides a narrowed glance toward Jensen behind me.

I can practically sense the careless shrug Jensen gives in return.

I like him. Would never want to be standing opposite him, but when he's in your corner, Jensen kicks ass.

The judge looks down at Ben and rolls his lips together. His blue eyes are hidden behind thick glasses and his overweight cheeks grow bigger when he smiles. It's kind, though, and that's all I care about. Despite the pressure he felt to do this, he seems like a good man, and fair.

"Do you have anything else to add to this other than the accounts I've read?"

Ben shakes his head. His palm grows sweaty in mine. "No, sir."

"Is everything you said the truth? No embellishing just because you're pissed at some unfair grounding?"

I gasp, squeeze Ben's hand, and open my mouth to speak.

Donovan beats me. "With all due respect, your honor—"

He silences him with a glance and holds one palm up. "With all due respect, I've had two hours to look over this case and I'm not interrogating, simply asking."

Ben shuffles in his seat. My fear begins to bubble to the surface. He can see the bruises on his cheek and eye, for crying out loud. He's seen the video.

"No, sir. It's all true."

"Very well." He nods and licks his lips. "If I were to grant you full emancipation, I'm not sure you have the financial means to care for yourself. Based on what I've read, it's unlikely I can trust you to meet the emancipation requirements that we like to see for being able to live on your own. However," he says, with a kind smile when he sees my jaw drop.

The color feels like it's draining from my face.

"In order to get you out of your current home environment, I'm willing to grant temporary guardianship to Mr. Lore here, seeing as he's an upstanding member of the community with the means to take you in, and someone it seems you're comfortable with. In six months, if you'd like to reapply for full emancipation as a minor, you will need to show me a bank account with more than lunch money in it, and proof of your ability to live on your own, pay your own bills, pay rent, etcetera. Does that make sense?"

I wait for Ben's response with bated breath. Donovan and I are more than willing to take Ben in. Now it just has to be his choice.

Seconds tick by on the clock hanging behind Judge Cochran and I squeeze Ben's hand, silently pleading with him to take the offer.

It's the best he's going to get, and far better than going to the streets, which is where I know he'll end up.

"Ben," Donovan says, his voice low and quiet, completely nonthreatening. "Please. Let us take care of you."

Tears begin forming in my eyes as he stiffens next to me, and when I slide my glance in Ben's direction, I see his eyes mirroring mine.

"My mom," he chokes out, his voice thick. "Doesn't she have to sign that away or something? Give me up?"

I close my eyes tightly. He doesn't know that Jensen convinced her to do this already—showed up at her house, apparently, with his investigator. And I don't know the specifics… don't want to know them…but I know when he left, he had her signature on a document stating that she's willing to surrender parental rights. I didn't know if she would, considering also late last night, once we sent a copy of the video to Jensen, he sent on another copy to the county's police department. Dick was arrested by members of the police force from his own squad. Sweet justice and good riddance, I say.

At some point Ben might have to testify, and we haven't told him that, either. We were waiting until we knew more about his situation.

The judge's kind but quiet look speaks for itself, and next to me, Ben brushes his fingers across his cheeks.

"Okay," he says, inhaling quickly. "I'll stay with them."

Sweet, beautiful relief floods my veins and I choke on a thankful sob.

It's one thing for him to be forced to stay with us. It's another for him to choose us.

And it seems like he has.

We hash out the specifics, sign enough paperwork to kill a small forest, and leave the office.

As happy as I am, as thrilled as I am, I know not everything is going to be simple; and while we drive back to Donovan's house, we're all silent, and I'm sure we're all wondering the same thing.

Ben jumps out of the car almost as soon as it pulls to a stop in the garage.

"Where are you going?" I ask, climbing out after him. He's halfway to his truck and turns around, keys spinning around his thumb.

"Sorry…" He shakes his head, looking confused. "Am I always going to have to tell you where I'm going and when I'll be home?"

He doesn't sound defensive. Surprised. Confused, maybe.

I smile and shrug. "It'd be nice, so I don't worry about you."

"We just care," Donovan says, walking toward him. "We can talk about rules later, but I also understand you're sixteen and you've essentially been living on your own and taking care of yourself for a long time now. I don't want to make you feel forced to be here, but yeah…letting us know when you're leaving and when you'll be home, so Talia isn't worried you're drowning in a ditch somewhere, would be nice."

I scowl at him throwing me under the bus, but in reality I don't mind. Much.

"I just want to go for a drive. Clear my head a bit, I guess. I'll be back…"

"Around four?" Donovan supplies. It's only eleven in the morning now. Four seems generous. "I'd like for us to be together for dinner tonight."

"Okay," he says, shuffling on his feet. His hair blows a bit with the cold breeze, and I wrap my arms around my stomach, warming myself. He turns toward his truck, and when he gets to the front of it, he slams a hand down on the hood and spins on his heels to face us. "Thanks. For everything."

"Welcome," I murmur, although he can't hear me.

Donovan and I watch as he peels out of the driveway much too quickly and I scrunch my nose.

"Come on," Donovan says, and wraps his arm around my waist. "We've got four hours before Jeremiah is home from school and we have to fill him in."

"What do you want to do?" I ask, raising a brow and feeling the stress of the day evaporate into the chilly air. "Anything in mind?"

He nods seriously. "I want to do you. In the kitchen. The living room. The game room…maybe in our bed, too."

"That sounds like you have your work cut out for you."

He smirks and opens the door to the house. "I think I can manage. And I think I have the rest of our lives to prove it to you."

A lump forms in my throat and my jaw drops. It's not the first mention of a permanent future for the two of us, but for the first time, there is the absence of any fear or nerves.

This is Donovan.

I've been his for eight years…I'll be his for eighty more.

Chapter Twenty-Four

Epilogue
Christmas

"We have to get up," I whisper, nudging Donovan on the shoulder.

The sun hasn't risen, but that's common in late December in Michigan.

What isn't common is the fact that in just a few hours we'll have a house full of guests celebrating Christmas with us. There's still so much to do, and I want to get started before Jeremiah and Ben wake up.

"Hmm." Donovan rolls to his side, pulling me to him as he wraps an arm over my waist. "I can get up."

His erection pressing to my backside is proof of his words.

He nuzzles into the crook of my shoulder, tickling my skin with his scruffy jaw. I push on his chest as he rolls on top of me. "I'm serious," I say, fighting a smile.

My thighs separate, letting him fall in between my legs, and I feel the truth of the fact that he can definitely get it up resting along my bare skin.

"Do you know what I want for Christmas?" he asks, his lips brushing against mine.

"What?" I arch into him, feeling his hardness slide along my wet, sensitive flesh.

In the months we've lived together and in the many more to come, I don't think I'll ever get used to how much Donovan wants me.

I want him just as much, if not more.

"I want to taste you." His fingers trail down my stomach until they're sliding through my sex, dipping in and pulling out. My lower stomach flips and heats at his teasing. "I want you to come on my mouth and around my fingers. And then I want you coming around my cock."

My hips arch into him and a heavy breath falls from my lips. "I think that sounds like a lot of work."

He licks his lips before he claims mine with a kiss. It's slow and sleepy, but full of passion as his fingers return to teasing me. It takes moments before he's sliding into me, his thumb brushing against my clit. My fingers dig into his hair as our tongues tangle together and I'm left breathless, my chest heaving when he pulls away, sliding down the bed.

He pauses, cupping my breast with his free hand while his other continues to drive me crazy. Wrapping his lips around my nipple, he sucks and licks on one, then the other, pulling both into hardened, needy peaks. His thumb on my clit sends sparks through my body and I gasp, lifting into him.

"Donovan," I gasp, pulling on his hair when he slides lower. His tongue trails lazily through my folds, licking my moisture and driving me crazy. "I love you."

His soft green eyes meet my half-lidded ones and he presses a kiss to my clit, sucking it into his mouth.

"I love you too," he whispers against my skin.

With his fingers and his tongue he brings me quickly to the cliff, and as I tumble over, gasping for breath and muffling my cries into my pillow, turning my head and biting down, I can't help but feel overwhelmed by not only his love, but everything he's given me in the last two months.

I have more than I could ever possibly imagine, but it's not because of his bank account.

It's because of his generosity.

It's because my dad will be joining us today—in a wheelchair and brought by a nurse from Rolling Oaks, but it's that he's going to be here that's important.

It's because Ben is still with us, flourishing in his new school, where Jeremiah also attends. The two boys have become friends, and both are happy, doing well in school. Both have their times where they pull back into themselves as if they're afraid of the goodness they've been given, but for the most part they're both showing signs of healing.

Ben rarely mentions his dad, and even though he was convicted of child abuse, where Ben managed to testify at his trial, he will also only serve six months in prison for his crimes. He never speaks to or of his mother, as if she never existed. We're becoming one big merry band of misfits.

And finally, it's because my new teen center is set to open after the first of the year. It's finally finished and it's incredible. And while I've given up my therapist's license, I'm still the business manger—but Marisa handles most of the daily operations, overseeing the kids who come through our doors and managing the four therapists who are now working for us.

Life is good. I have absolutely nothing to complain about, nothing I could possibly want.

Which is why, once I come down from my climax, I'm shocked as hell when Donovan slides back up my body. He kneels back onto his heels, pulling me so my thighs drape over his.

With one hand wrapped around his erection, he teases my slit, sliding it through my wetness.

I gasp at the sensation, my core still throbbing for more.

"I have a question for you," he says, his voice deep and husky.

Leaning over me, he reaches into his bedside table and comes back out with something wrapped in his tight fist.

I blink rapidly, my brow furrowed, when he lifts my left hand to his lips and presses kisses along my knuckles. "There's something I want to give you."

I look down at our bodies, at his cock resting against the top of my core, and smirk. "There's something I want you to give me."

"Woman," he growls playfully, "your wish is my command."

He adjusts us, his one hand still wrapped around something I can't see, but I forget all about it as he lifts and pulls me to him, sliding himself to the hilt in one slow but powerful thrust.

Rolling his hips, he asks, "This what you want?"

Always. "Yes."

He rocks himself inside me, never once breaking the connection with our eyes that grows more heated with every thrust until my breath is coming in quick pants, his own pulse pumping in his neck.

He lifts his hand, grabs onto my left one, and before I know it, he's sliding a ring onto my finger.

The finger.

My eyes burst wide in shock, and then I whimper from his quickening movements.

"What the hell?" I ask, grabbing his hips and forcing him to stop his wicked, mind-bending ministrations.

"Marry me."

"Are you asking or telling?" I ask, surprise evident in my voice. I wasn't expecting this.

"Do you love me?" He rolls his hips.

My eyes almost roll back into my head.

"Of course I love you," I whisper, gasping for breath. From the sex or the ring, I'm not certain.

He leans forward, presses himself further into me, and I can only groan from the tightness, how full he makes me feel. Everywhere.

My heart is bursting as he rocks into me, pulling out slowly and pushing in with determination.

"Then marry me."

I lick my lips and lift my head up, seeking his mouth. His lips fall to mine and he devours me. Soon the question is unanswerable because our groans and moans fill each other's mouths as we swallow the pleasured cries.

He's too much.

This is too much.

"Donovan!" I shout as he slams into me, his thumb moves to my clit and it takes one…then two more thrusts as my orgasm coils at the tops of my thighs and spreads out throughout my body. Everything explodes, my skin heated, and I cling to him, crying in ecstasy while I chant "Yes! Yes, I'll marry you!"

He slams into me, seating himself one last time, and I feel him pulsing inside of me, his own climax barreling down on him just as quickly as mine did.

"I'll marry you," I say, panting, still clinging to him.

He wraps his arms around me and pulls me up so I'm sitting on his lap, his cock still inside me, my flesh still clenching around him. "I'll make you the happiest wife in the world," he whispers against my lips.

"I love you," I murmur against him.

"I love you more," he teases, and shifts his position on the bed. Then he stands up, walks us to the shower with me still clinging to him, all arms and legs wrapped around him, and sets me down on the bathroom counter. "Now we can get ready for the day."

Which reminds me.

I smile. "Merry Christmas, Donovan."

"Merry Christmas, Talia." His lips seal over mine in a slow and languid kiss, and I release my hold on him to run my hands down his chest. "I love you so much."

I catch sight of the ring and gasp, shoving it in front of my face. It's huge. And sparkly. A great, giant diamond on a simple band. "This is beautiful," I say in awe, tearing my gaze off my finger and meeting his eyes. "Thank you."

"You're welcome. Jeremiah helped pick it out."

"You asked him?"

Donovan grins. "Of course I did. And Ben. And…" He lowers his head and slowly slides his lips over mine. My body spasms again, heating and coiling and burning for him. God, I love him. "I also got your dad's permission."

He pulls back, pleased with himself, and I can only thank him by dropping to my knees on the cold tile floor, opening my mouth, and sucking him inside.

He's too much. And perfect.

And I get to spend every day showing this amazing man how much I love him.

* * * * *

"This has been the best Christmas I could ever imagine," I tell everyone, raising my champagne flute high in the air. As I look around the table, I smile with tear-filled eyes as everyone does the same.

James and Laurie are sitting to my left, visiting from Ann Arbor for the dinner. Next to them are Mrs. Bartol and her husband, Harold. Donovan grins at me from the other end of the table, and filling out the other side are Ben, his new girlfriend Amanda, Jeremiah, and Jensen—who is here only because when I learned he was going to be spending the holiday alone, I insisted he come.

To my right, my dad sits in his wheelchair, not holding onto a champagne flute because he can't grip things for too long in his hand, but it's within his reach as soon as my toast is done.

Between a pile of Christmas presents larger than anything I've ever seen in my life for Ben and Jeremiah, and fixing Christmas dinner for so many people, I've been rushing around all day, barely able to sit and relax.

But now it's time, and as I survey our crazy crowd of friends and family, I can't even begin to count my blessings for what I've been given throughout this last year.

"Thank you, so much, to everyone for coming today. Thank you, Donovan and Jeremiah, for bringing me into your family and loving me, and thank you, Ben…for trusting us."

He blushes slightly but nods with a small smile. His girlfriend wraps her hand over his at the table, and in front of me, Donovan laughs.

"I believe we have you to thank for all of that."

"Potatoes-potahtoes," I say. "Merry Christmas, everyone. Cheers!"

We clink glasses, sip champagne, and dig into an incredible Christmas ham and turkey dinner.

We've celebrated Christmas.

We've celebrated and announced our engagement.

And through the laughter and the jokes, several times, I catch Donovan's eyes on me, watching me with a love that I can feel searing into my heart with unbridled intensity.

After clearing the plates, Laurie and I are in the middle of serving up pie for everyone when the doorbell rings.

I look at Donovan, pie spatula raised in the air. "Want me to get it?"

He slides back from his chair. "Nope," he says, grasping my shoulders and pressing a kiss to my forehead. "Get my food ready, wench."

"Hey!" I jump when he slaps my behind and keeps walking toward the door.

"That's some man you have there," Laurie says, choking down

laughter.

I sigh dramatically, waving my ring in the air. "And he's all mine."

She bumps my hip with hers and slides a clean plate in front of me. "You seem happy."

I grin, catching a sight of James watching his wife. He hasn't taken his eyes off her all day, and he keeps getting this goofy grin on his face. I like it. "You guys seem happy, too."

She shrugs, look at James, and her cheeks turn hot pink. "Yes…well…we've had an exciting day ourselves."

My eyes widen at her tone. I can't help but glance down at her flat belly. "Are you?"

"No," she whispers sheepishly. "But we decided to start trying. I think James is just anxious to get home and get to work on making one."

I snort, shaking my head. "Men."

"Talia? Jeremiah and Ben?" I snap my head toward Donovan's serious voice. He's standing in the doorway, and as if everyone suddenly senses something serious, the chatter stops. "Can you three come here, please?"

I nod, handing the spatula to Laurie. "Can you finish up?"

"Of course, get going."

I wait for Jeremiah and Ben to reach me, and then the three of us head toward Donovan.

"Everything okay?" I ask, seeing a line deep between his brows. He looks tense, or angry. I haven't decided. "Who's here?"

"My mother," he growls, low enough for only the three of us to hear him.

Jeremiah stiffens, but Donovan quickly pulls him to his side. "It's going to be okay, trust me." His eyes meet mine. "She wants to talk."

"Well, by all means…" I roll my eyes but follow him. We

haven't heard from Claire for months, other than when Donovan has to see her at board meetings. A part of me isn't surprised at all she's here today, of all days. Why wouldn't she want to take the opportunity to ruin someone's Christmas when she's most likely miserable and alone?

"Mom," Donovan says as we reach her in the entryway, "you remember, Talia. My fiancée."

Claire's eyes widen at the announcement, but she recovers quickly. I scoot closer to Donovan, Jeremiah on his other side, Ben on my other side.

"Hello, Claire."

She nods briskly, her eyes dipping to my exposed left hand before she meets my eyes. "Merry Christmas, Talia."

"This is Ben," Donovan says, nodding his head. "He's a friend of ours, staying with us indefinitely."

"Yes," his mom says, nodding. "I heard you've become a foster parent. That's…well…congratulations."

Her voice is tight, her eyes sad, and by the way she's wringing her hands together, I almost feel bad for her.

Almost.

"You have something you wanted to say?"

She shuffles on her feet and I bite back a smile. I've never seen this horrible woman looking so uncomfortable. "Yes. Well…it occurs to me that I might not have always supported you like you need a mom to do. It was only because I wanted the best for you, truly, but well…you're old enough to make your own decisions about your life. So I plan to stay out of it from now on."

"Do you?" Donovan doesn't bother hiding the bite or the doubt in his tone. His shoulders are stiff, arms crossed over his chest.

He stands as protector, watching out for his family. It makes him even sexier in my eyes and I slide closer, resting my hand on his lower back.

Claire notices, her eyes pinching minutely before she nods. "I would simply like to be able to see you occasionally, and you—Jeremiah," she says, nodding toward him. "If you'd like."

My heart softens. Damn it. She truly does seem sincere…and it's Christmas.

"And Talia?"

Claire nods at Donovan's question. "Yes, of course. I'd like that, too."

I glance at Donovan and watch as he debates whether this is a ploy, but then I decide enough is enough: she'll show her true colors eventually, and she shouldn't be alone.

"We're just about ready to have dessert," I say, stepping forward. "Would you care to join us?"

Her hands go to the tied belt at the front of her coat and she begins undoing the knot. "Thank you. That'd be kind."

"Well, it is Christmas." I take her coat from her, spin around to see a grateful smile on Donovan's lips, and I know I've done the right thing. He hates the distance with his mom, knowing she has no one else, and he hasn't enjoyed waiting for her apology. Me making the effort speaks volumes to him, and I can see it glimmering in his eyes. "Jeremiah and Ben? Why don't you take Claire into the kitchen, find her a chair, and get her some pie. We have dinner too, if you haven't eaten."

She shakes her head, a thankful smile on her own lips. "No. Thank you, pie is just fine."

"We'll be right there," Donovan says as Claire passes us.

When she's gone, he cups my cheeks with his hands and steals my breath with a kiss.

"Have I told you how amazing you are?"

I grin. "Not since I did that trick with my tongue the other day."

Throwing his head back, he laughs and pulls me to him,

wrapping his arms around me. "Thank you. For today, for yesterday, and for every day for the rest of our lives."

I wiggle my eyebrows. "You can show me how thankful you are later."

"Oh, I will," he replies. "Today, tonight…tomorrow…"

"Come on." I pull out of his embrace and tug him toward the kitchen. "We've got family and food waiting for us."

"Hmm…everything I could possibly want."

I squeeze Donovan's hand, raise it to my lips, and with my kiss, I silently agree with him.

Acknowledgements

To my first readers and betas, thank you so much for your insight to improving this story. Heather Carver, Amanda Maxlyn, Samien Newcomb, and Brittainy C. Cherry – I love you all!

To my favorite Bad Ass CP's. You ladies are the absolute bestest of the best. Thanks for loving my brand of crazy.

To Shannon, - Lady…I love you. You completely keep me sane and go well and above any assistant. I think you're absolutely amazing!

To Amy Jackson and Emily Lawrence…someday, I swear I will learn all these rules that you constantly correct me for. Thanks for making this manuscript shine.

To my readers: You're the best. Thanks for taking a chance on me and I hope I can provide you all with many more books for years to come.

To all the blogs, especially Love Between The Sheets for your promotional help. Every review, every cover reveal, I'm amazed with your support. Thanks just isn't enough but it's all I have to give you.

To my husband…thank you for always being there for me to encourage me and support me, and most importantly, thanks for all the great brainstorming ideas.

Other Books by Stacey Lynn

Crazy Love Series - 2018
Fake Wife
Knocked Up

The Rough Riders Series
Dirty Player
Filthy Player

The Luminous Series
Dominate Me
Crave Me
Long For Me

The Fireside Series
His to Love
His to Protect
His to Cherish
His to Seduce

The Tangled Love Series
Entice
Embrace
Enflame

Just One Series
Just One Song
Just One Week
Just One Regret
Just One Moment

The Nordic Lords Series
Point of Return
Point of Redemption
Point of Freedom
Point of Surrender

Standalones
Captive – The Fidelity Kindle World
Remembering Us
Don't Lie To Me
Try Me – A Don't Lie To Me Novella

About the Author

Stacey Lynn currently lives in Minnesota with her husband and four children. When she's not conquering mountains of laundry and fighting a war against dust bunnies and cracker crumbs, you can find her playing with her children, curled up on the couch with a good book, or on the boat with her family enjoying Minnesota's beautiful, yet too short, summer.

She lives off her daily pot of coffee, can only write with a bowlful of Skittles nearby, and has been in love with romance novels since before she could drive herself to the library.

If you would like to know more about Stacey Lynn, follow her here:

Website: www.staceylynnbooks.com
Facebook: www.facebook.com/staceylynnbooks
Twitter: www.twitter.com/staceylynnbooks
Instagram: www.instagram.staceylynn.author

If you enjoyed this book, please leave a review on the site where it was purchased.

Made in the USA
Las Vegas, NV
11 October 2021